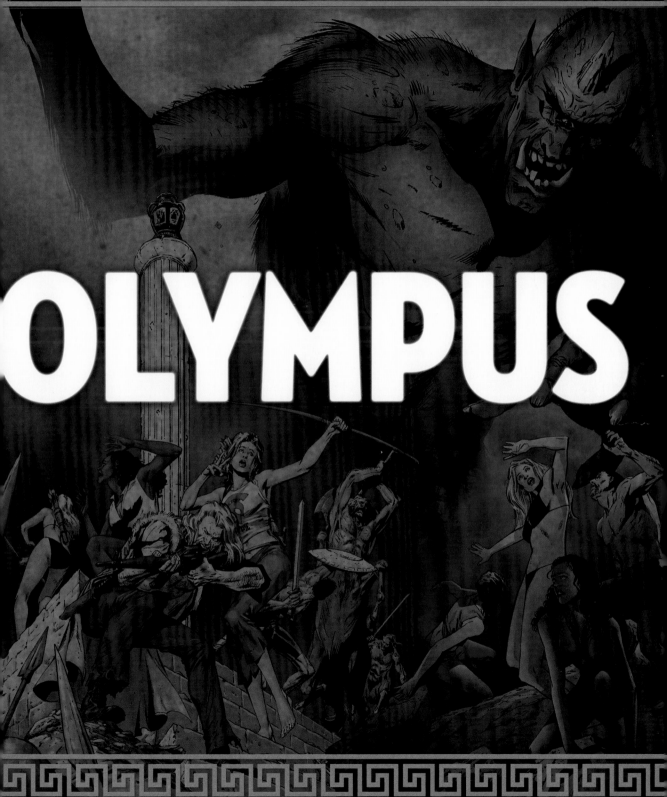

GEOFF JOHNS - KRIS GRIMMINGER - BUTCH GUICE

OLYMPUS

HUMANOIDS

GEOFF JOHNS & **KRIS GRIMMINGER**
WRITERS

BUTCH GUICE
ARTIST

DAN BROWN
COLORIST

•••

ALEX DONOGHUE
EDITOR

JERRY FRISSEN
BOOK DESIGNER

FABRICE GIGER, PUBLISHER

RIGHTS & LICENSING - LICENSING@HUMANOIDS.COM
PRESS AND SOCIAL MEDIA - PR@HUMANOIDS.COM

OLYMPUS
This title is a publication of Humanoids, Inc. 8033 Sunset Blvd. #628, Los Angeles, CA 90046.

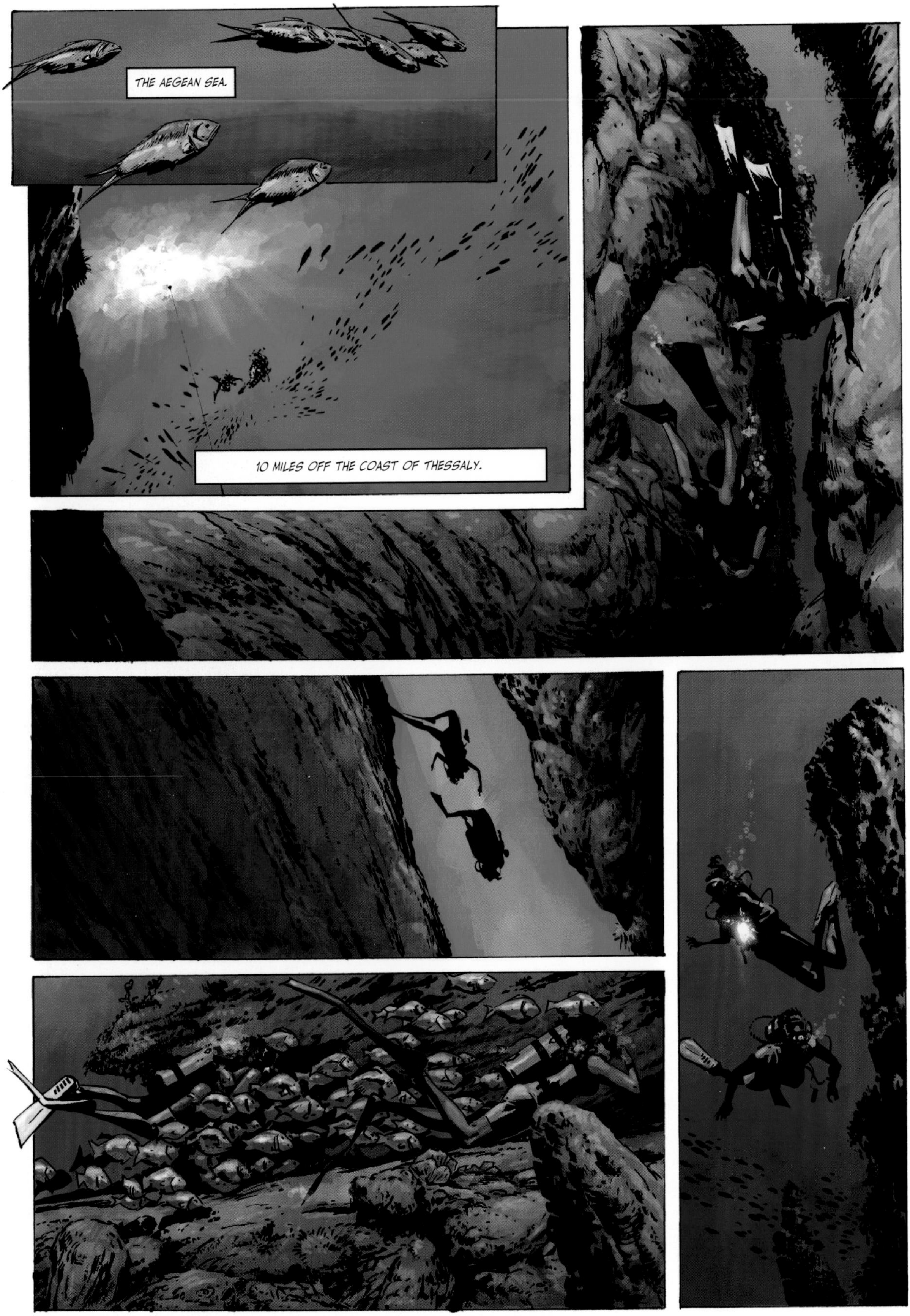
THE AEGEAN SEA.
10 MILES OFF THE COAST OF THESSALY.

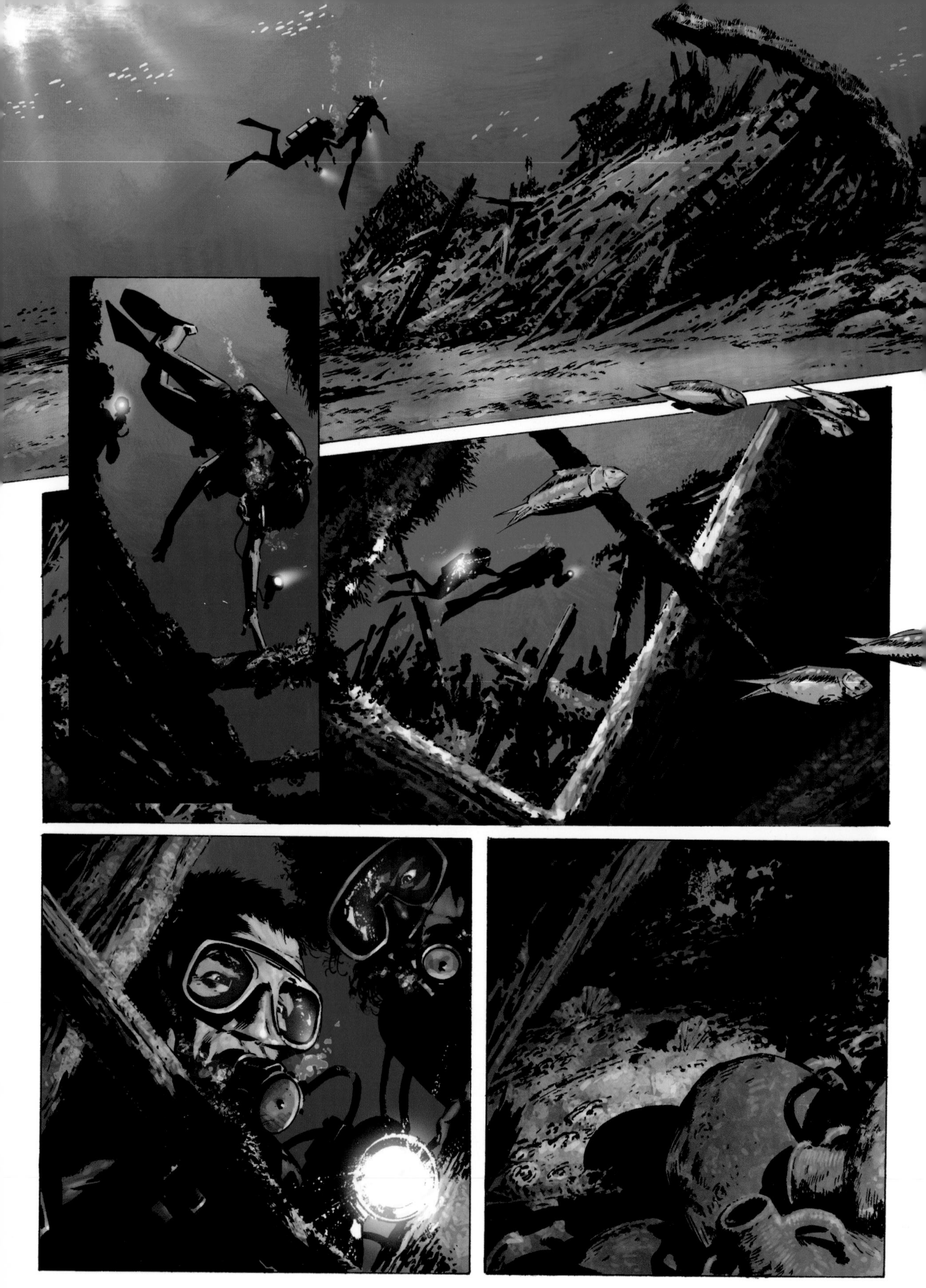

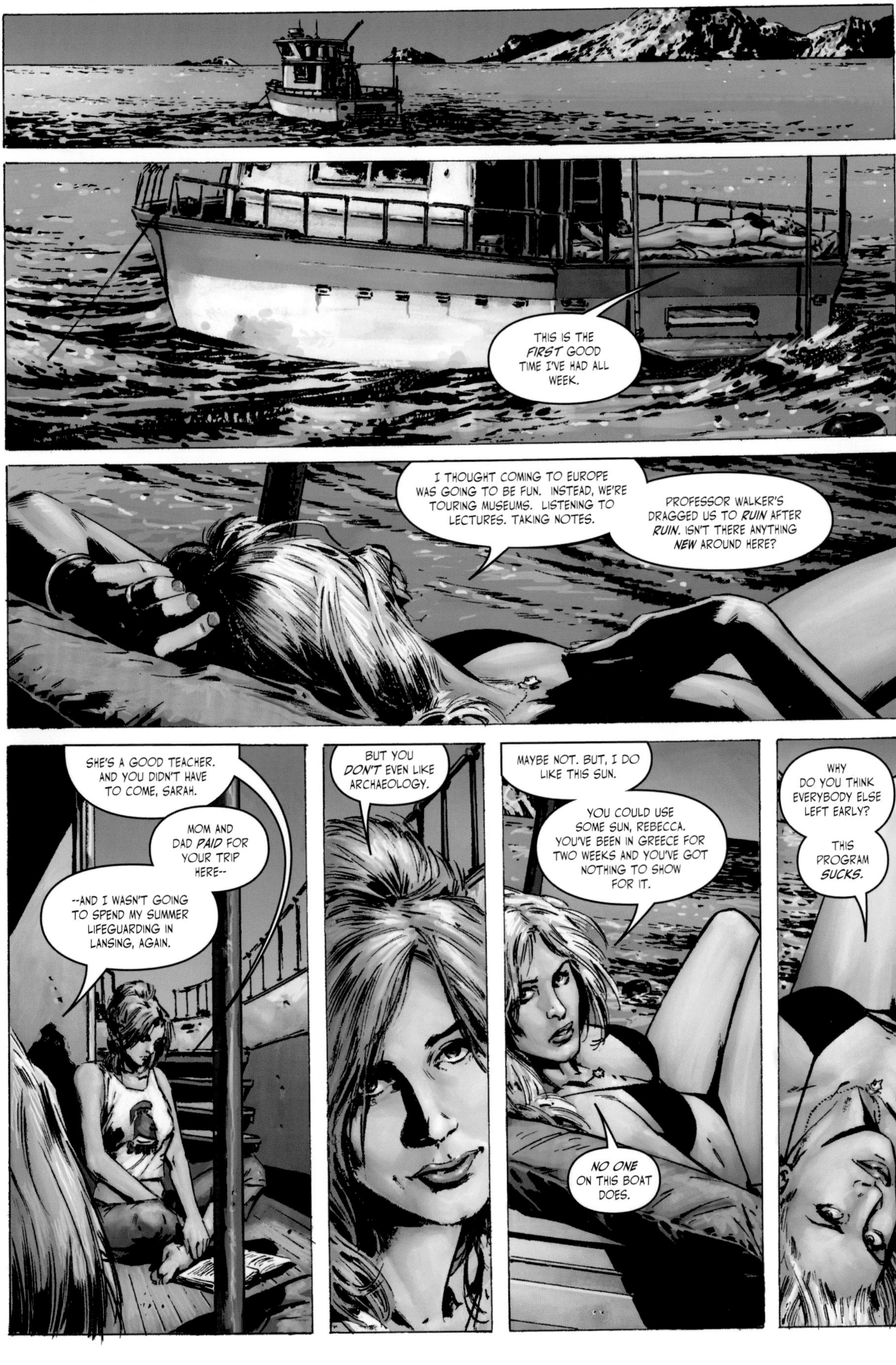
THIS IS THE FIRST GOOD TIME I'VE HAD ALL WEEK.
I THOUGHT COMING TO EUROPE WAS GOING TO BE FUN. INSTEAD, WE'RE TOURING MUSEUMS. LISTENING TO LECTURES. TAKING NOTES.
PROFESSOR WALKER'S DRAGGED US TO RUIN AFTER RUIN. ISN'T THERE ANYTHING NEW AROUND HERE?
SHE'S A GOOD TEACHER. AND YOU DIDN'T HAVE TO COME, SARAH.
MOM AND DAD PAID FOR YOUR TRIP HERE--
--AND I WASN'T GOING TO SPEND MY SUMMER LIFEGUARDING IN LANSING, AGAIN.
BUT YOU DON'T EVEN LIKE ARCHAEOLOGY.
MAYBE NOT. BUT, I DO LIKE THIS SUN.
YOU COULD USE SOME SUN, REBECCA. YOU'VE BEEN IN GREECE FOR TWO WEEKS AND YOU'VE GOT NOTHING TO SHOW FOR IT.
NO ONE ON THIS BOAT DOES.
WHY DO YOU THINK EVERYBODY ELSE LEFT EARLY?
THIS PROGRAM SUCKS.

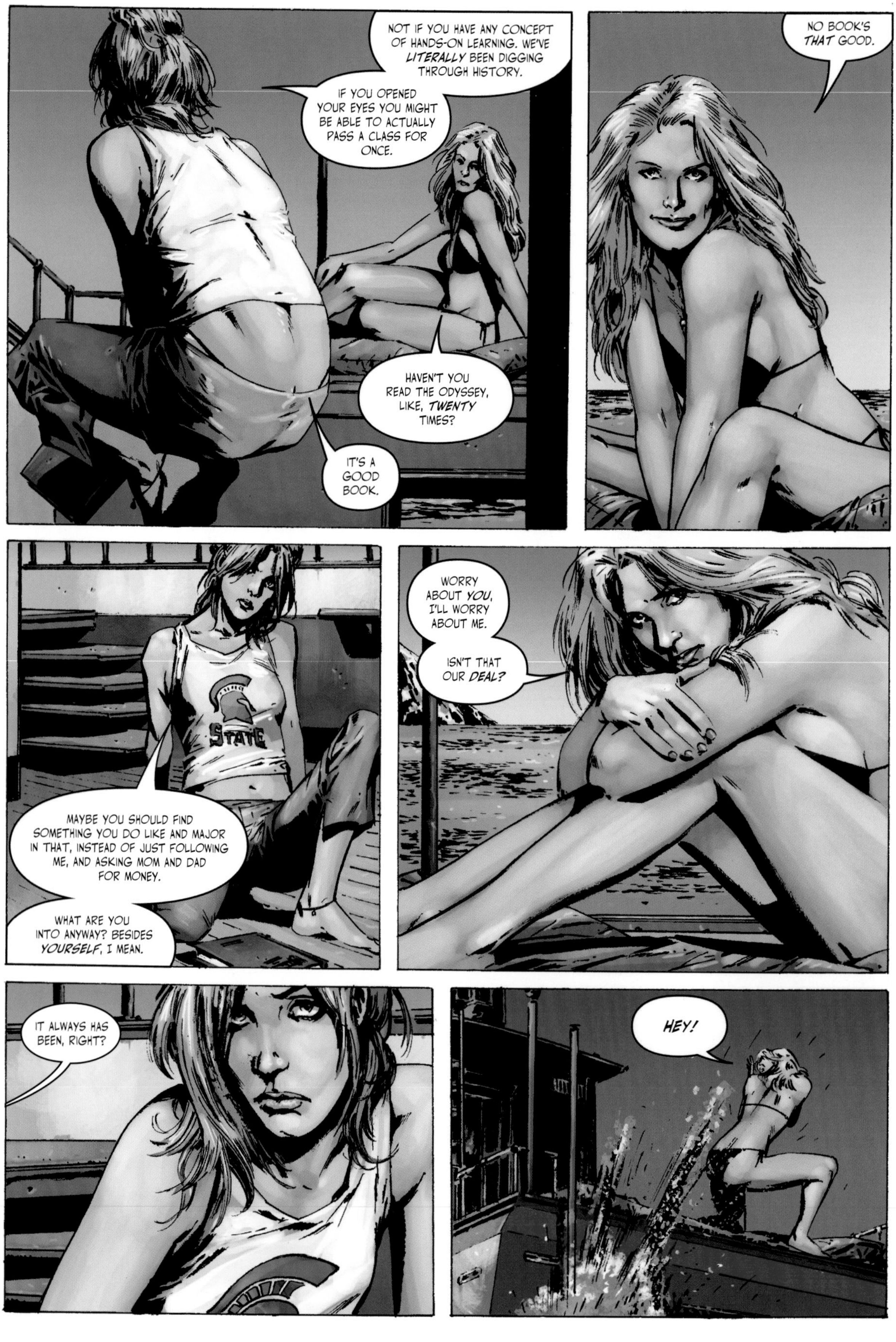
NOT IF YOU HAVE ANY CONCEPT OF HANDS-ON LEARNING. WE'VE *LITERALLY* BEEN DIGGING THROUGH HISTORY.
IF YOU OPENED YOUR EYES YOU MIGHT BE ABLE TO ACTUALLY PASS A CLASS FOR ONCE.
HAVEN'T YOU READ THE ODYSSEY, LIKE, *TWENTY* TIMES?
IT'S A GOOD BOOK.
NO BOOK'S *THAT* GOOD.
MAYBE YOU SHOULD FIND SOMETHING YOU DO LIKE AND MAJOR IN THAT, INSTEAD OF JUST FOLLOWING ME, AND ASKING MOM AND DAD FOR MONEY.
WHAT ARE YOU INTO ANYWAY? BESIDES *YOURSELF*, I MEAN.
WORRY ABOUT *YOU*, I'LL WORRY ABOUT ME.
ISN'T THAT OUR *DEAL?*
IT ALWAYS HAS BEEN, RIGHT?
HEY!

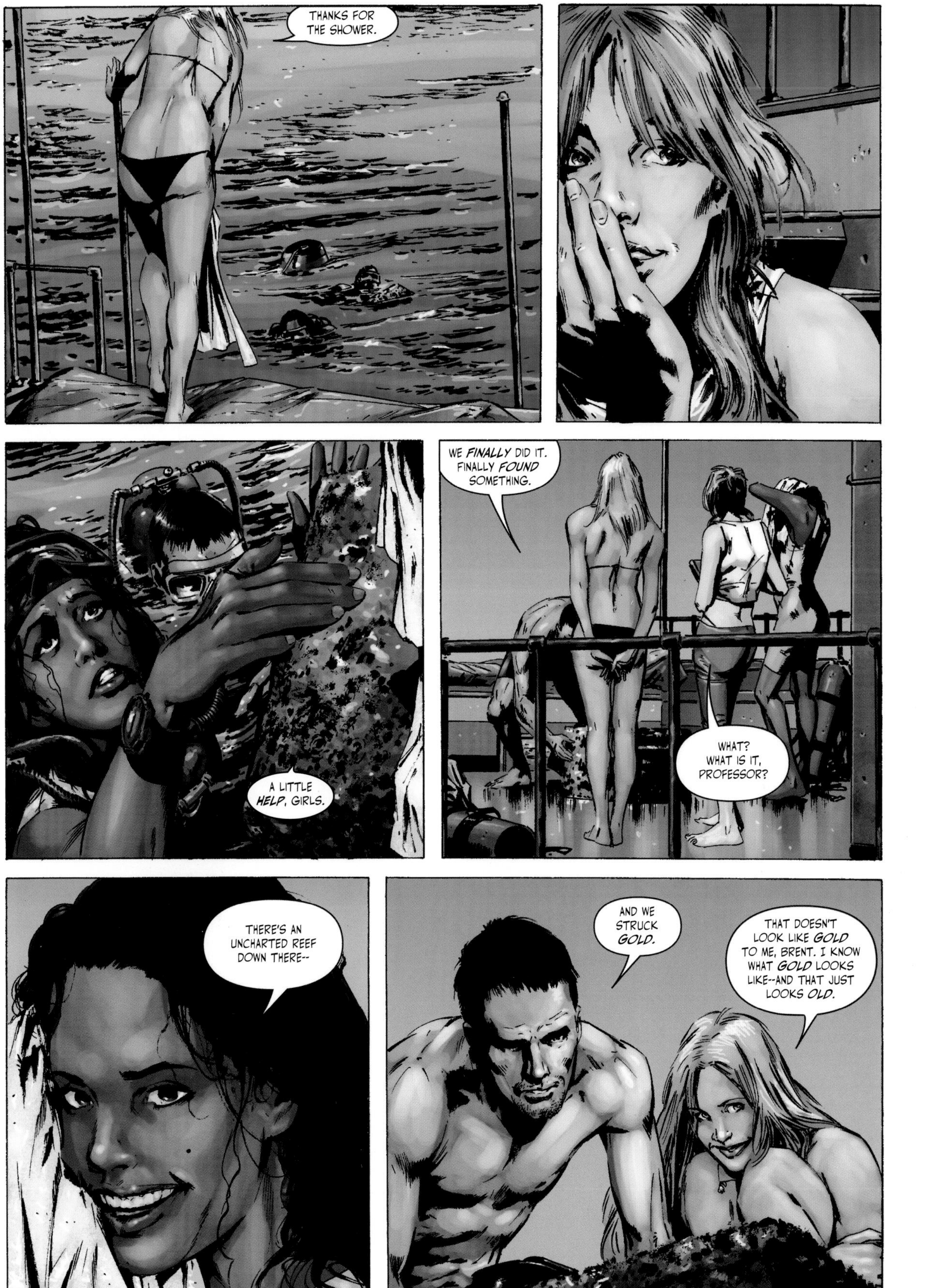
THANKS FOR THE SHOWER.
A LITTLE *HELP*, GIRLS.
WE *FINALLY* DID IT. FINALLY *FOUND* SOMETHING.
WHAT? WHAT IS IT, PROFESSOR?
THERE'S AN UNCHARTED REEF DOWN THERE--
AND WE STRUCK *GOLD*.
THAT DOESN'T LOOK LIKE *GOLD* TO ME, BRENT. I KNOW WHAT *GOLD* LOOKS LIKE--AND THAT JUST LOOKS *OLD*.

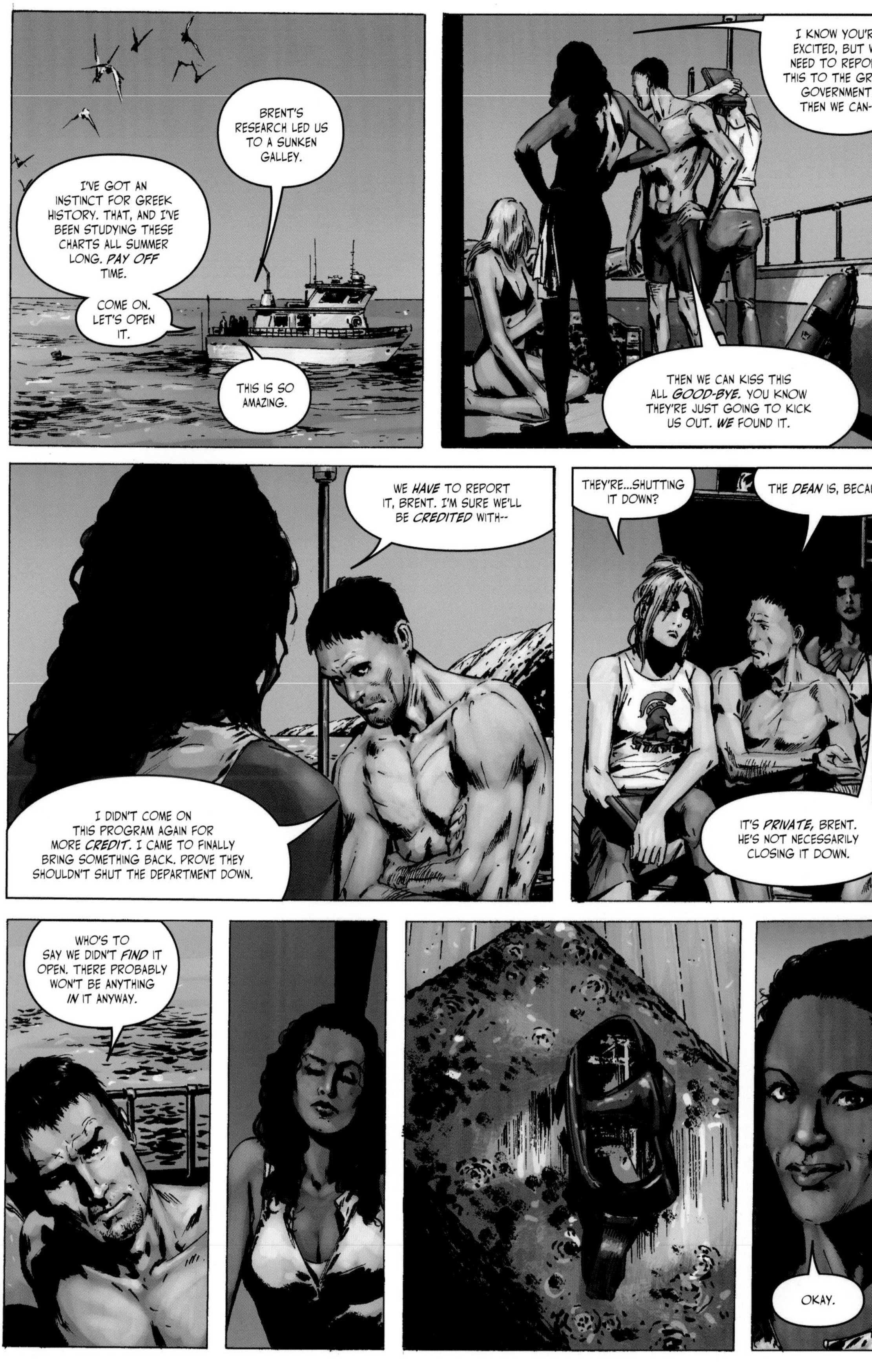
BRENT'S RESEARCH LED US TO A SUNKEN GALLEY.
I'VE GOT AN INSTINCT FOR GREEK HISTORY. THAT, AND I'VE BEEN STUDYING THESE CHARTS ALL SUMMER LONG. *PAY OFF* TIME.
COME ON. LET'S OPEN IT.
THIS IS SO AMAZING.
I KNOW YOU'RE EXCITED, BUT WE NEED TO REPORT THIS TO THE GREEK GOVERNMENT. THEN WE CAN--
THEN WE CAN KISS THIS ALL *GOOD-BYE.* YOU KNOW THEY'RE JUST GOING TO KICK US OUT. *WE* FOUND IT.
WE *HAVE* TO REPORT IT, BRENT. I'M SURE WE'LL BE *CREDITED* WITH--
I DIDN'T COME ON THIS PROGRAM AGAIN FOR MORE *CREDIT*. I CAME TO FINALLY BRING SOMETHING BACK. PROVE THEY SHOULDN'T SHUT THE DEPARTMENT DOWN.
THEY'RE...SHUTTING IT DOWN?
THE *DEAN* IS, BECAUSE--
IT'S *PRIVATE,* BRENT. HE'S NOT NECESSARILY CLOSING IT DOWN.
WHO'S TO SAY WE DIDN'T *FIND* IT OPEN. THERE PROBABLY WON'T BE ANYTHING *IN* IT ANYWAY.
OKAY.

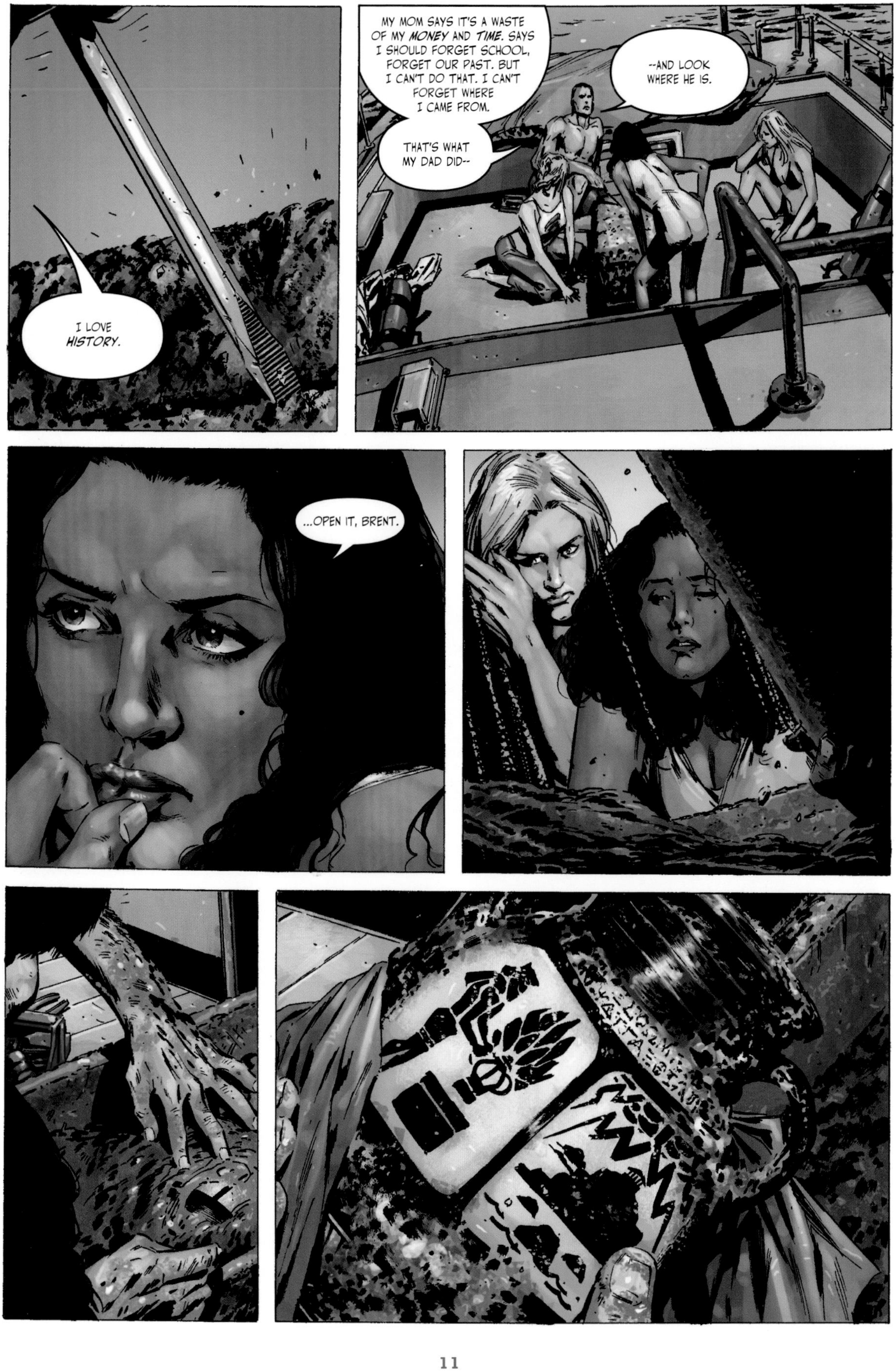
I LOVE HISTORY.
MY MOM SAYS IT'S A WASTE OF MY MONEY AND TIME. SAYS I SHOULD FORGET SCHOOL, FORGET OUR PAST. BUT I CAN'T DO THAT. I CAN'T FORGET WHERE I CAME FROM.
THAT'S WHAT MY DAD DID--
--AND LOOK WHERE HE IS.
...OPEN IT, BRENT.

IT'S JUST AN OLD POT.

REBECCA, YOUR SECOND MAJOR IS ART HISTORY--

HER *THIRD* IS OVER-ACHIEVING.

IT IS OLD...*REALLY* OLD. THIS FIGURE ON THE BOTTOM...

IT LOOKS LIKE THE CHARIOTEER. THE ANCIENT GREEK ATHLETE FROM THE PYTHIAN GAMES. SO, THIS COULDN'T HAVE BEEN MADE BEFORE 480 B.C.

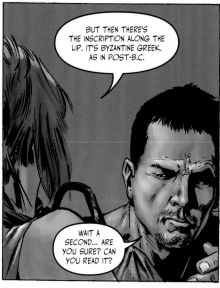

BUT THEN THERE'S THE INSCRIPTION ALONG THE LIP. IT'S BYZANTINE GREEK. AS IN POST-B.C.

WAIT A SECOND... ARE YOU SURE? CAN YOU READ IT?

"HEREIN CONTAINS... THE MISFORTUNES... OF MAN."

...SHE'S RIGHT.

WHAT'S THAT SUPPOSED TO MEAN?

THE FIRST WOMAN, THE *GREEK EVE*, WAS CREATED AND SENT BY *ZEUS* TO LIVE AMONGST MEN. SHE WAS GIVEN A SEALED JAR CONTAINING ALL THE *MISFORTUNES OF EXISTENCE.*

"THE MISFORTUNES OF MEN," AND ALL THE SORROWS OF *MANKIND*, WERE CONTAINED WITHIN *PANDORA'S BOX.*

BUT IT'S NOT EVEN A BOX...

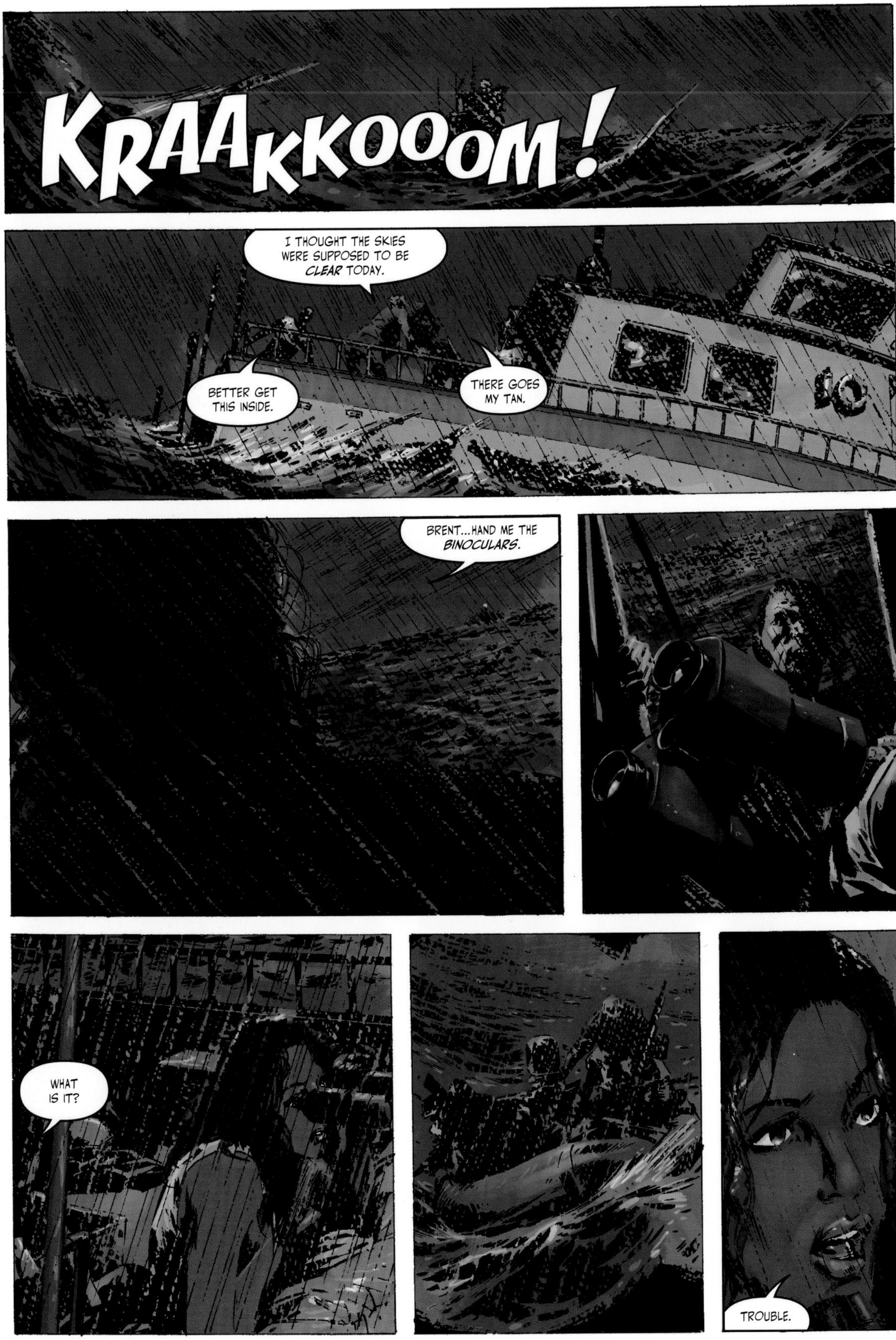
KRAAKKOOOM!
I THOUGHT THE SKIES WERE SUPPOSED TO BE CLEAR TODAY.
BETTER GET THIS INSIDE.
THERE GOES MY TAN.
BRENT...HAND ME THE BINOCULARS.
WHAT IS IT?
TROUBLE.

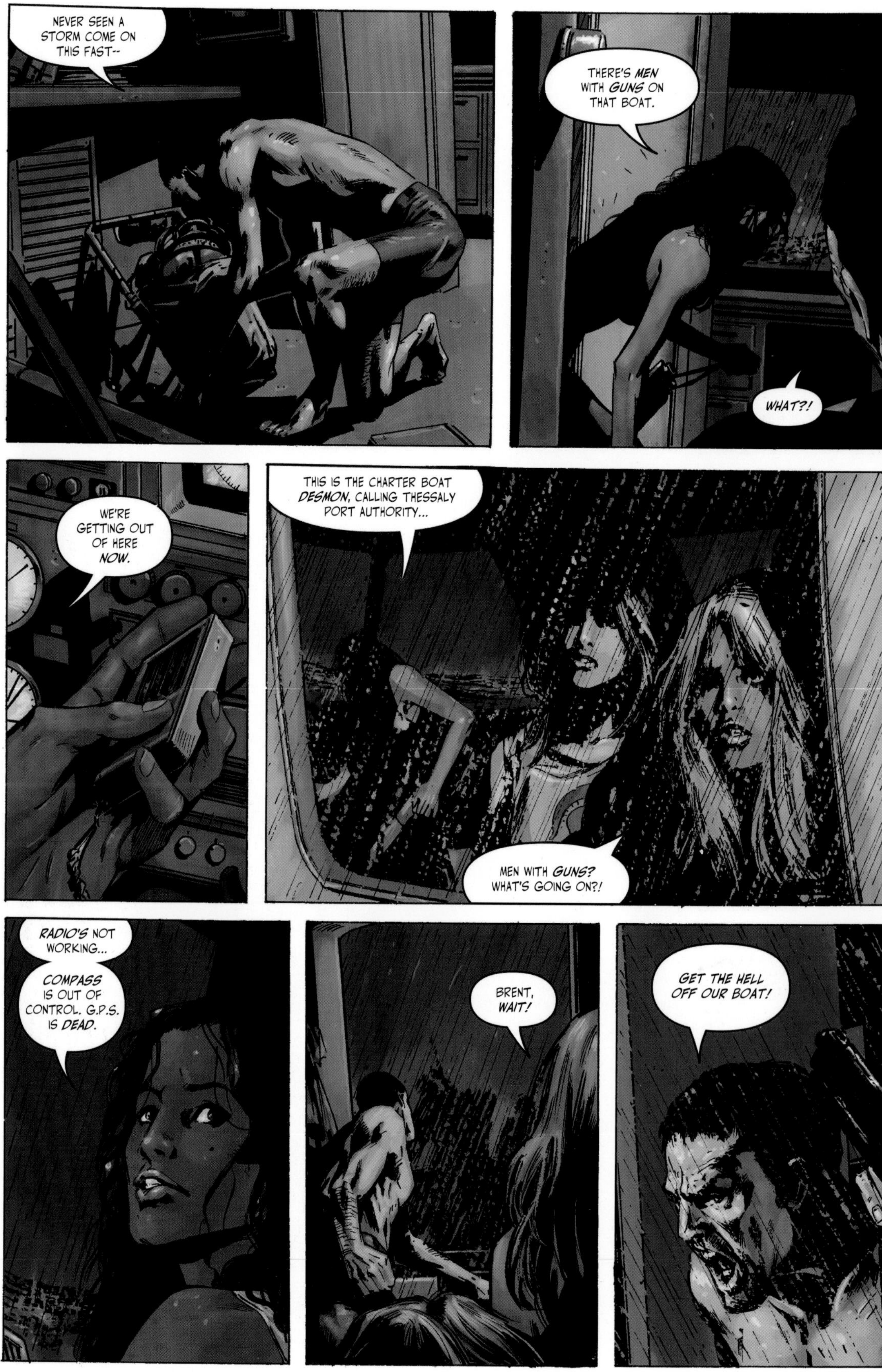
NEVER SEEN A STORM COME ON THIS FAST--
THERE'S MEN WITH GUNS ON THAT BOAT.
WHAT?!
WE'RE GETTING OUT OF HERE NOW.
THIS IS THE CHARTER BOAT DESMON, CALLING THESSALY PORT AUTHORITY...
MEN WITH GUNS? WHAT'S GOING ON?!
RADIO'S NOT WORKING...
COMPASS IS OUT OF CONTROL. G.P.S. IS DEAD.
BRENT, WAIT!
GET THE HELL OFF OUR BOAT!

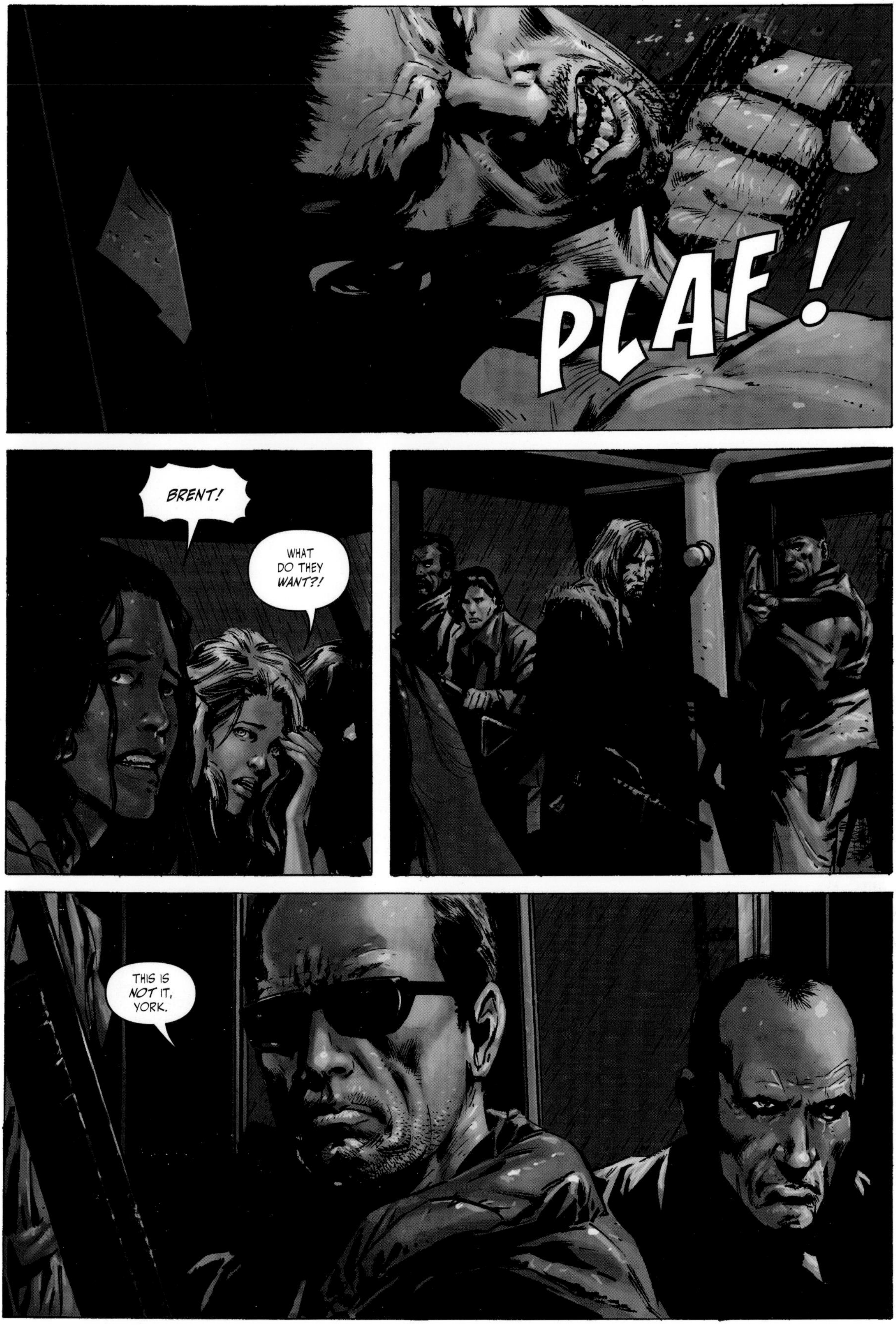
PLAF!
BRENT!
WHAT DO THEY *WANT?!*
THIS IS *NOT* IT, YORK.

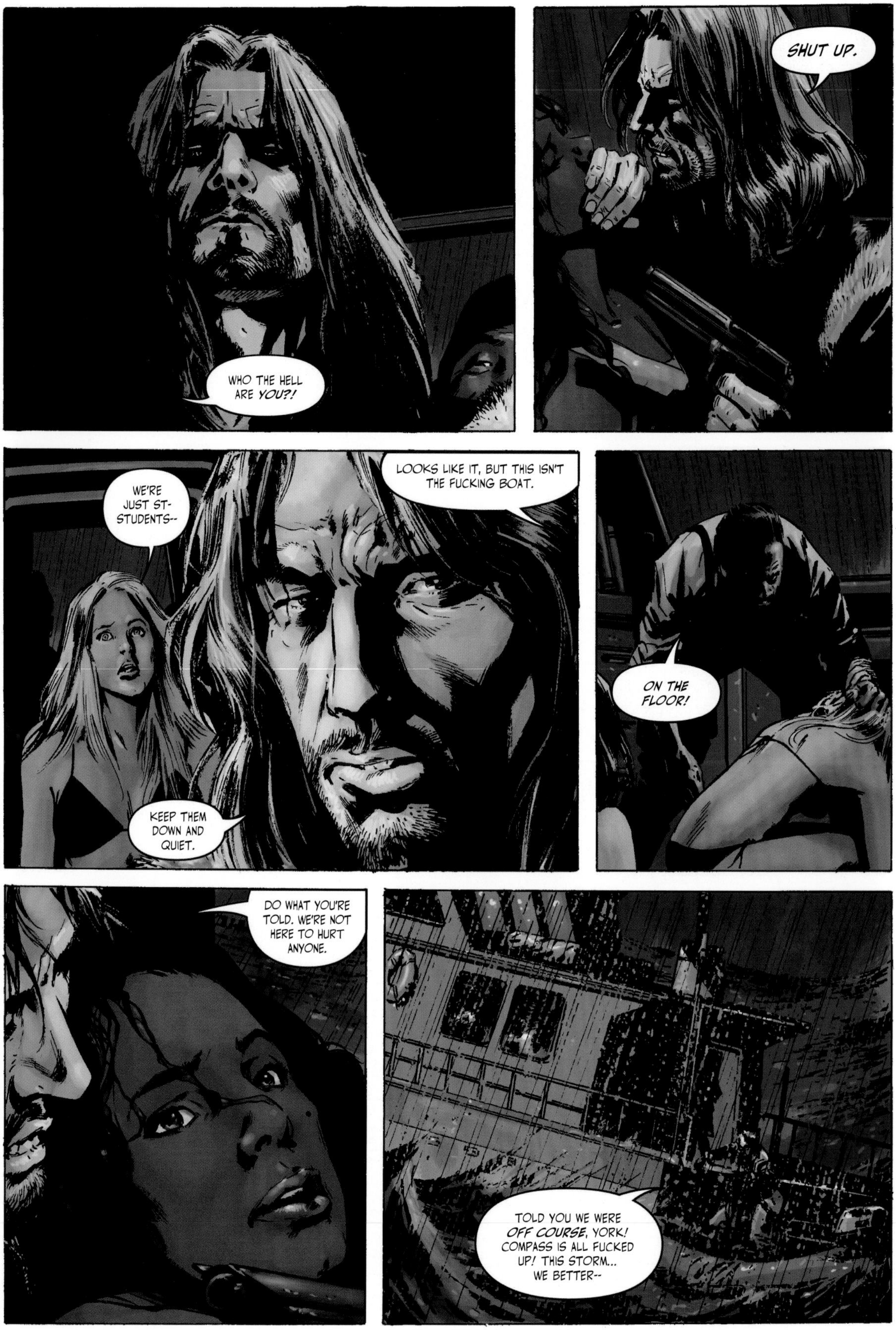

WHO THE HELL ARE YOU?!
SHUT UP.
WE'RE JUST ST- STUDENTS--
LOOKS LIKE IT, BUT THIS ISN'T THE FUCKING BOAT.
KEEP THEM DOWN AND QUIET.
ON THE FLOOR!
DO WHAT YOU'RE TOLD. WE'RE NOT HERE TO HURT ANYONE.
TOLD YOU WE WERE OFF COURSE, YORK! COMPASS IS ALL FUCKED UP! THIS STORM... WE BETTER--

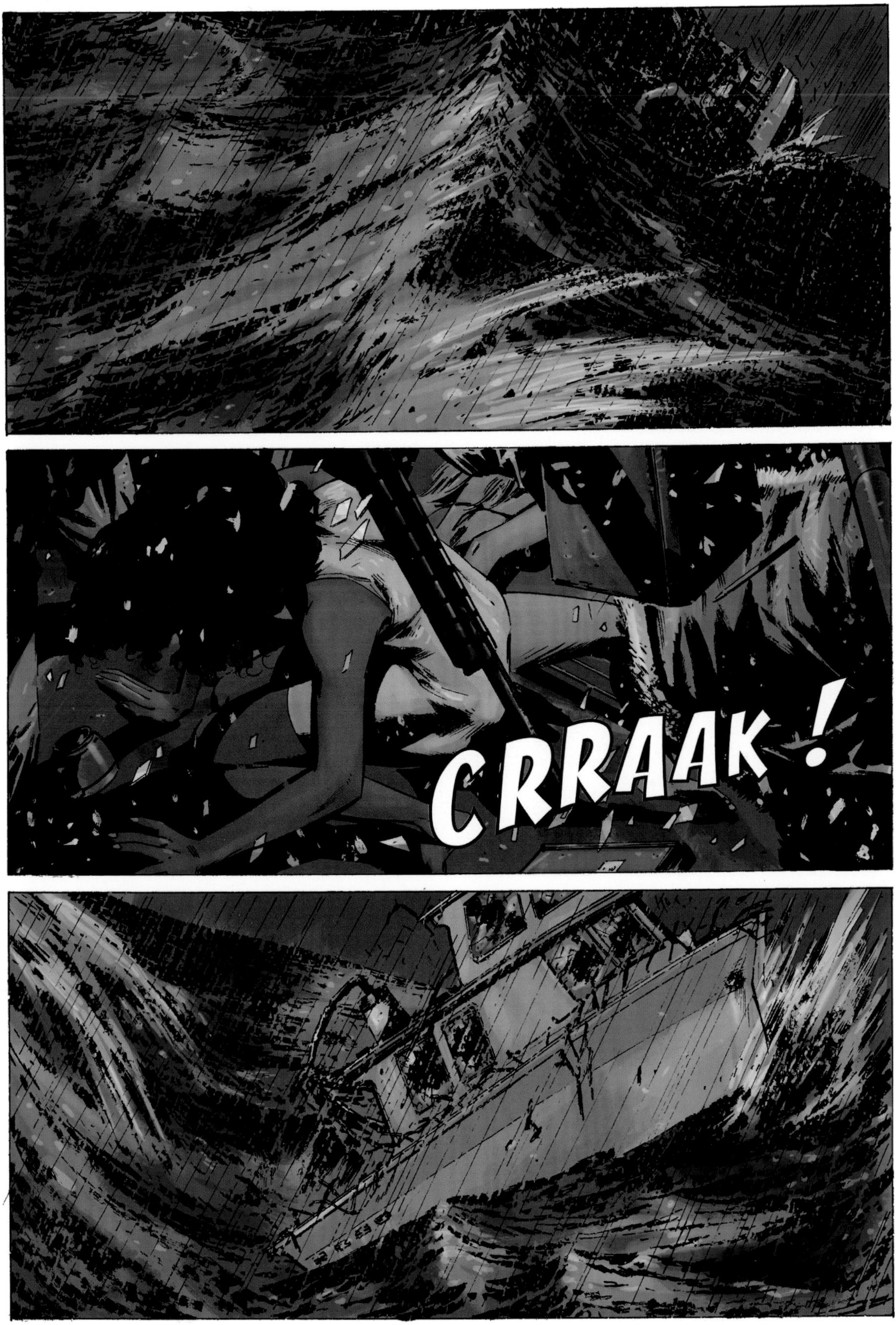
CRRAAK !

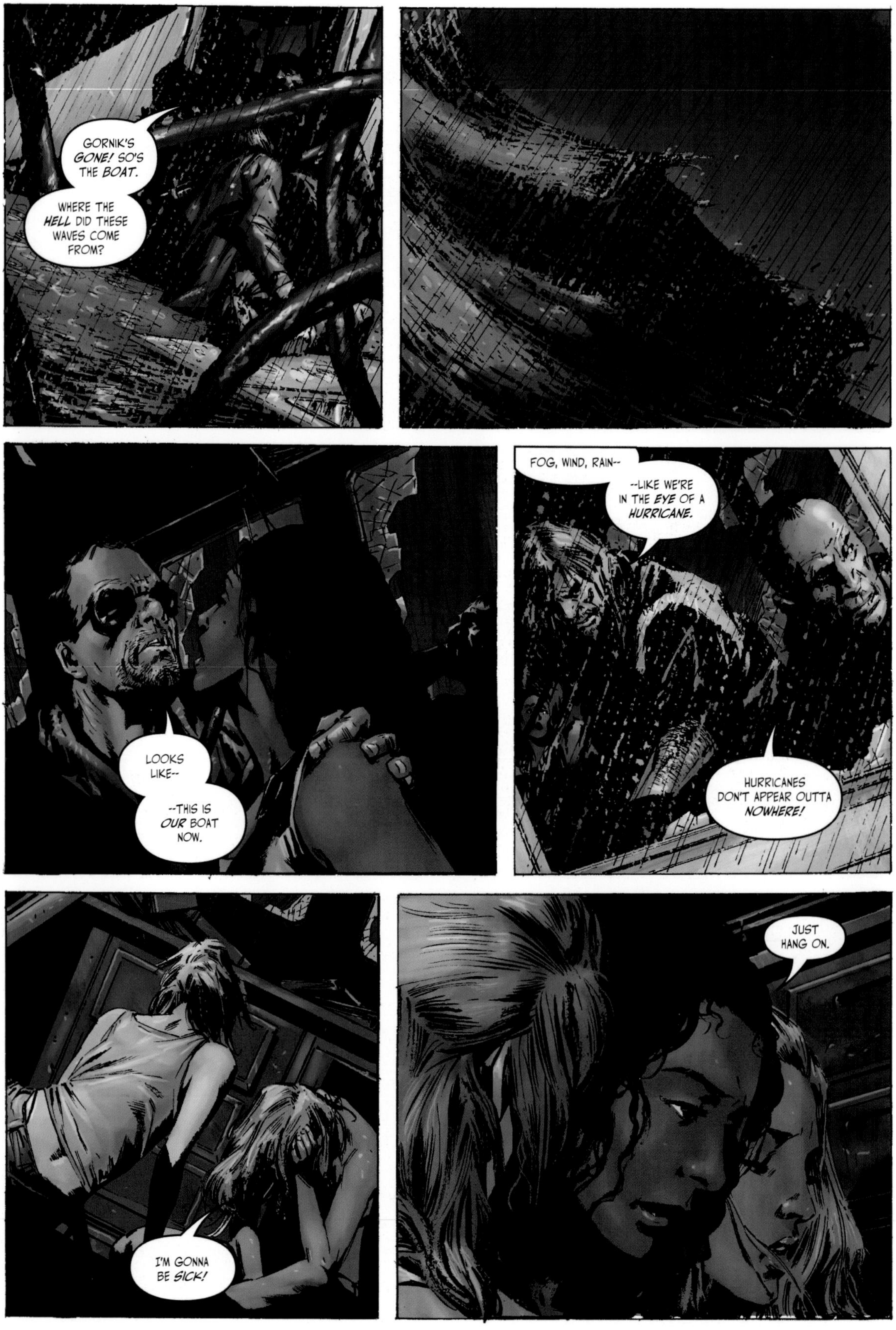
GORNIK'S GONE! SO'S THE BOAT.
WHERE THE HELL DID THESE WAVES COME FROM?
LOOKS LIKE--
--THIS IS OUR BOAT NOW.
FOG, WIND, RAIN--
--LIKE WE'RE IN THE EYE OF A HURRICANE.
HURRICANES DON'T APPEAR OUTTA NOWHERE!
I'M GONNA BE SICK!
JUST HANG ON.

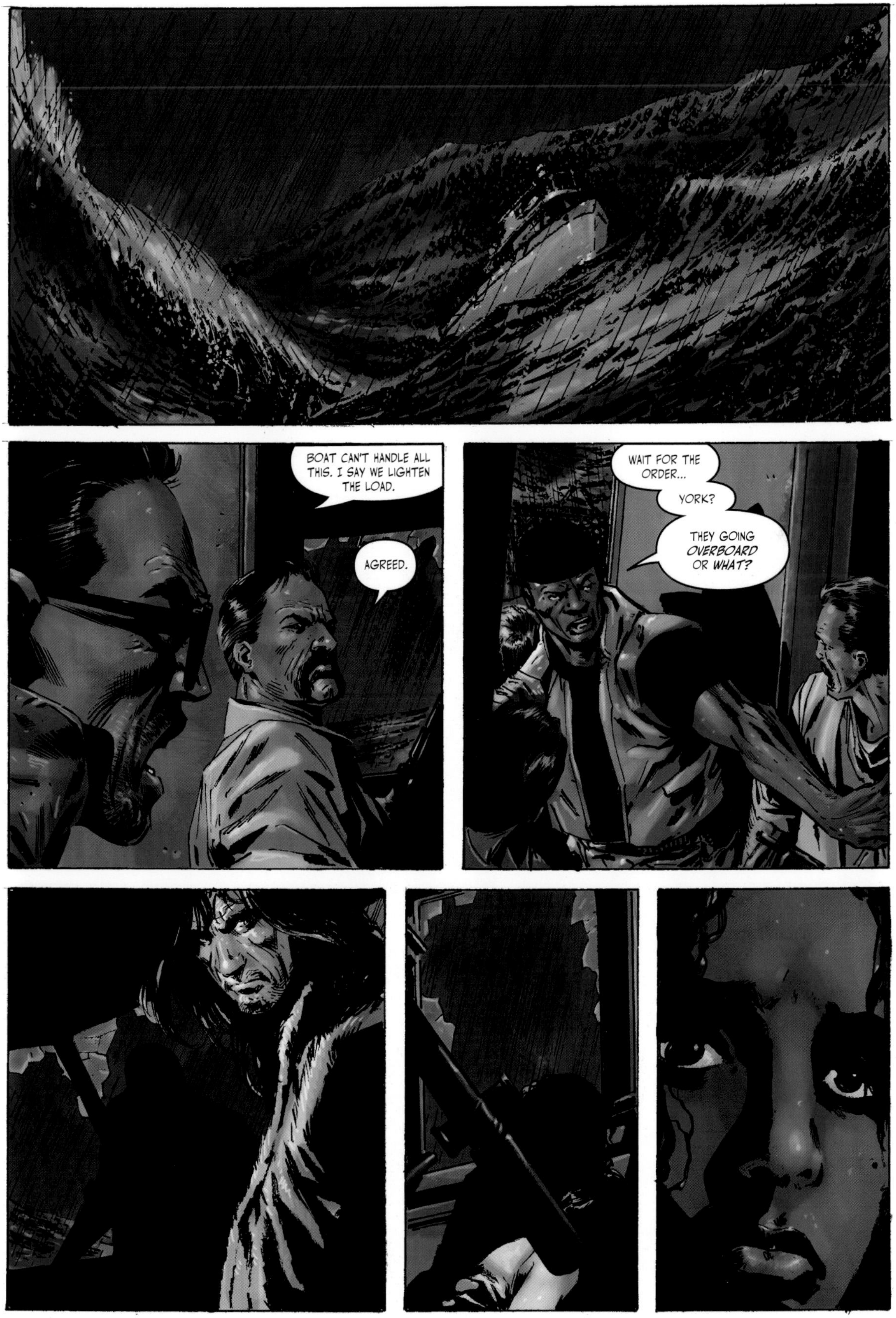
BOAT CAN'T HANDLE ALL THIS. I SAY WE LIGHTEN THE LOAD.
AGREED.
WAIT FOR THE ORDER...
YORK?
THEY GOING *OVERBOARD* OR *WHAT?*

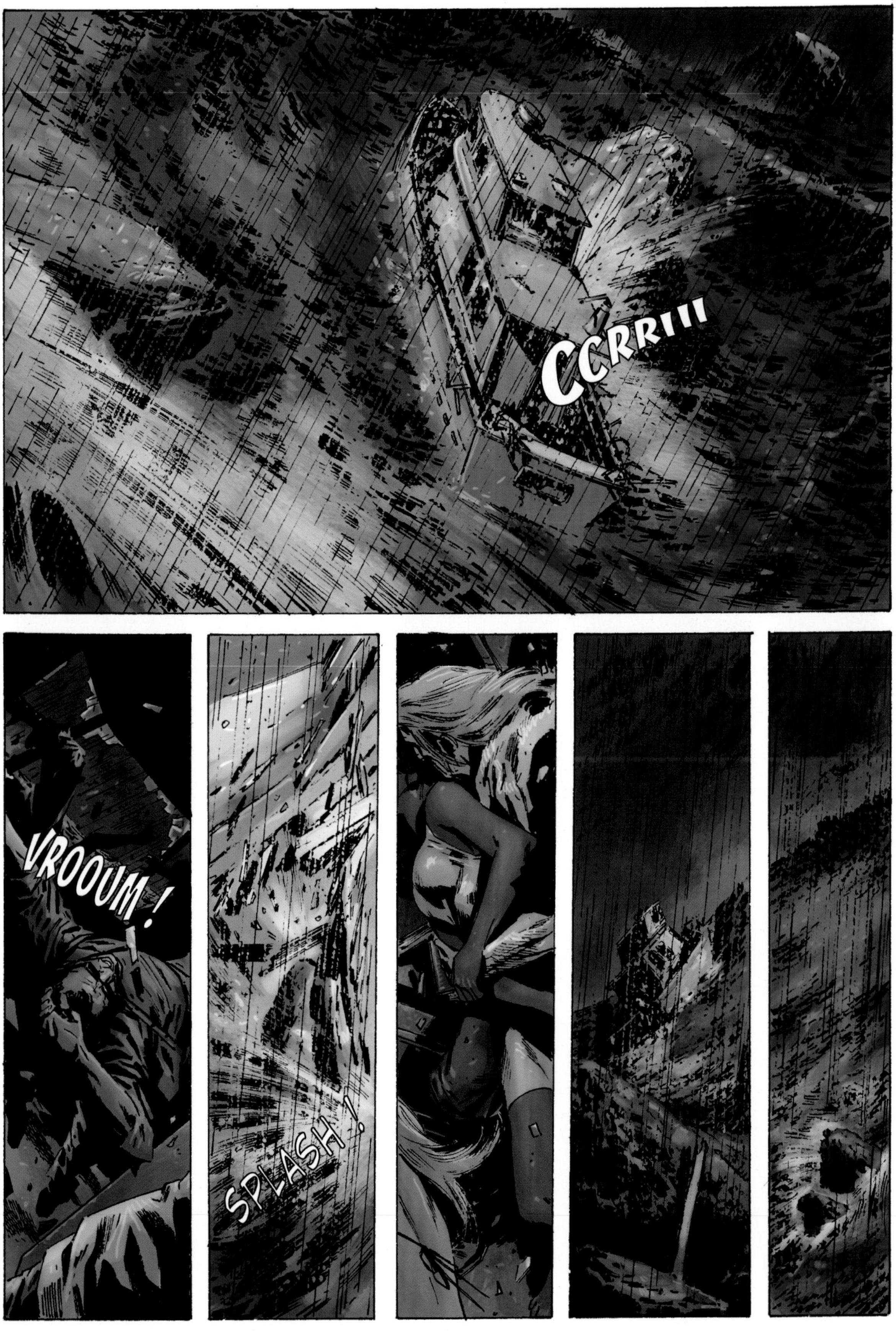
CCRRIII
VROOUM !
SPLASH !

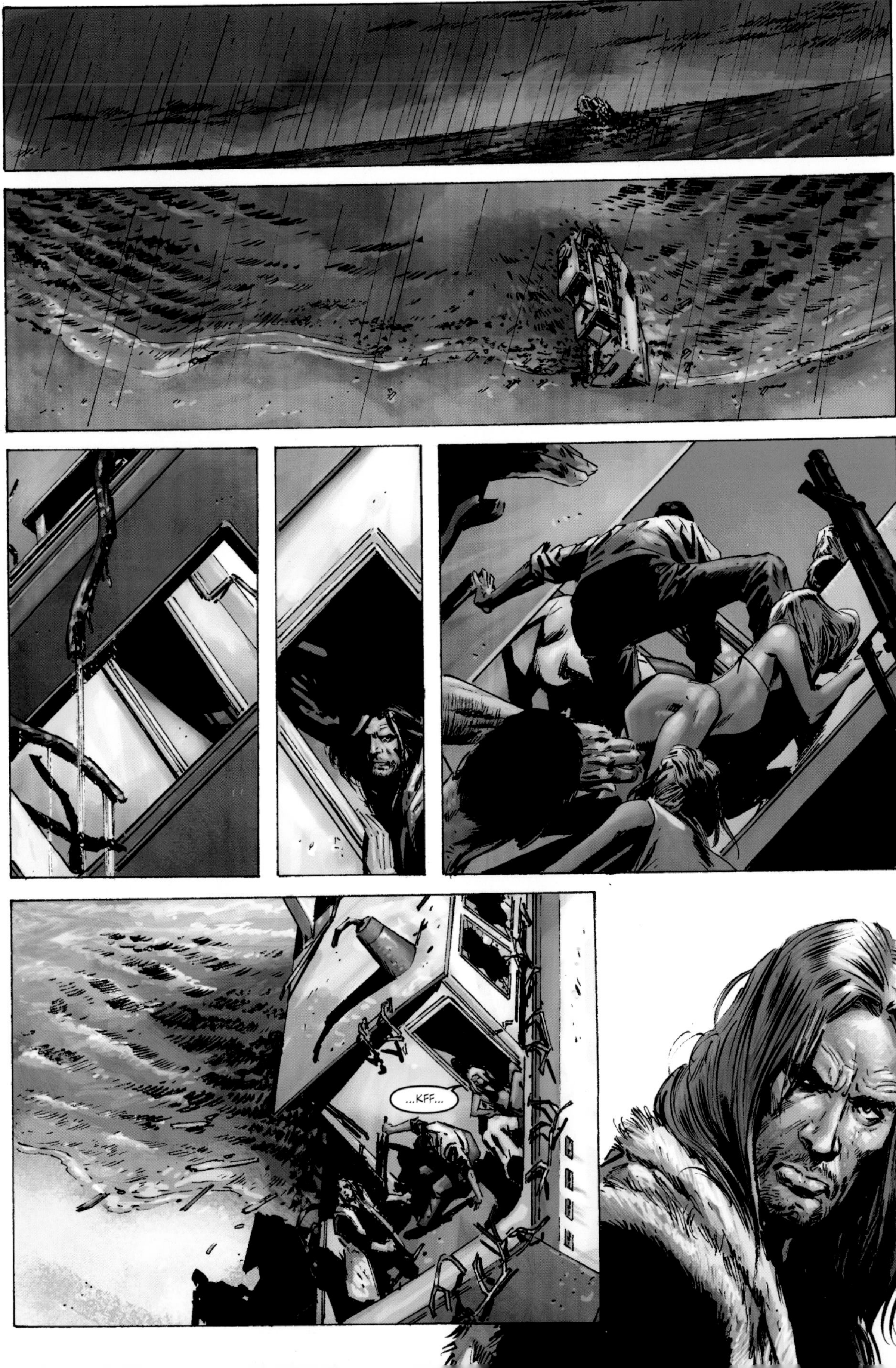
...KFF...

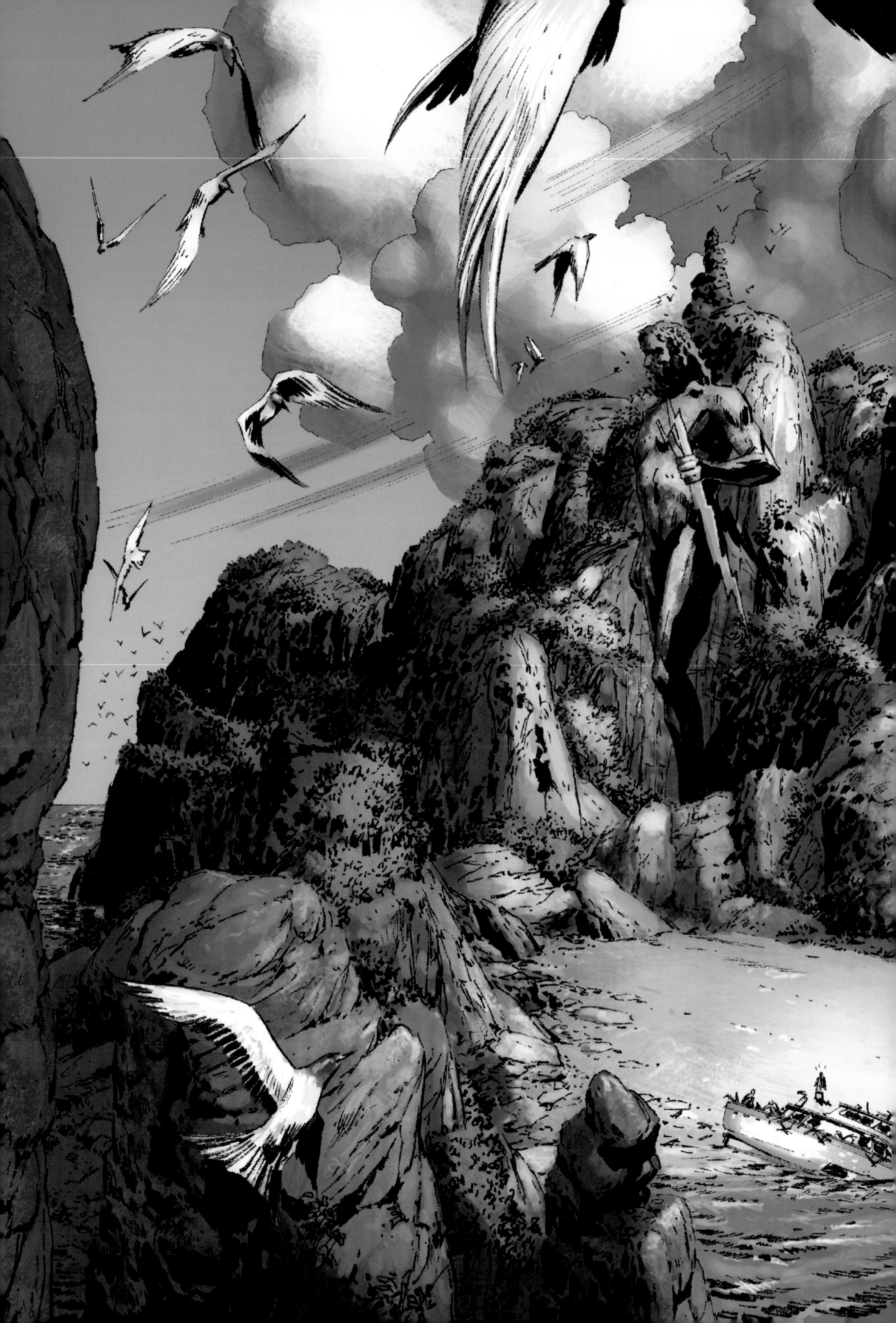

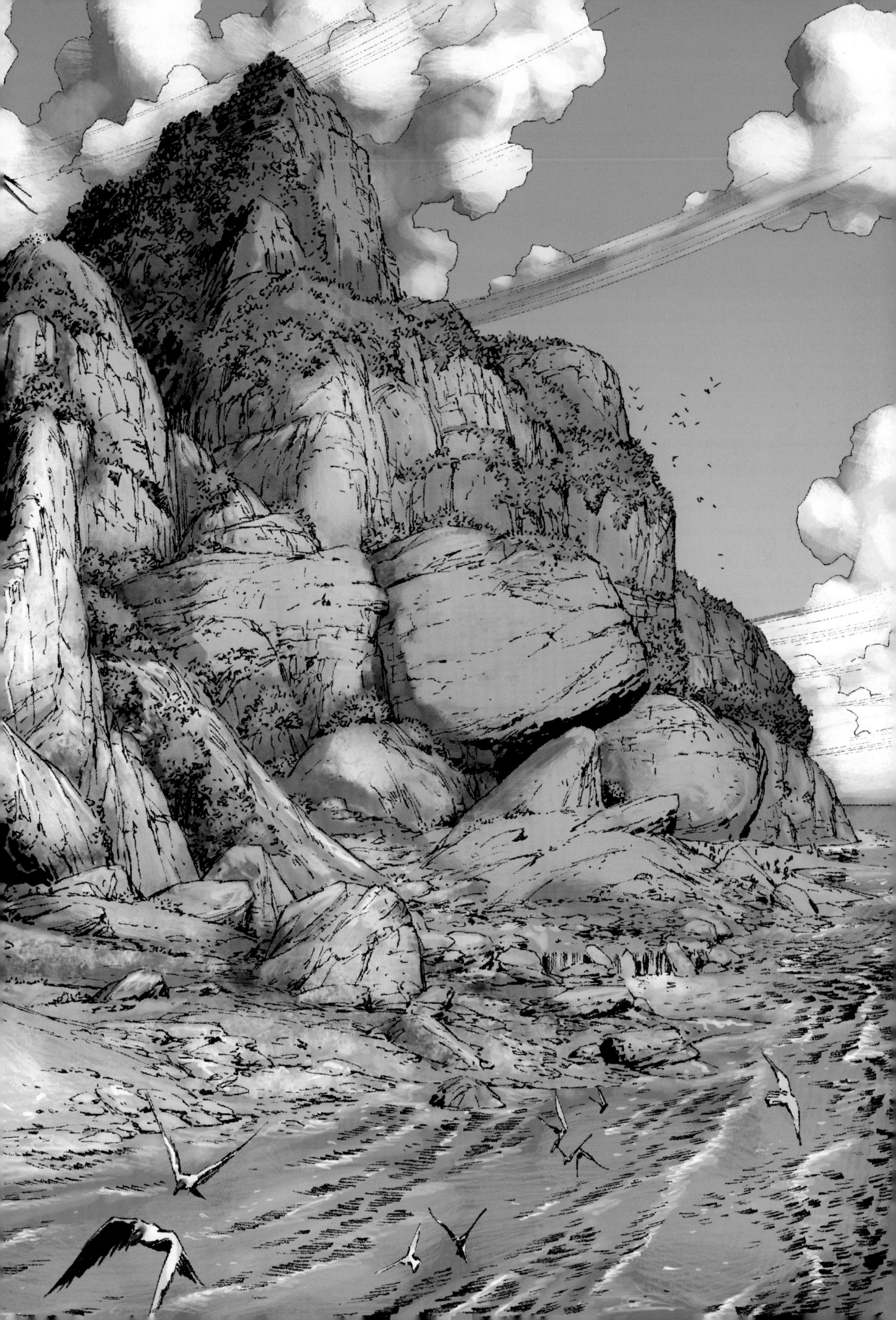

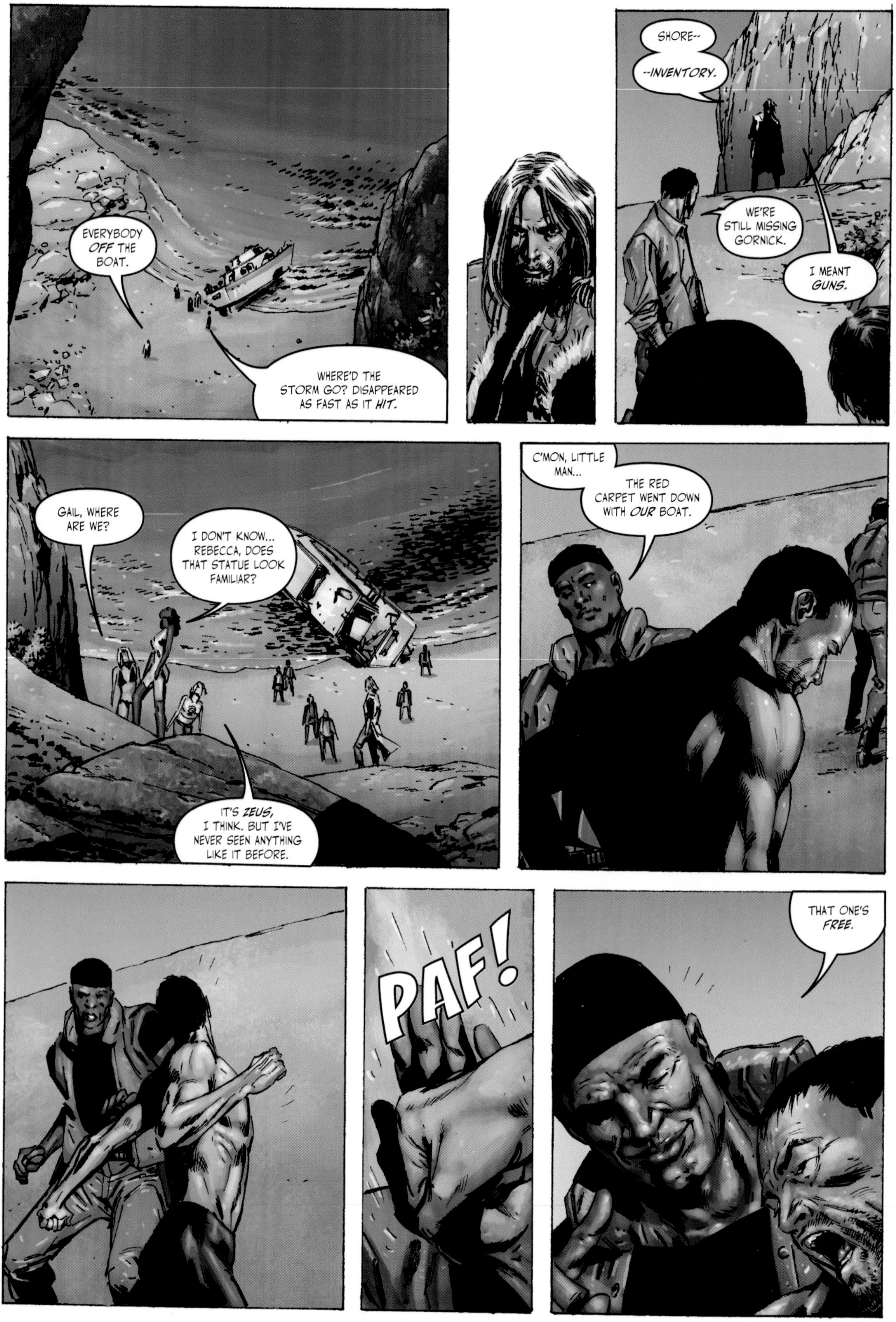
EVERYBODY OFF THE BOAT.
WHERE'D THE STORM GO? DISAPPEARED AS FAST AS IT HIT.
SHORE--
--INVENTORY.
WE'RE STILL MISSING GORNICK.
I MEANT GUNS.
GAIL, WHERE ARE WE?
I DON'T KNOW... REBECCA, DOES THAT STATUE LOOK FAMILIAR?
IT'S ZEUS, I THINK. BUT I'VE NEVER SEEN ANYTHING LIKE IT BEFORE.
C'MON, LITTLE MAN...
THE RED CARPET WENT DOWN WITH OUR BOAT.
PAF!
THAT ONE'S FREE.

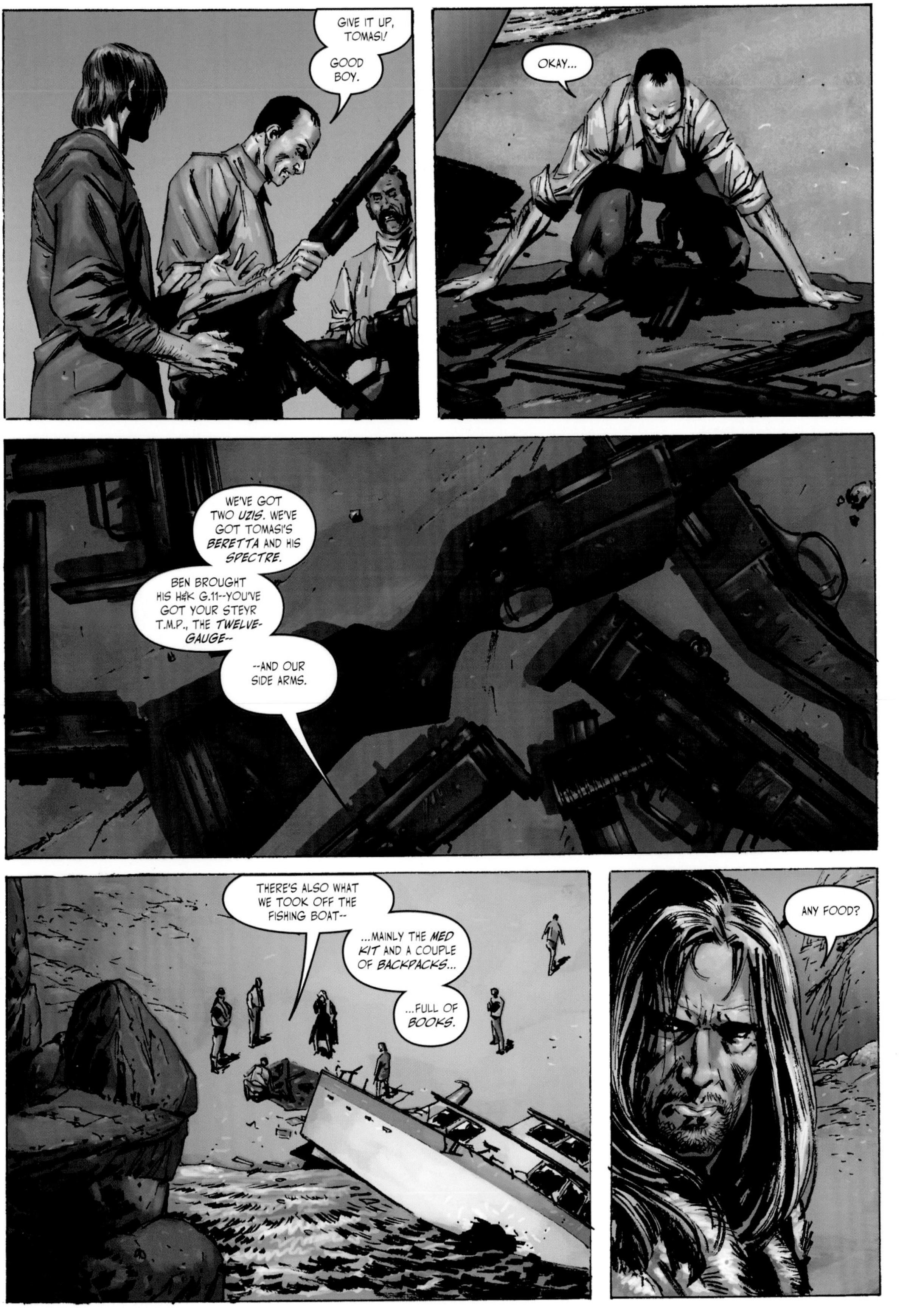
GIVE IT UP, TOMASI!
GOOD BOY.
OKAY...
WE'VE GOT TWO *UZIS*. WE'VE GOT TOMASI'S *BERETTA* AND HIS *SPECTRE*.
BEN BROUGHT HIS H&K G.11--YOU'VE GOT YOUR STEYR T.M.P., THE *TWELVE-GAUGE*--
--AND OUR SIDE ARMS.
THERE'S ALSO WHAT WE TOOK OFF THE FISHING BOAT--
...MAINLY THE *MED KIT* AND A COUPLE OF *BACKPACKS*...
...FULL OF *BOOKS*.
ANY FOOD?

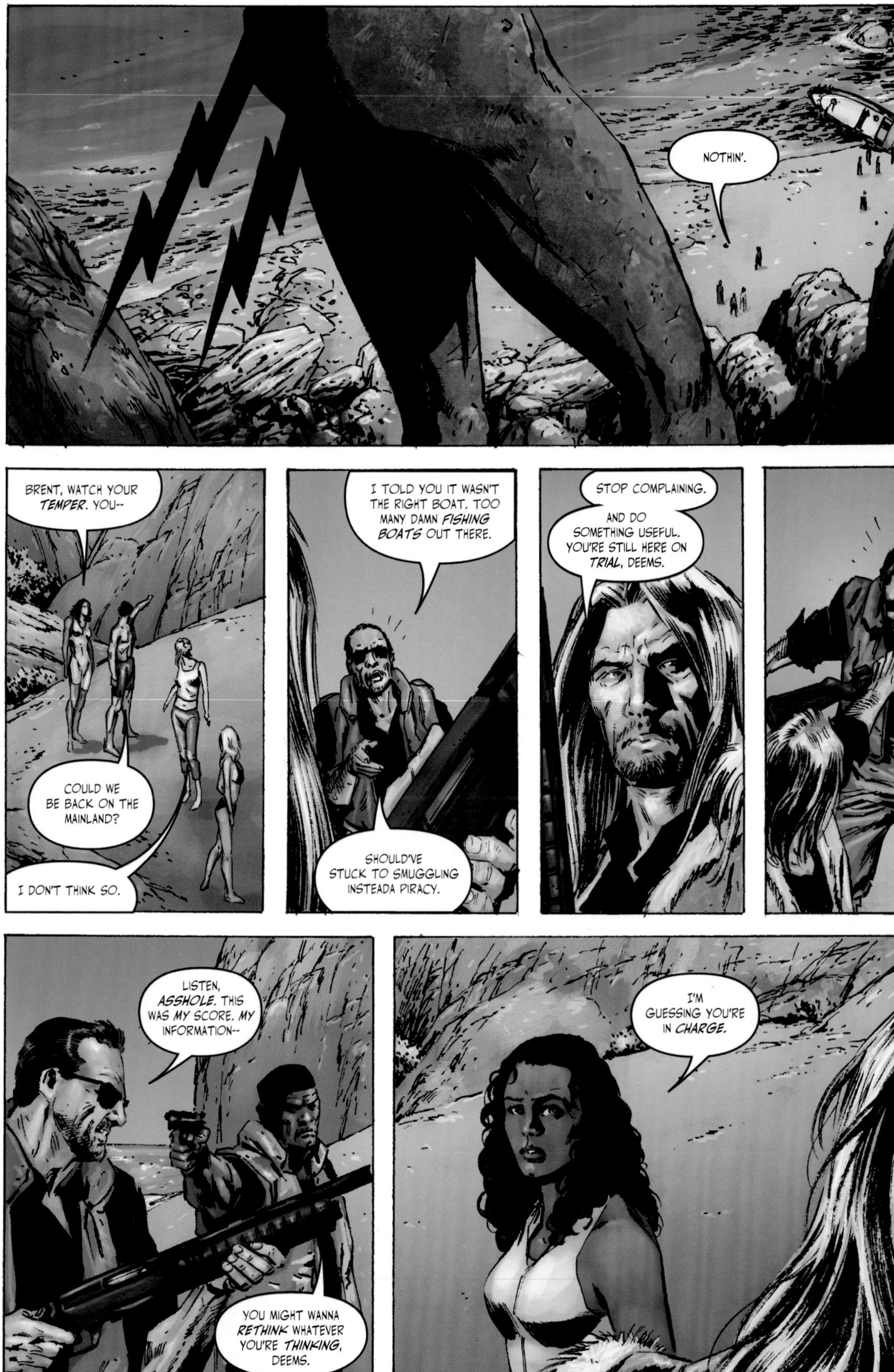
NOTHIN'.
BRENT, WATCH YOUR *TEMPER*. YOU--
COULD WE BE BACK ON THE MAINLAND?
I DON'T THINK SO.
I TOLD YOU IT WASN'T THE RIGHT BOAT. TOO MANY DAMN *FISHING BOATS* OUT THERE.
SHOULD'VE STUCK TO SMUGGLING INSTEADA PIRACY.
STOP COMPLAINING.
AND DO SOMETHING USEFUL. YOU'RE STILL HERE ON *TRIAL*, DEEMS.
LISTEN, *ASSHOLE*. THIS WAS *MY* SCORE. *MY* INFORMATION--
YOU MIGHT WANNA *RETHINK* WHATEVER YOU'RE *THINKING*, DEEMS.
I'M GUESSING YOU'RE IN *CHARGE*.

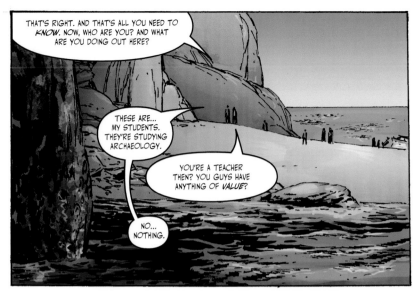

THAT'S RIGHT. AND THAT'S ALL YOU NEED TO *KNOW*. NOW, WHO ARE YOU? AND WHAT ARE YOU DOING OUT HERE?

THESE ARE... MY STUDENTS. THEY'RE STUDYING ARCHAEOLOGY.

YOU'RE A TEACHER THEN? YOU GUYS HAVE ANYTHING OF *VALUE*?

NO... NOTHING.

HEY...

WHAT'S THIS?

CAREFUL, THAT'S *PRICELESS!*

DOESN'T LOOK IT--

--BUT I TRUST YA.

NICE JOB, *GENIUS.*

NOTHING OF *VALUE*, HUH?

PLEASE... THEY'RE JUST A BUNCH OF KIDS.

HEY--

--I SEE SOMEONE ON THE SHORE!

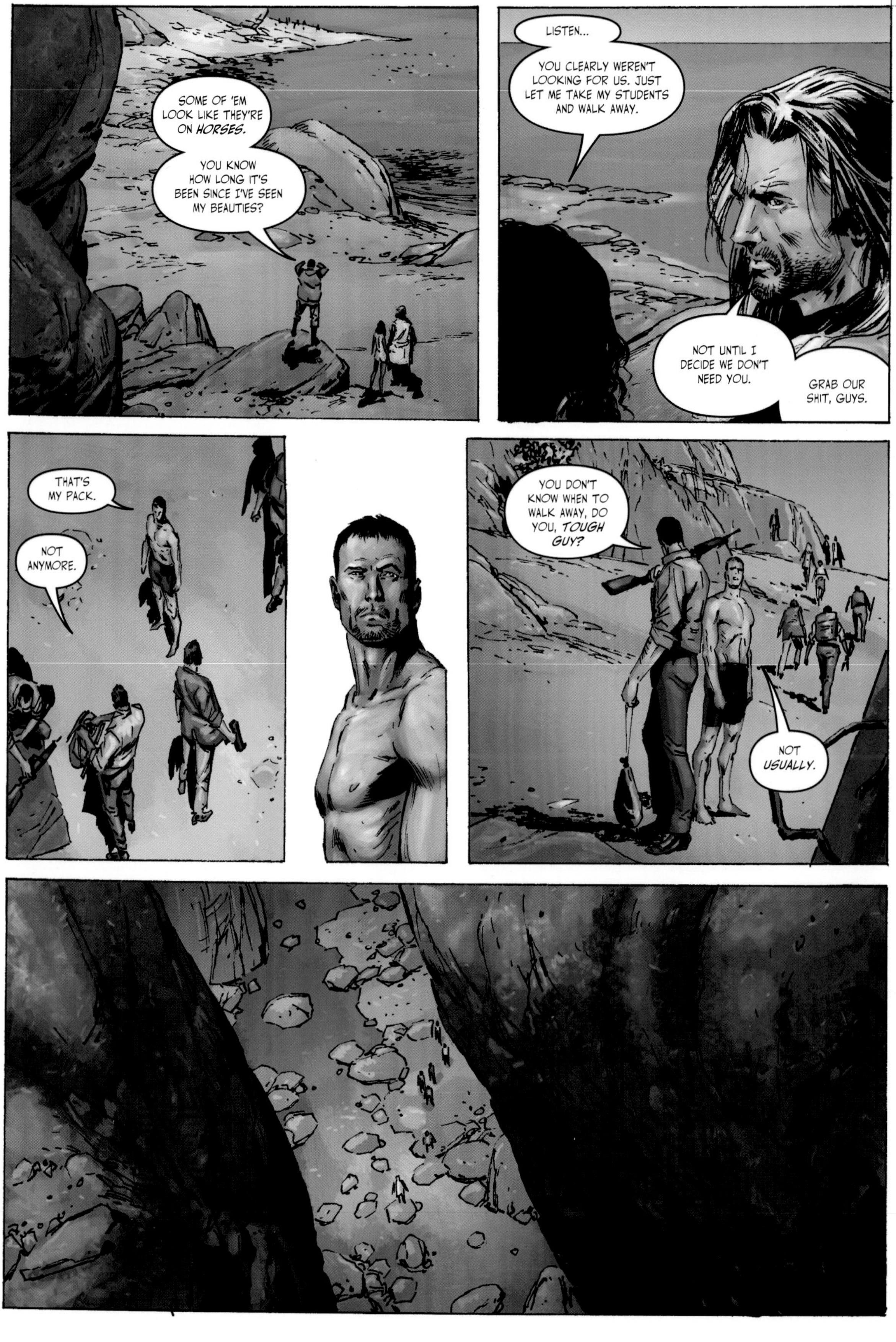
SOME OF 'EM LOOK LIKE THEY'RE ON *HORSES.*
YOU KNOW HOW LONG IT'S BEEN SINCE I'VE SEEN MY BEAUTIES?
LISTEN...
YOU CLEARLY WEREN'T LOOKING FOR US. JUST LET ME TAKE MY STUDENTS AND WALK AWAY.
NOT UNTIL I DECIDE WE DON'T NEED YOU.
GRAB OUR SHIT, GUYS.
THAT'S MY PACK.
NOT ANYMORE.
YOU DON'T KNOW WHEN TO WALK AWAY, DO YOU, *TOUGH GUY?*
NOT *USUALLY.*

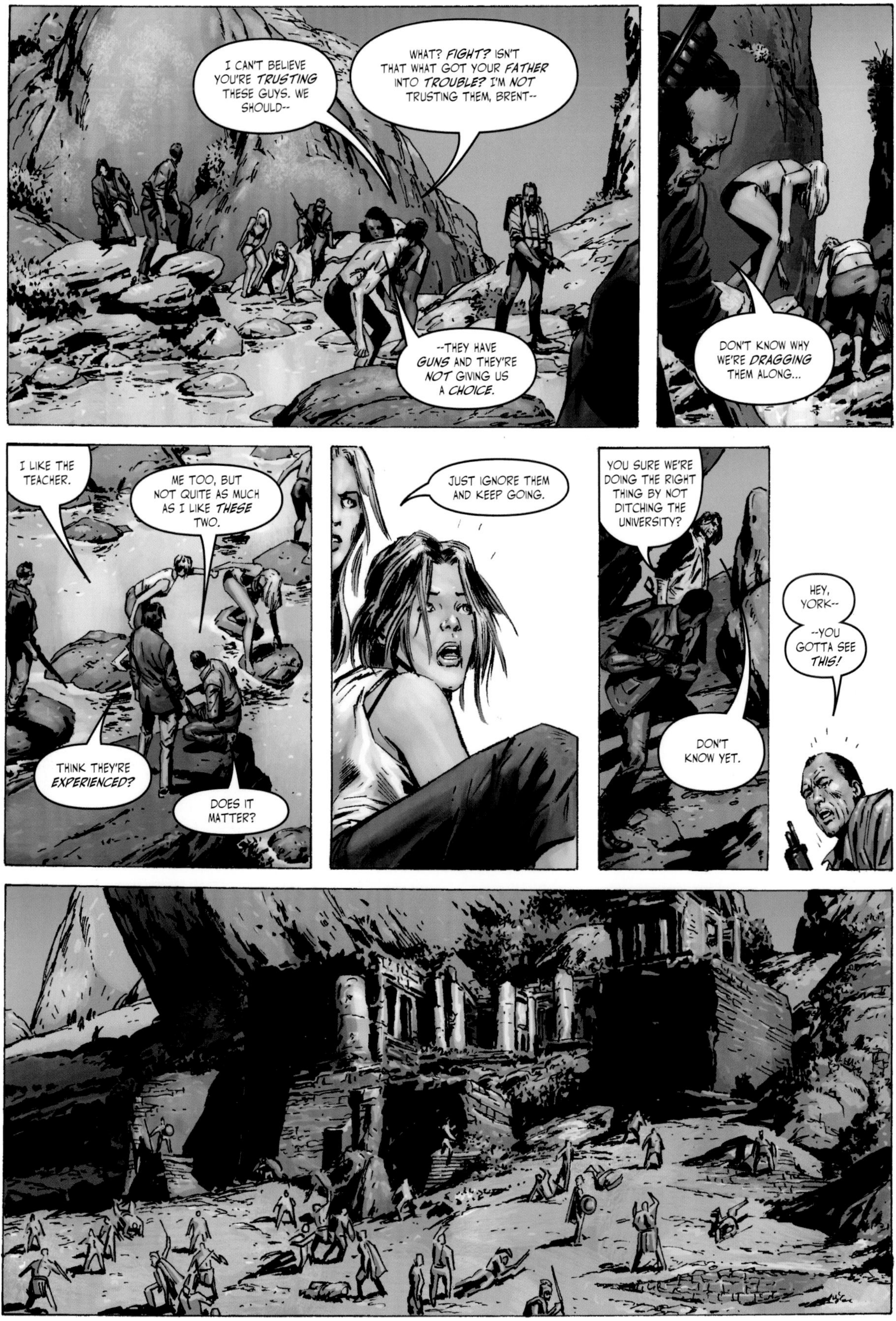
I CAN'T BELIEVE YOU'RE TRUSTING THESE GUYS. WE SHOULD--
WHAT? FIGHT? ISN'T THAT WHAT GOT YOUR FATHER INTO TROUBLE? I'M NOT TRUSTING THEM, BRENT--
--THEY HAVE GUNS AND THEY'RE NOT GIVING US A CHOICE.
DON'T KNOW WHY WE'RE DRAGGING THEM ALONG...
I LIKE THE TEACHER.
ME TOO, BUT NOT QUITE AS MUCH AS I LIKE THESE TWO.
THINK THEY'RE EXPERIENCED?
DOES IT MATTER?
JUST IGNORE THEM AND KEEP GOING.
YOU SURE WE'RE DOING THE RIGHT THING BY NOT DITCHING THE UNIVERSITY?
DON'T KNOW YET.
HEY, YORK--
--YOU GOTTA SEE THIS!

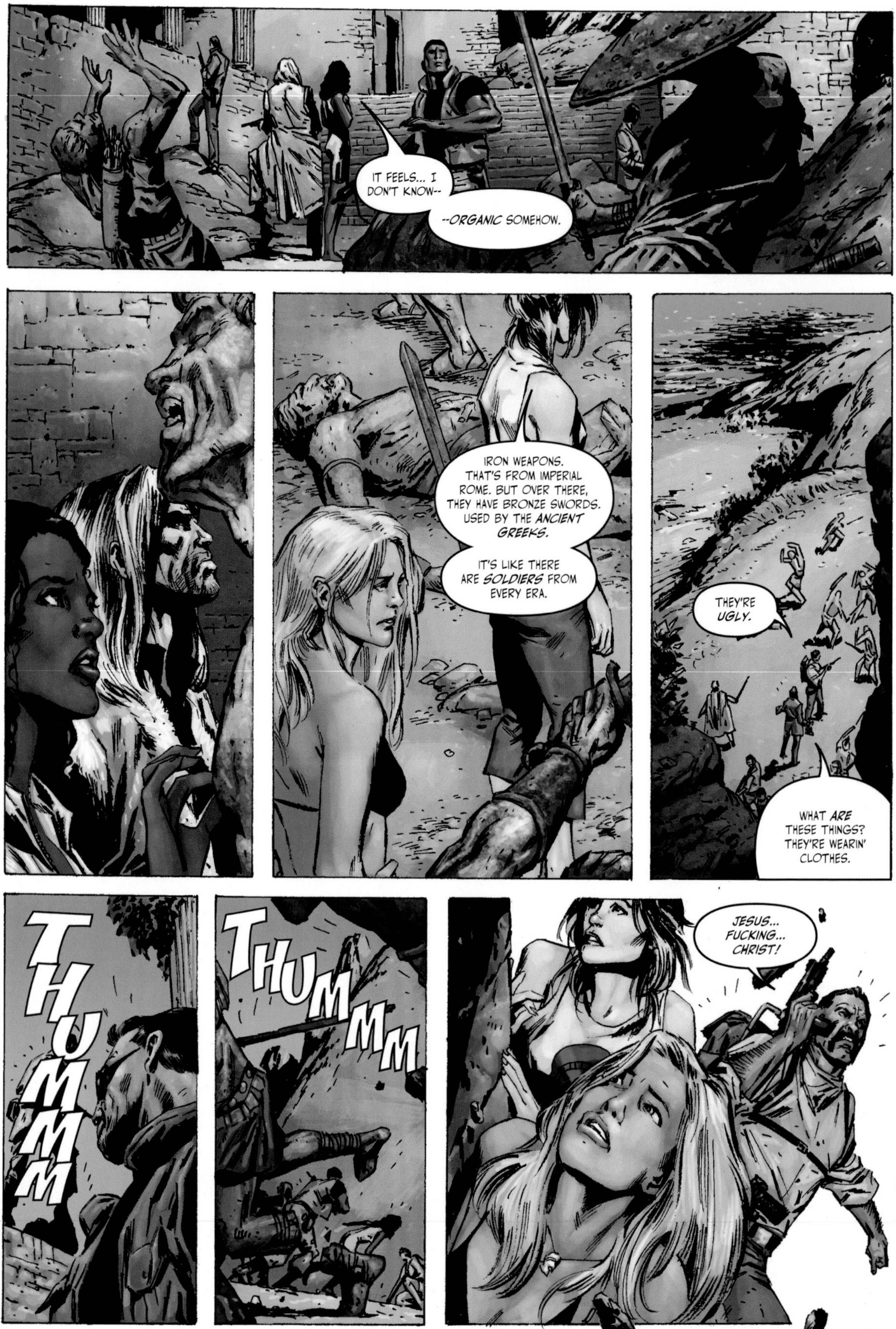
IT FEELS... I DON'T KNOW--
--ORGANIC SOMEHOW.
IRON WEAPONS. THAT'S FROM IMPERIAL ROME. BUT OVER THERE, THEY HAVE BRONZE SWORDS. USED BY THE ANCIENT GREEKS.
IT'S LIKE THERE ARE SOLDIERS FROM EVERY ERA.
THEY'RE UGLY.
WHAT ARE THESE THINGS? THEY'RE WEARIN' CLOTHES.
THUMMM
THUMMMM
JESUS... FUCKING... CHRIST!

RROOOAA!

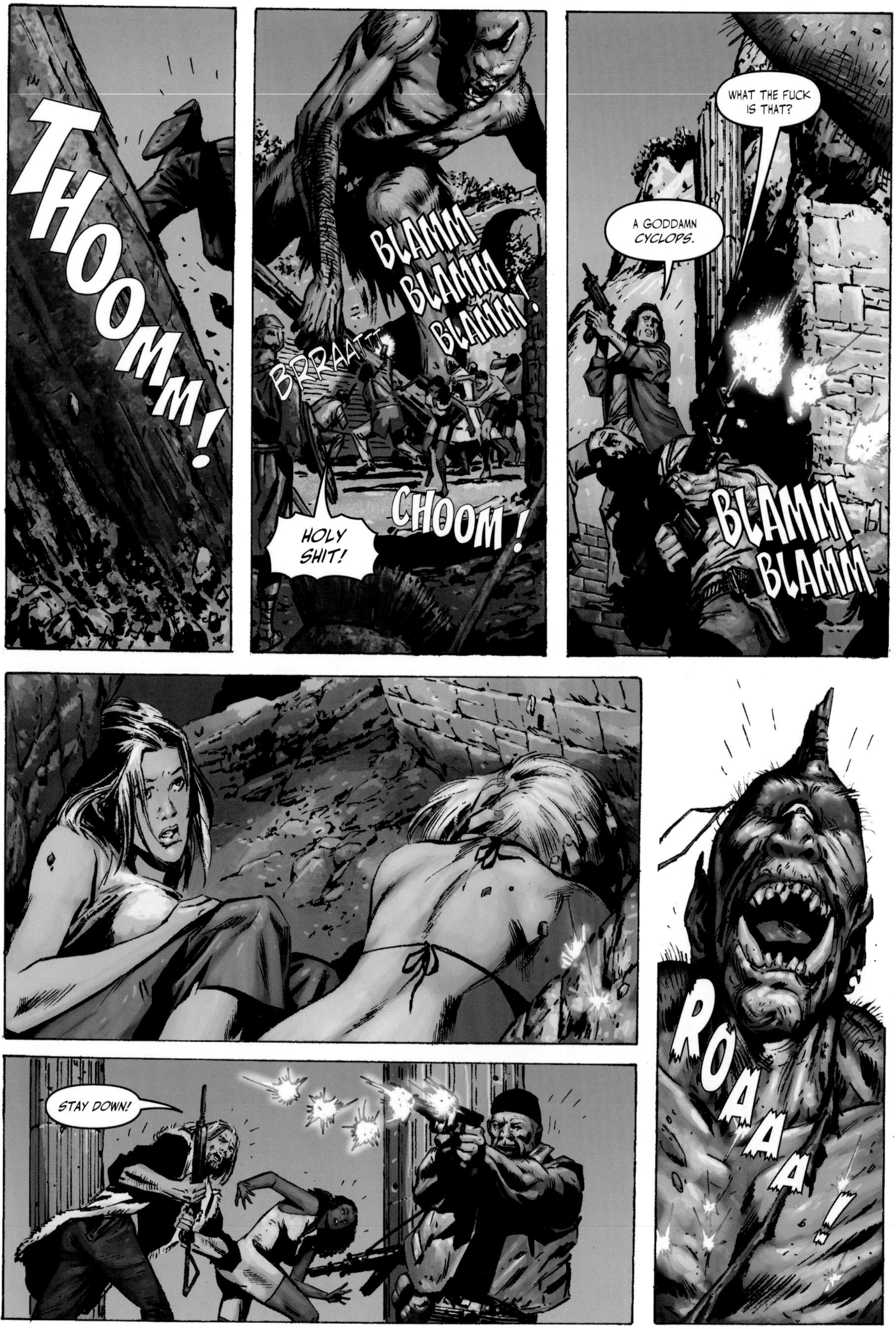
THOOMM!
BLAMM BLAMM BLAMM!
BRRAATT
HOLY SHIT!
CHOOM!
WHAT THE FUCK IS THAT?
A GODDAMN CYCLOPS.
BLAMM BLAMM
STAY DOWN!
ROAAAA!

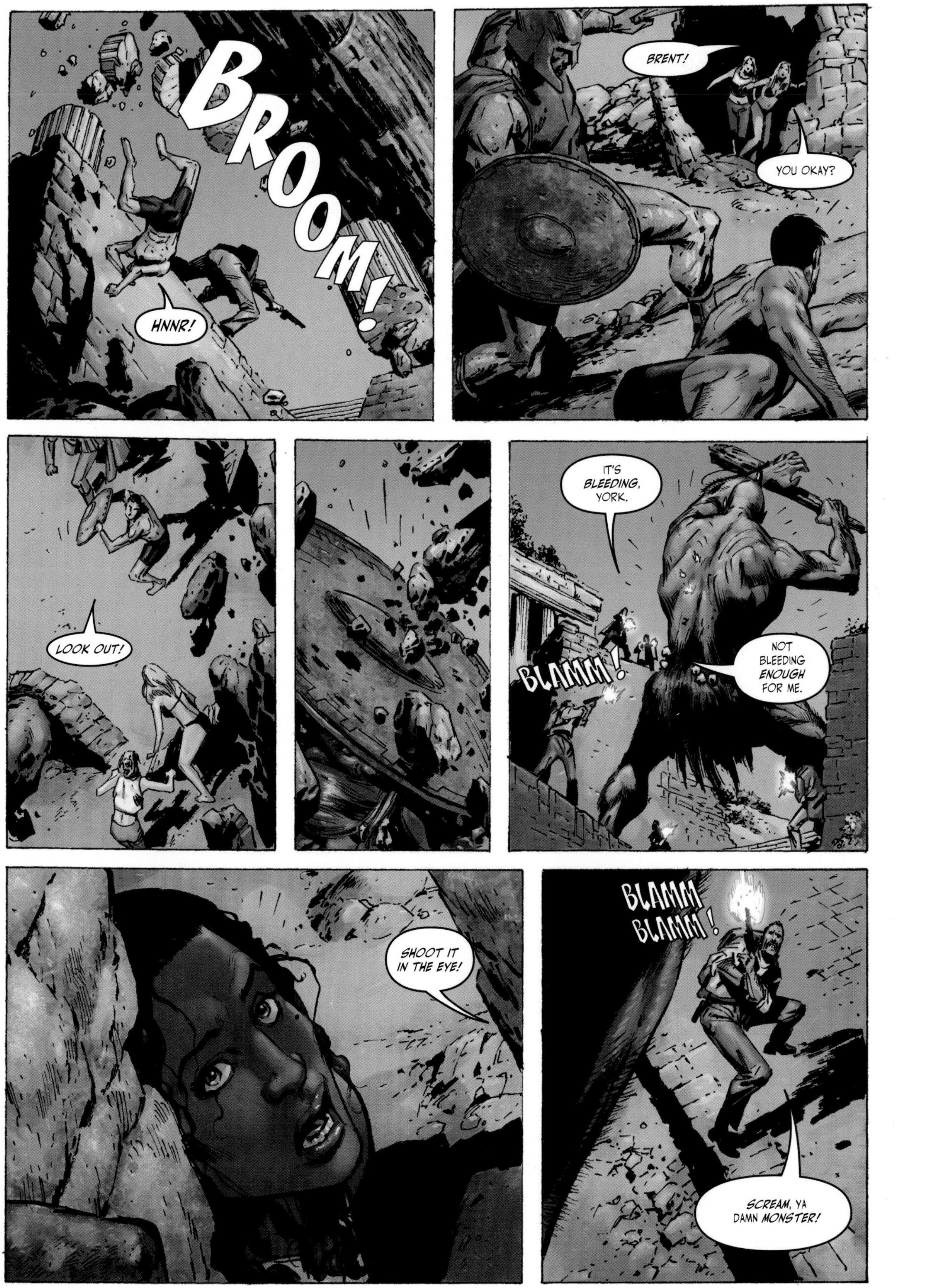
BROOM!
HNNR!
BRENT!
YOU OKAY?
LOOK OUT!
IT'S BLEEDING, YORK.
BLAMM!
NOT BLEEDING ENOUGH FOR ME.
SHOOT IT IN THE EYE!
BLAMM BLAMM!
SCREAM, YA DAMN MONSTER!

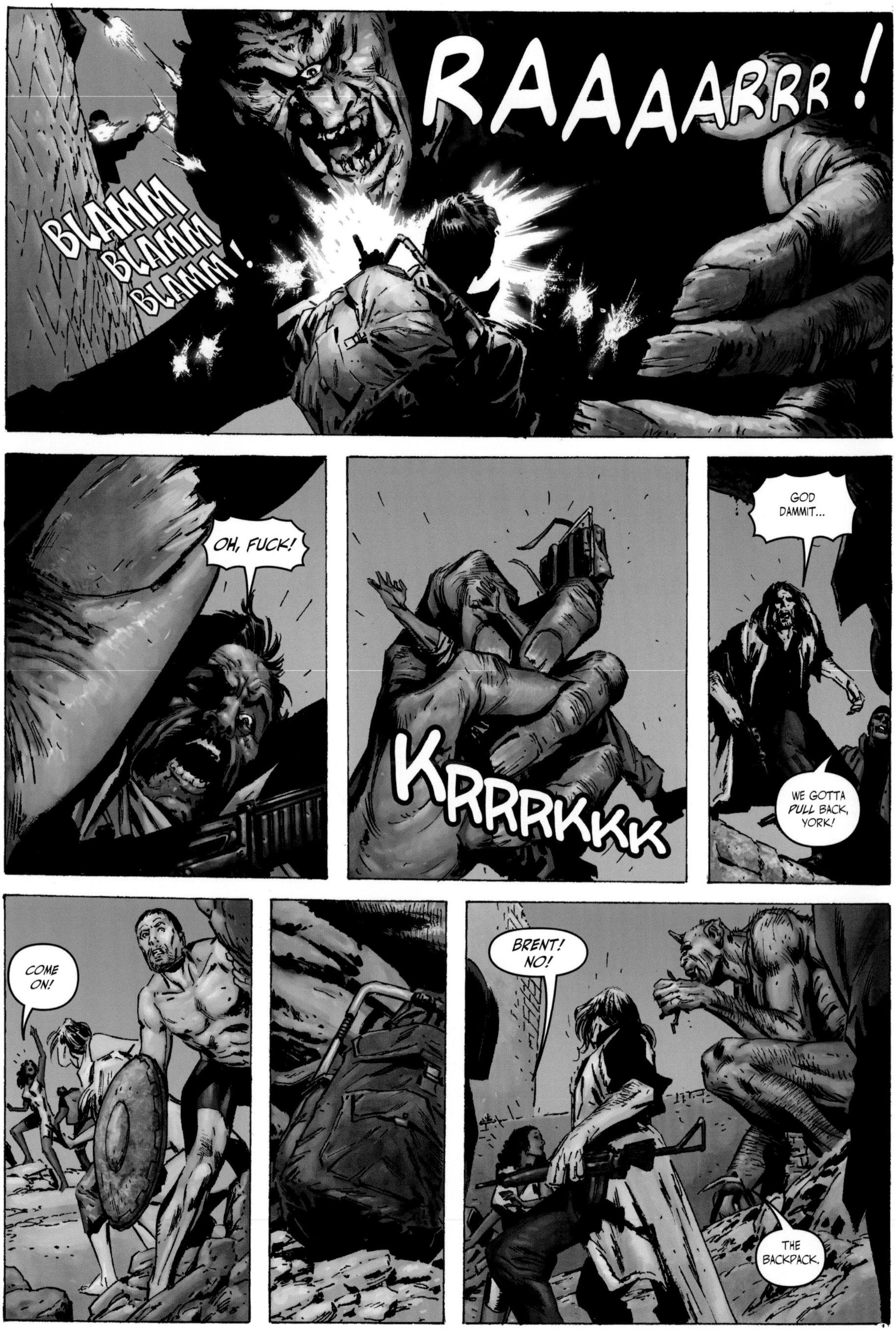
RAAAARRR!
BLAMM BLAMM BLAMM!
OH, FUCK!
KRRRKKK
GOD DAMMIT...
WE GOTTA PULL BACK, YORK!
COME ON!
BRENT! NO!
THE BACKPACK.

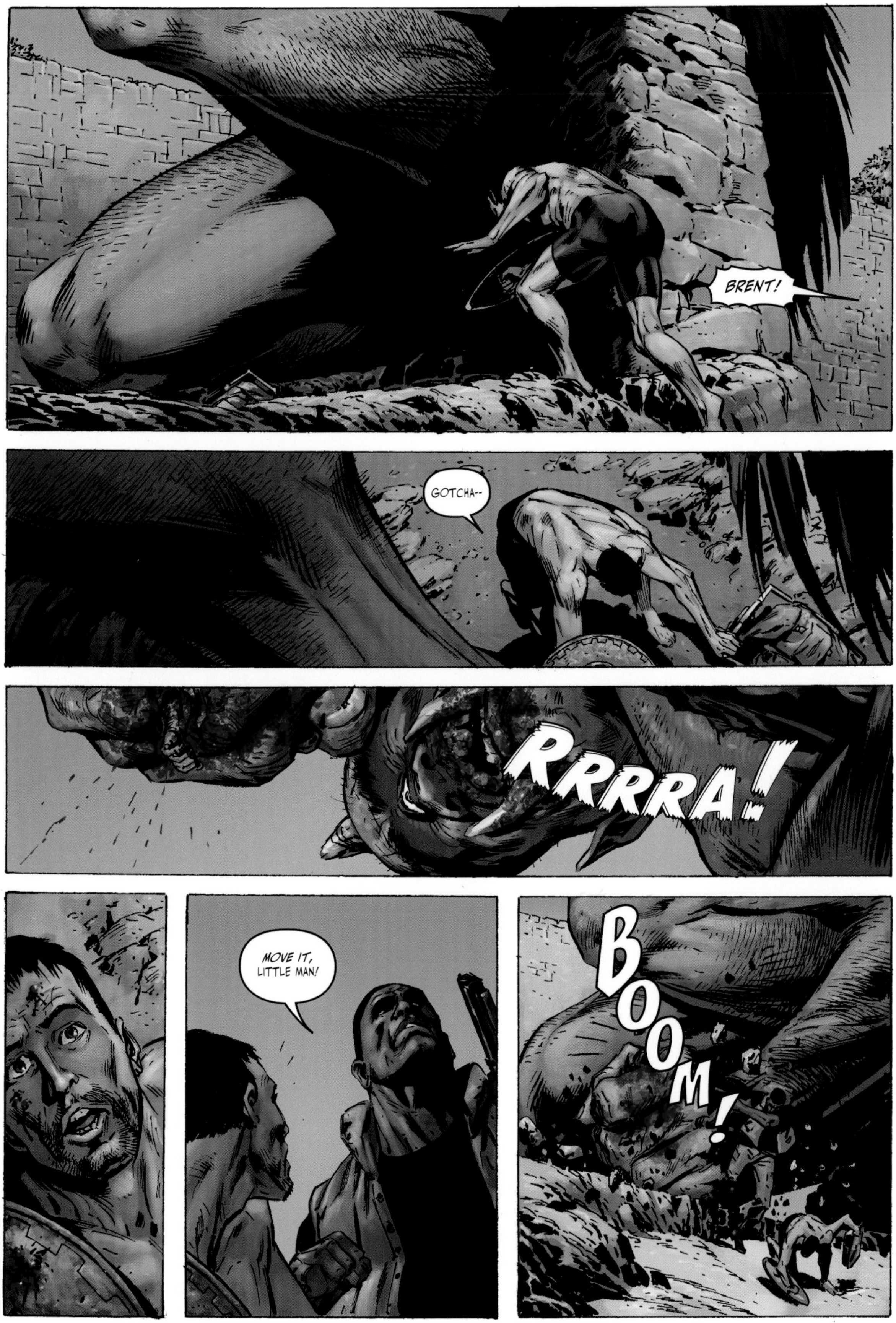
BRENT!
GOTCHA--
RRRRA!
MOVE IT, LITTLE MAN!
BOOM!

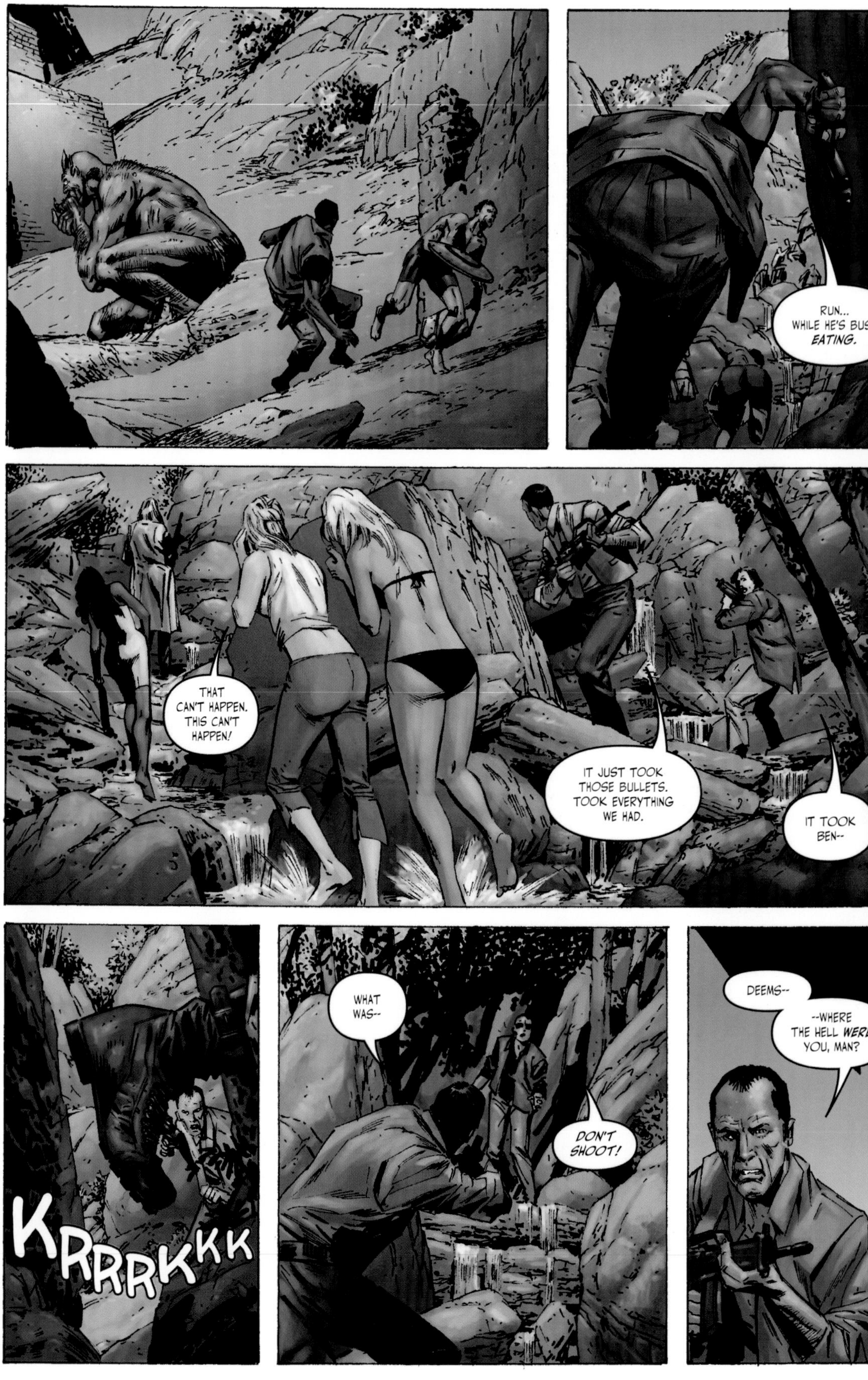
RUN...
WHILE HE'S BUSY
EATING.
THAT
CAN'T HAPPEN.
THIS CAN'T
HAPPEN!
IT JUST TOOK
THOSE BULLETS.
TOOK EVERYTHING
WE HAD.
IT TOOK
BEN--
KRRRKKK
WHAT
WAS--
*DON'T
SHOOT!*
DEEMS--
--WHERE
THE HELL *WERE*
YOU, MAN?

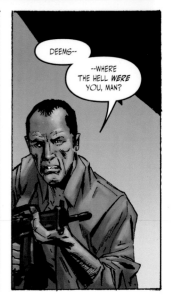

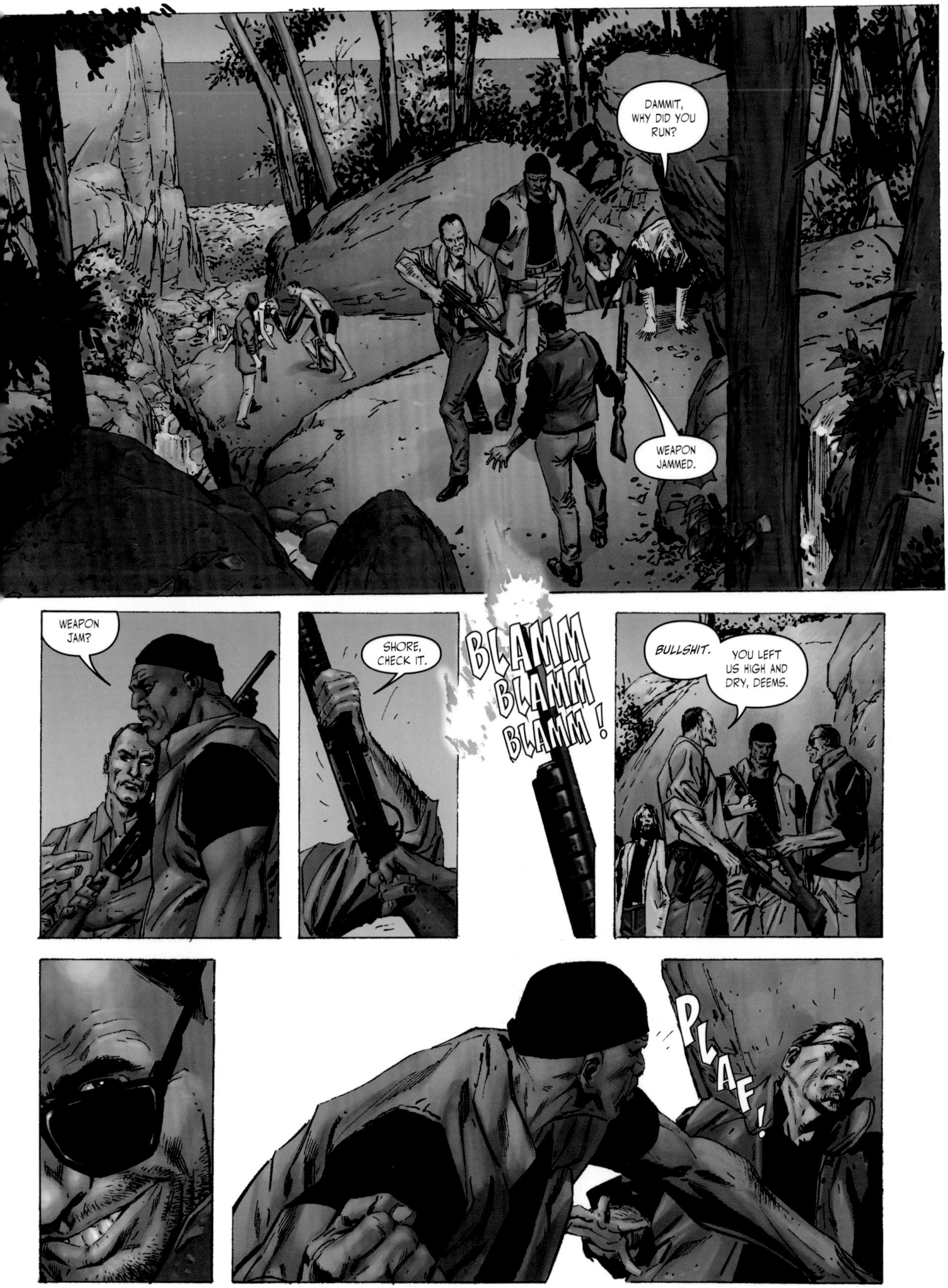
DAMMIT, WHY DID YOU RUN?
WEAPON JAMMED.
WEAPON JAM?
SHORE, CHECK IT.
BLAMM BLAMM BLAMM!
BULLSHIT.
YOU LEFT US HIGH AND DRY, DEEMS.
PLAF!

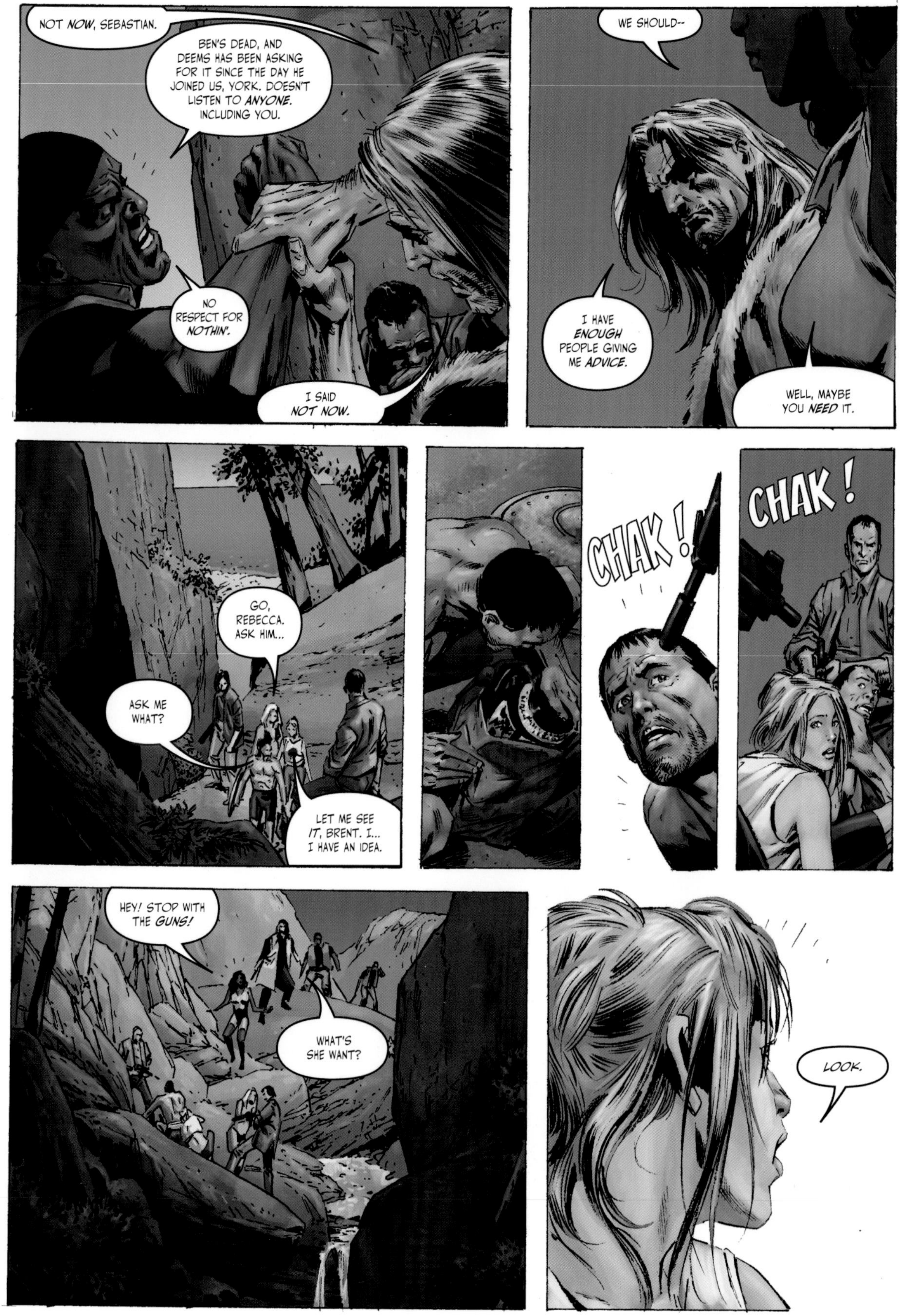

NOT NOW, SEBASTIAN.
BEN'S DEAD, AND DEEMS HAS BEEN ASKING FOR IT SINCE THE DAY HE JOINED US, YORK. DOESN'T LISTEN TO ANYONE. INCLUDING YOU.
NO RESPECT FOR NOTHIN'.
I SAID NOT NOW.
WE SHOULD--
I HAVE ENOUGH PEOPLE GIVING ME ADVICE.
WELL, MAYBE YOU NEED IT.
GO, REBECCA. ASK HIM...
ASK ME WHAT?
LET ME SEE IT, BRENT. I... I HAVE AN IDEA.
CHAK!
CHAK!
HEY! STOP WITH THE GUNS!
WHAT'S SHE WANT?
LOOK.

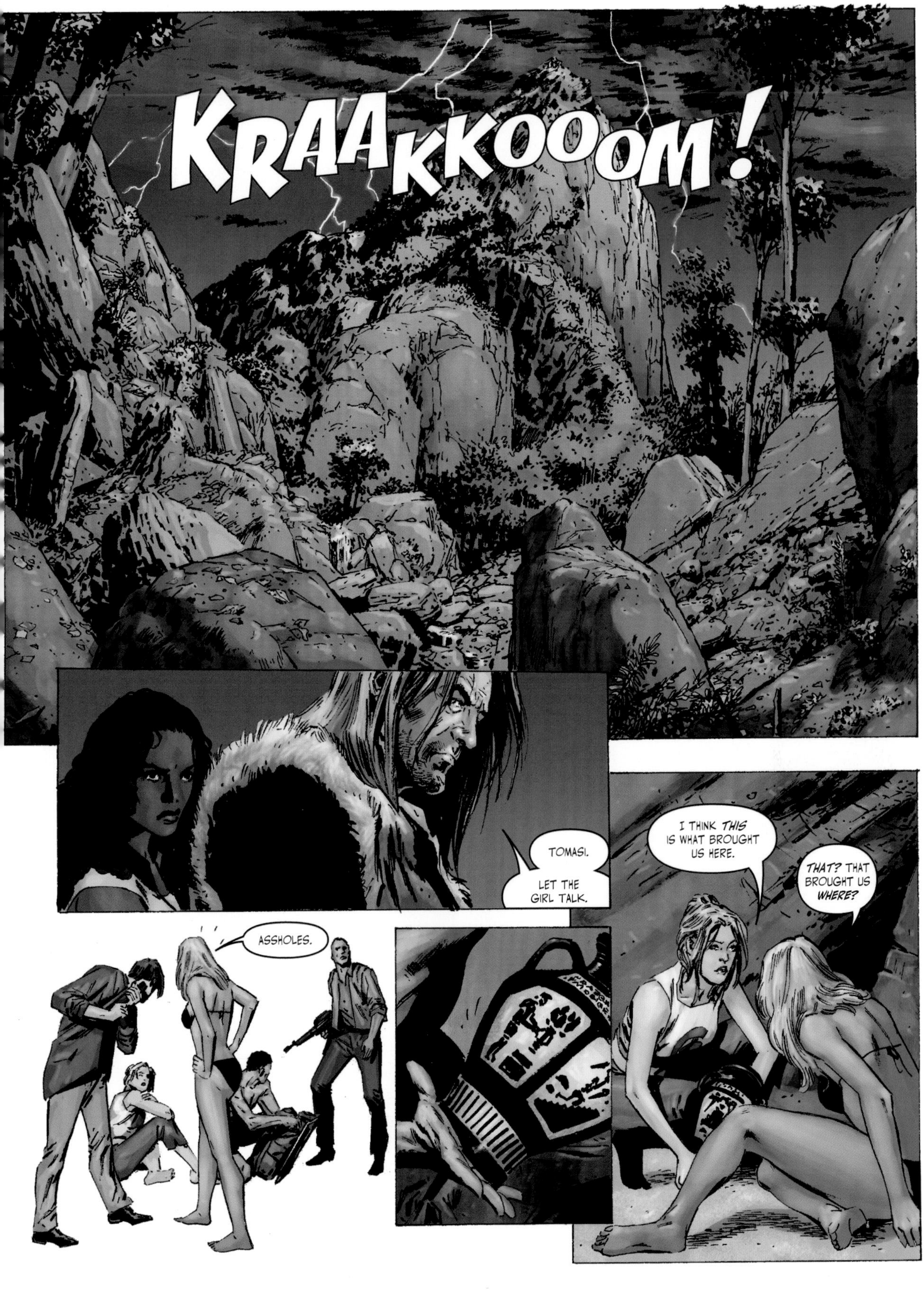
KRAAKKOOOM!
TOMASI.
LET THE GIRL TALK.
I THINK *THIS* IS WHAT BROUGHT US HERE.
THAT? THAT BROUGHT US *WHERE?*
ASSHOLES.

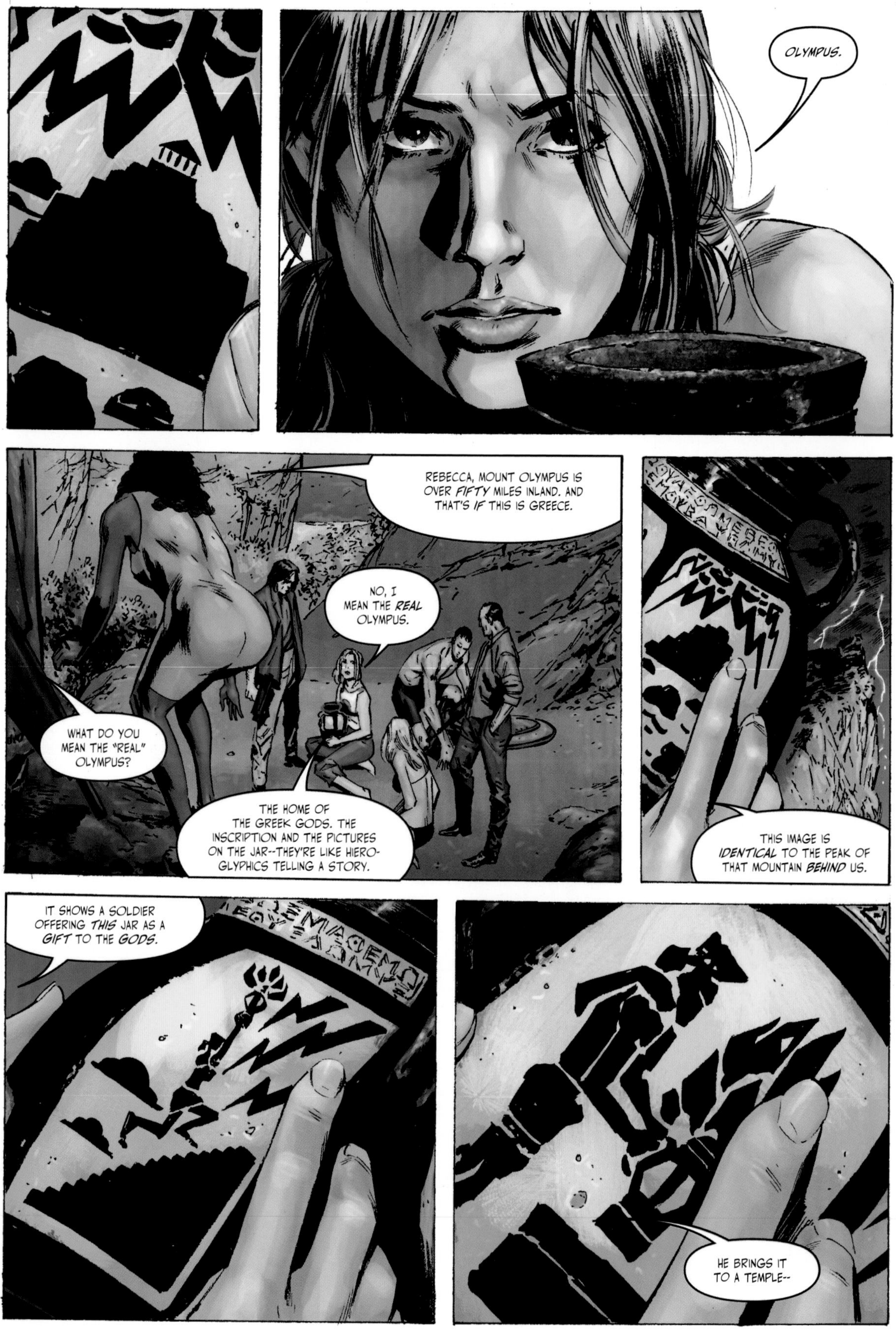
OLYMPUS.
REBECCA, MOUNT OLYMPUS IS OVER FIFTY MILES INLAND. AND THAT'S IF THIS IS GREECE.
NO, I MEAN THE REAL OLYMPUS.
WHAT DO YOU MEAN THE "REAL" OLYMPUS?
THE HOME OF THE GREEK GODS. THE INSCRIPTION AND THE PICTURES ON THE JAR--THEY'RE LIKE HIERO-GLYPHICS TELLING A STORY.
THIS IMAGE IS IDENTICAL TO THE PEAK OF THAT MOUNTAIN BEHIND US.
IT SHOWS A SOLDIER OFFERING THIS JAR AS A GIFT TO THE GODS.
HE BRINGS IT TO A TEMPLE--

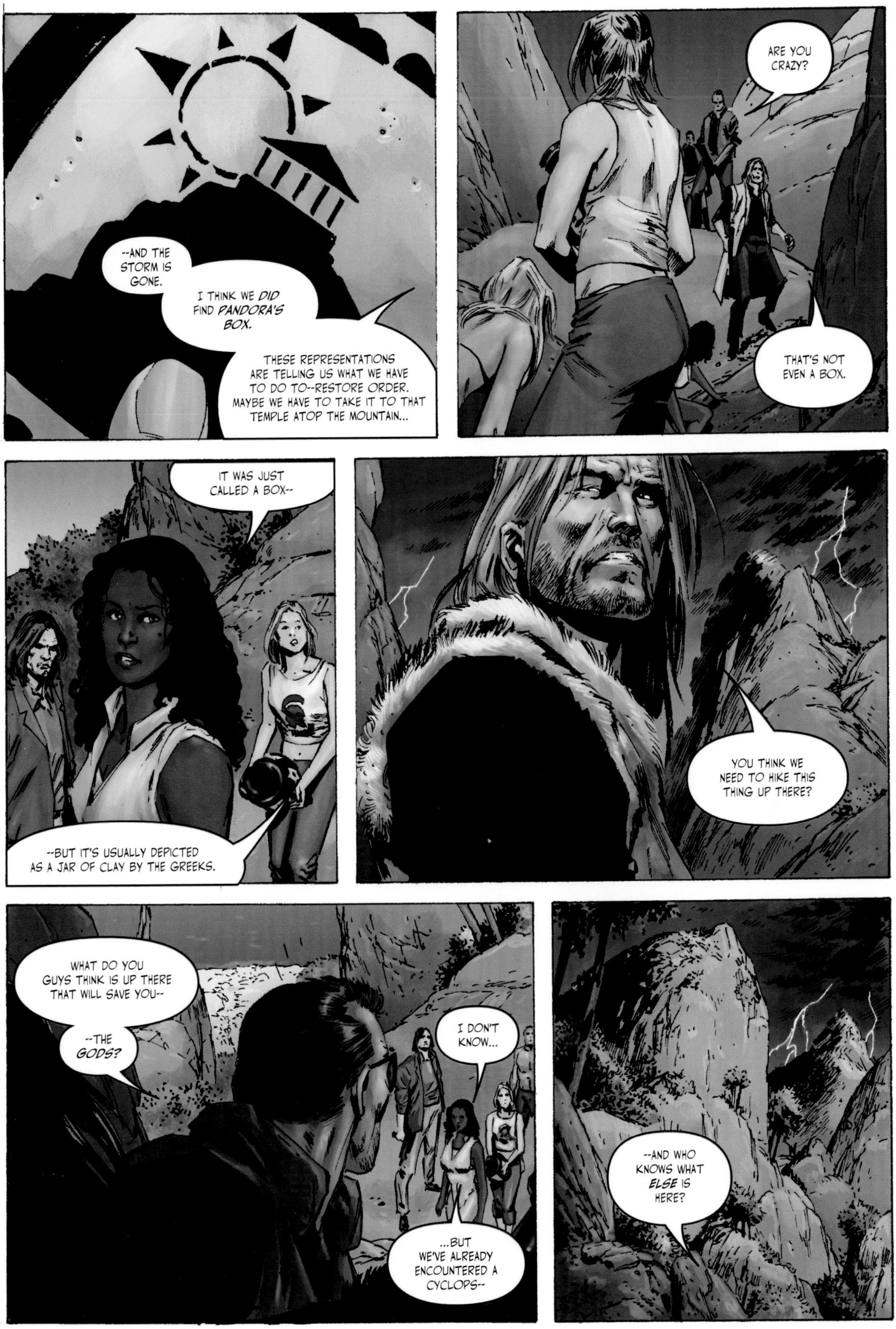
--AND THE STORM IS GONE.
I THINK WE DID FIND PANDORA'S BOX.
THESE REPRESENTATIONS ARE TELLING US WHAT WE HAVE TO DO TO--RESTORE ORDER. MAYBE WE HAVE TO TAKE IT TO THAT TEMPLE ATOP THE MOUNTAIN...
ARE YOU CRAZY?
THAT'S NOT EVEN A BOX.
IT WAS JUST CALLED A BOX--
--BUT IT'S USUALLY DEPICTED AS A JAR OF CLAY BY THE GREEKS.
YOU THINK WE NEED TO HIKE THIS THING UP THERE?
WHAT DO YOU GUYS THINK IS UP THERE THAT WILL SAVE YOU--
--THE GODS?
I DON'T KNOW...
...BUT WE'VE ALREADY ENCOUNTERED A CYCLOPS--
--AND WHO KNOWS WHAT ELSE IS HERE?

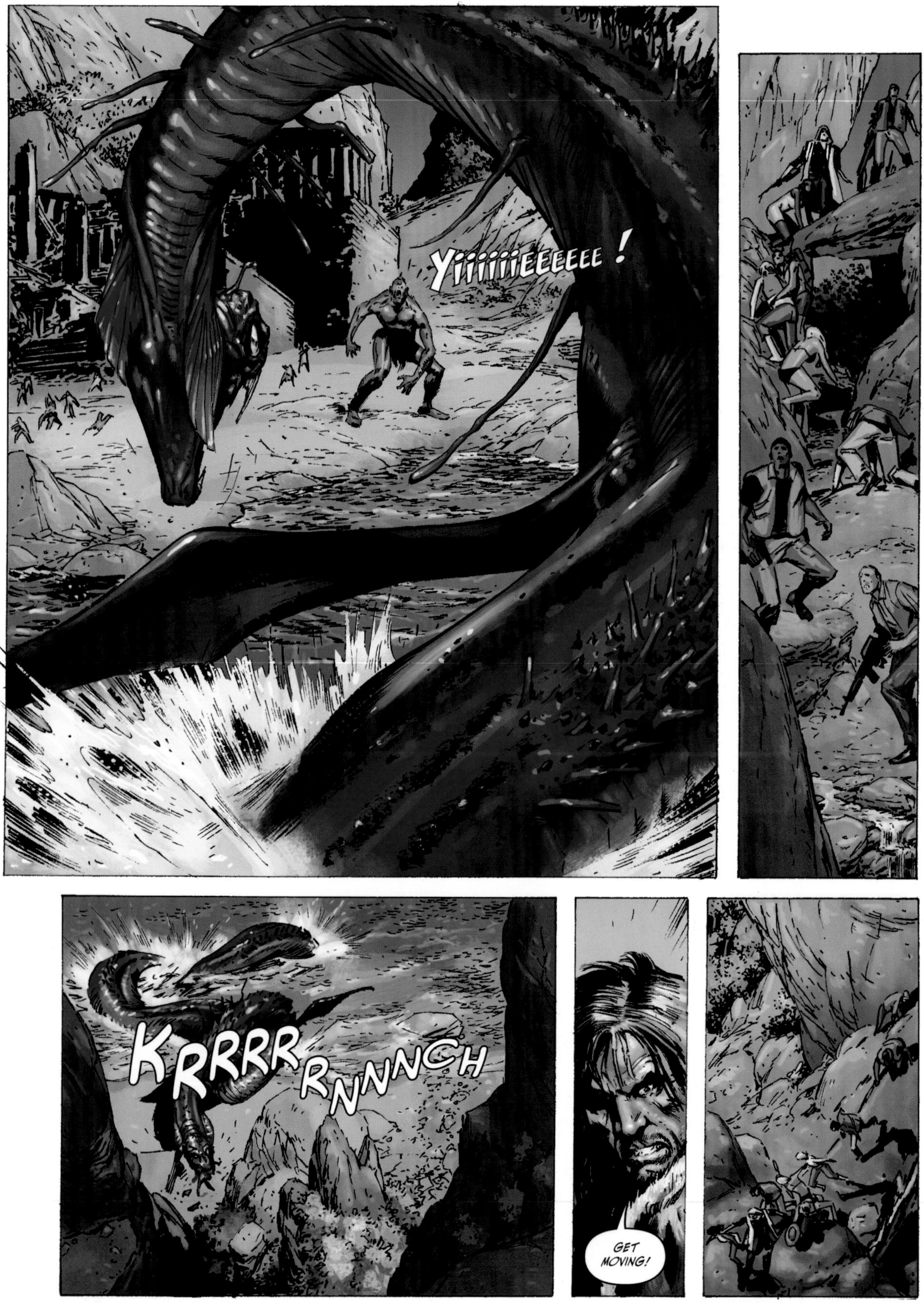
YiiiiiiEEEEEE !
KRRRRRNNNNCH
GET MOVING!

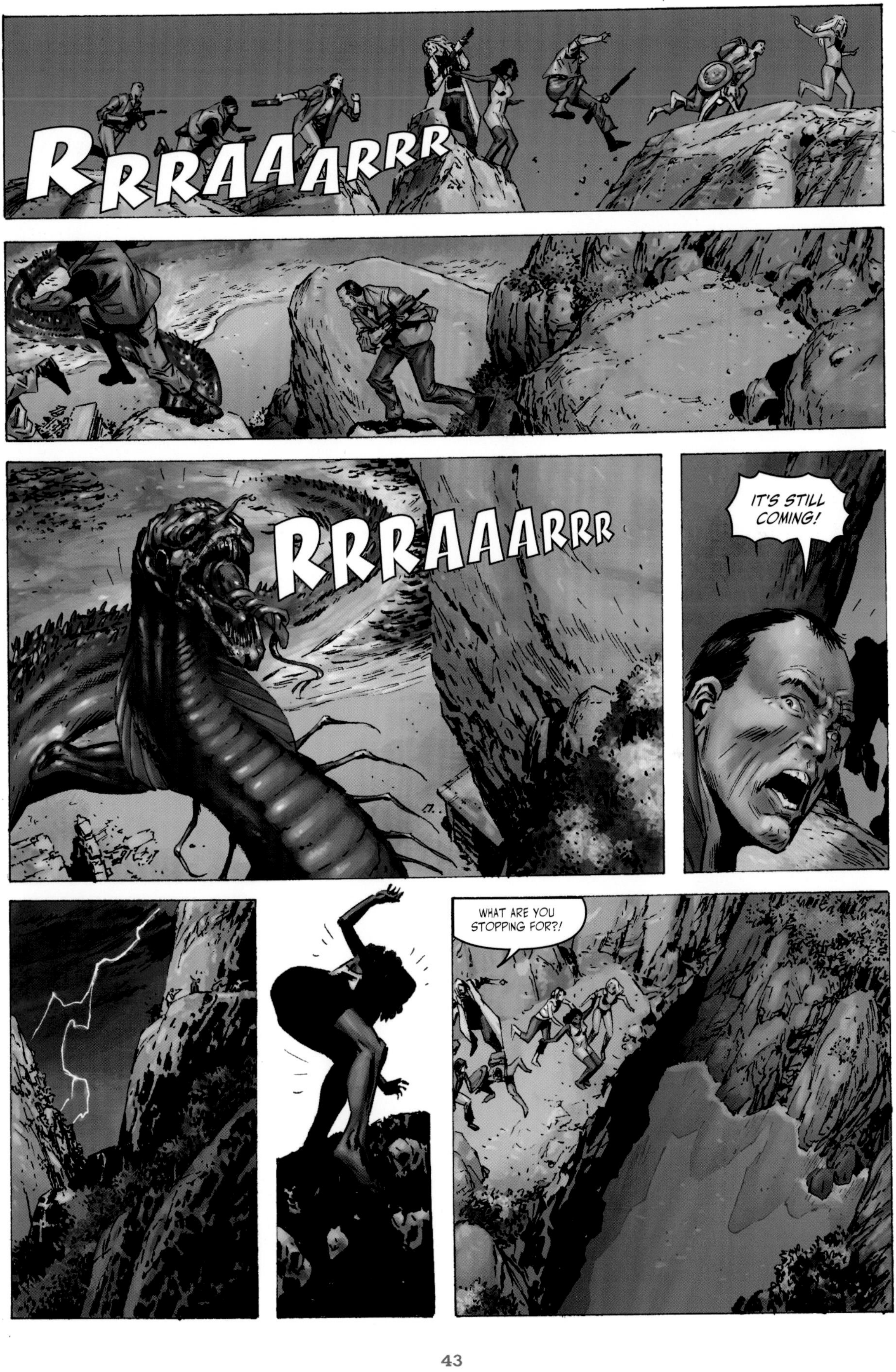
RRRAAARRR
RRRAAARRR
IT'S STILL COMING!
WHAT ARE YOU STOPPING FOR?!

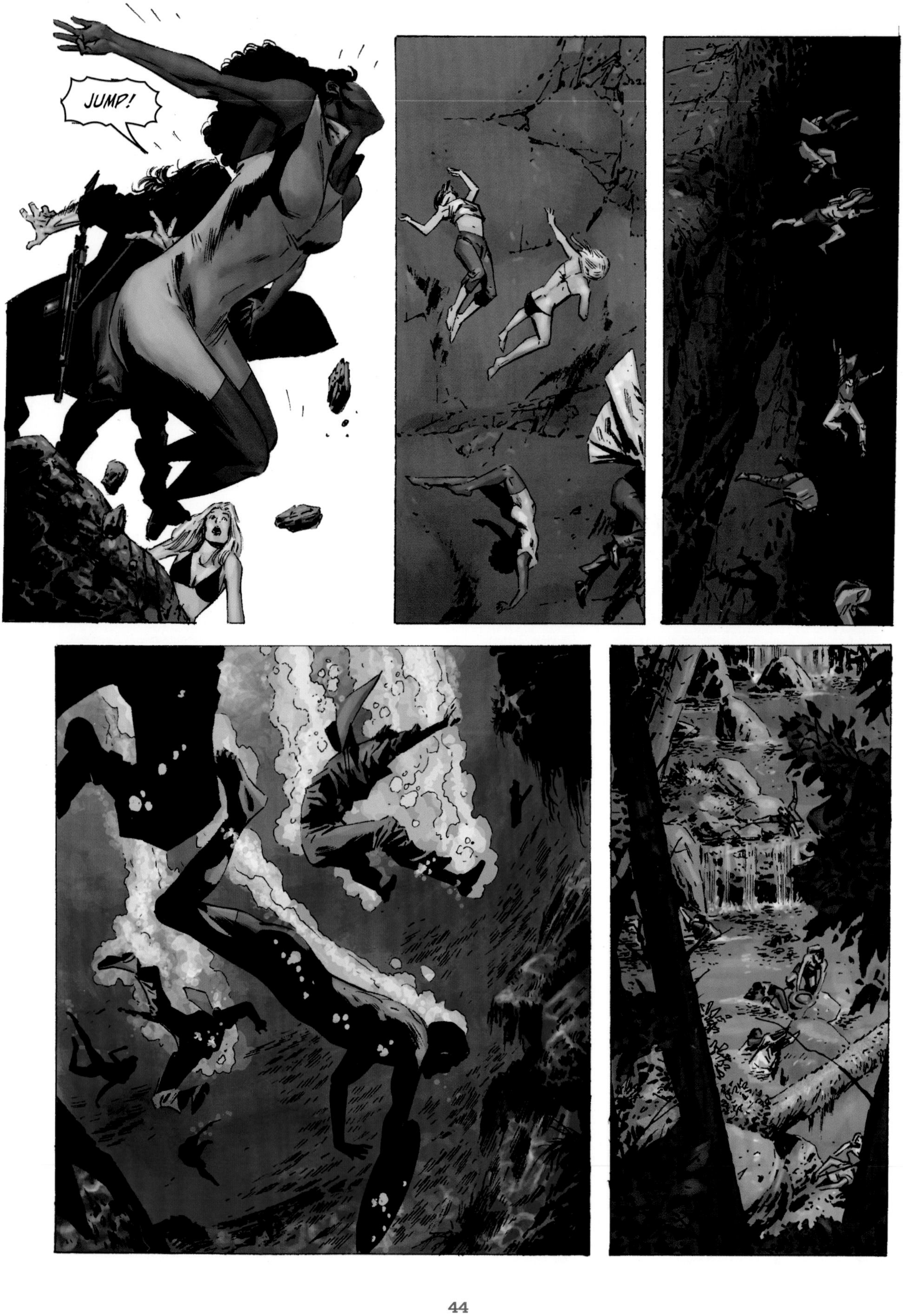
JUMP!

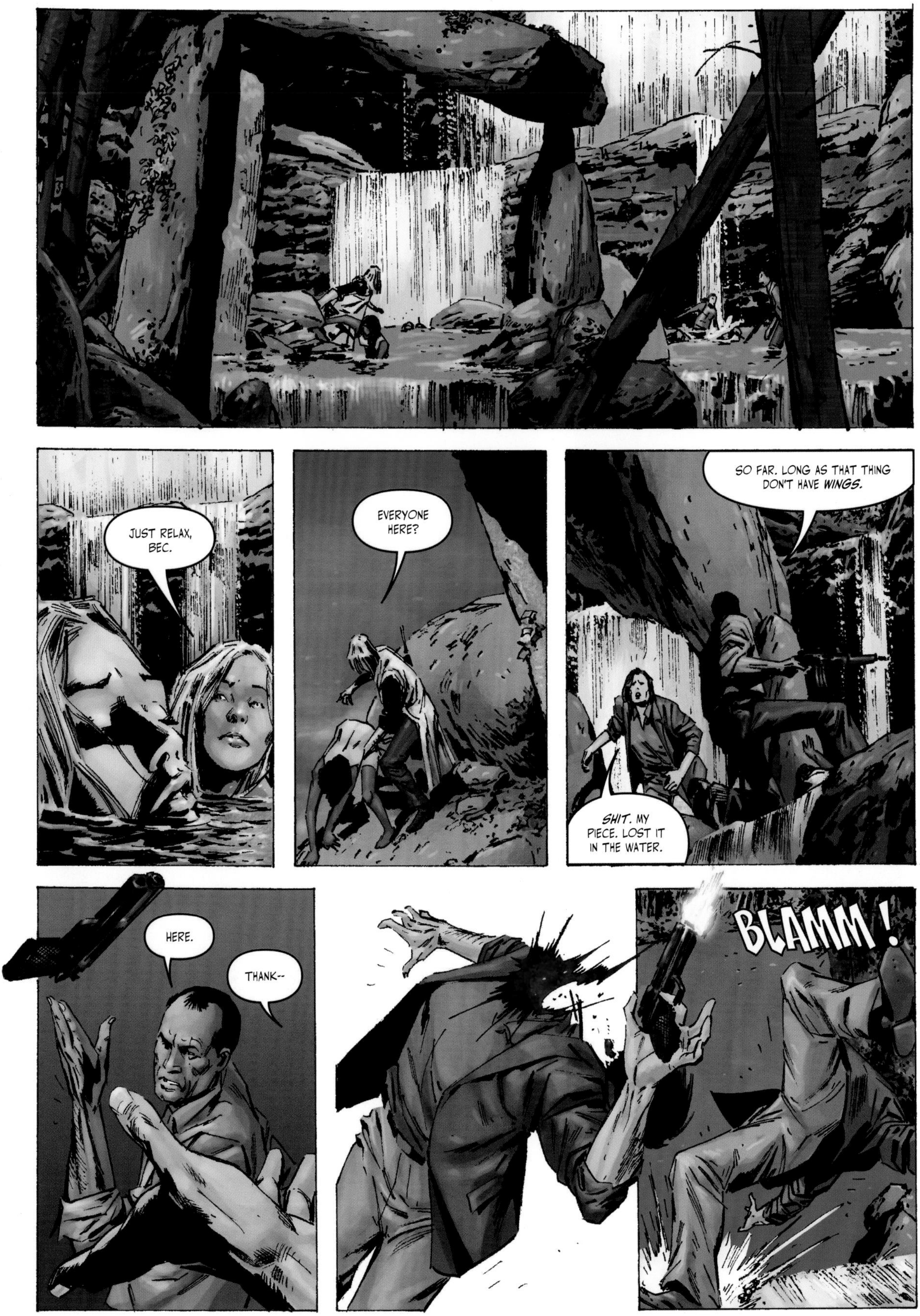
JUST RELAX, BEC.
EVERYONE HERE?
SO FAR. LONG AS THAT THING DON'T HAVE WINGS.
SHIT. MY PIECE. LOST IT IN THE WATER.
HERE.
THANK--
BLAMM!

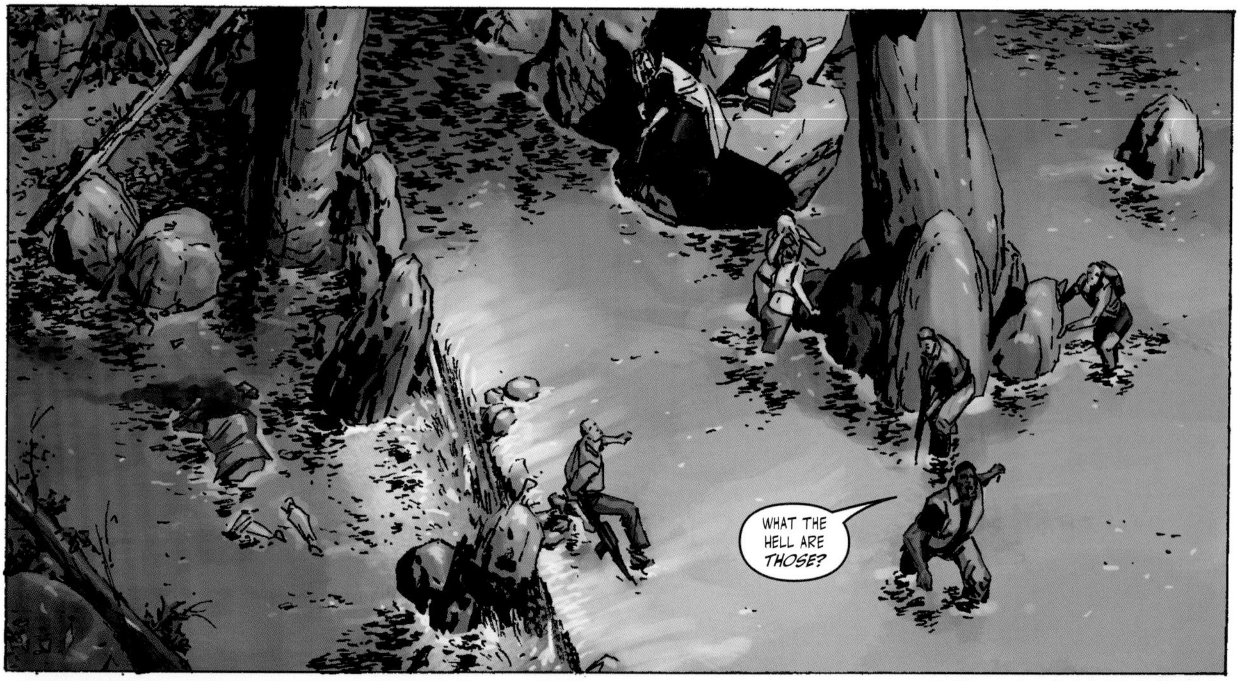
WHAT THE HELL ARE THOSE?

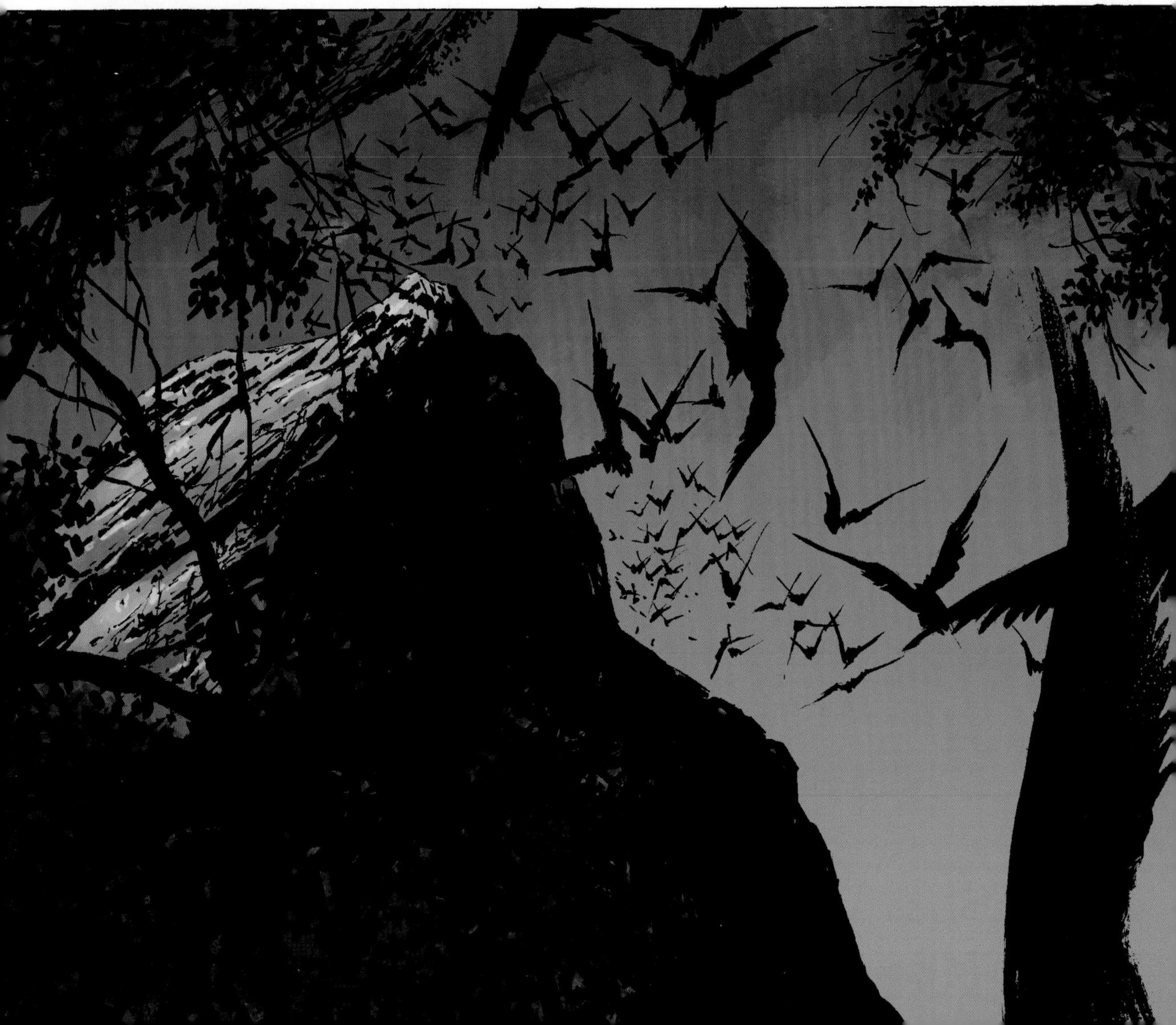

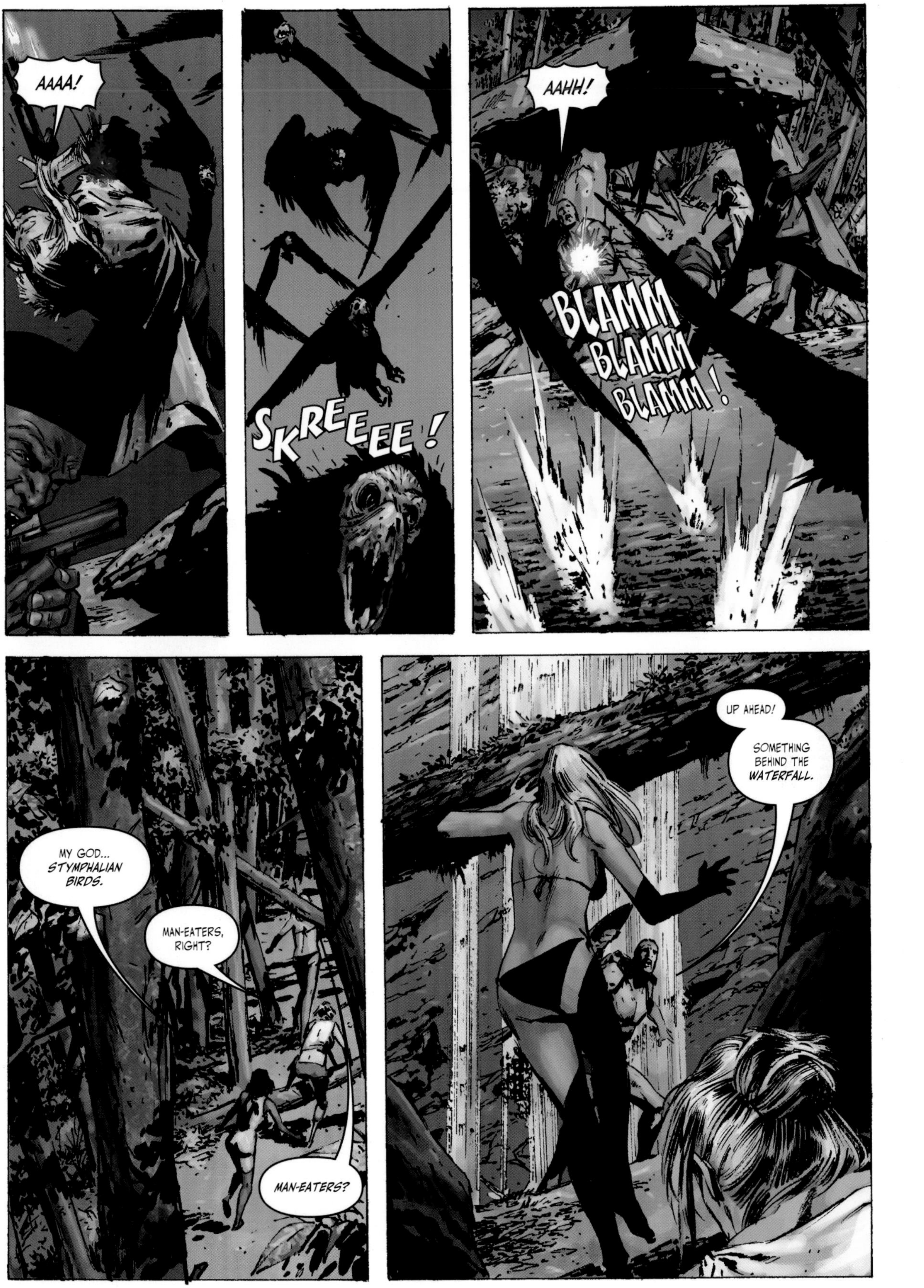
AAAA!
SKREEEEE!
AAHH!
BLAMM BLAMM BLAMM!
MY GOD... STYMPHALIAN BIRDS.
MAN-EATERS, RIGHT?
MAN-EATERS?
UP AHEAD!
SOMETHING BEHIND THE WATERFALL.

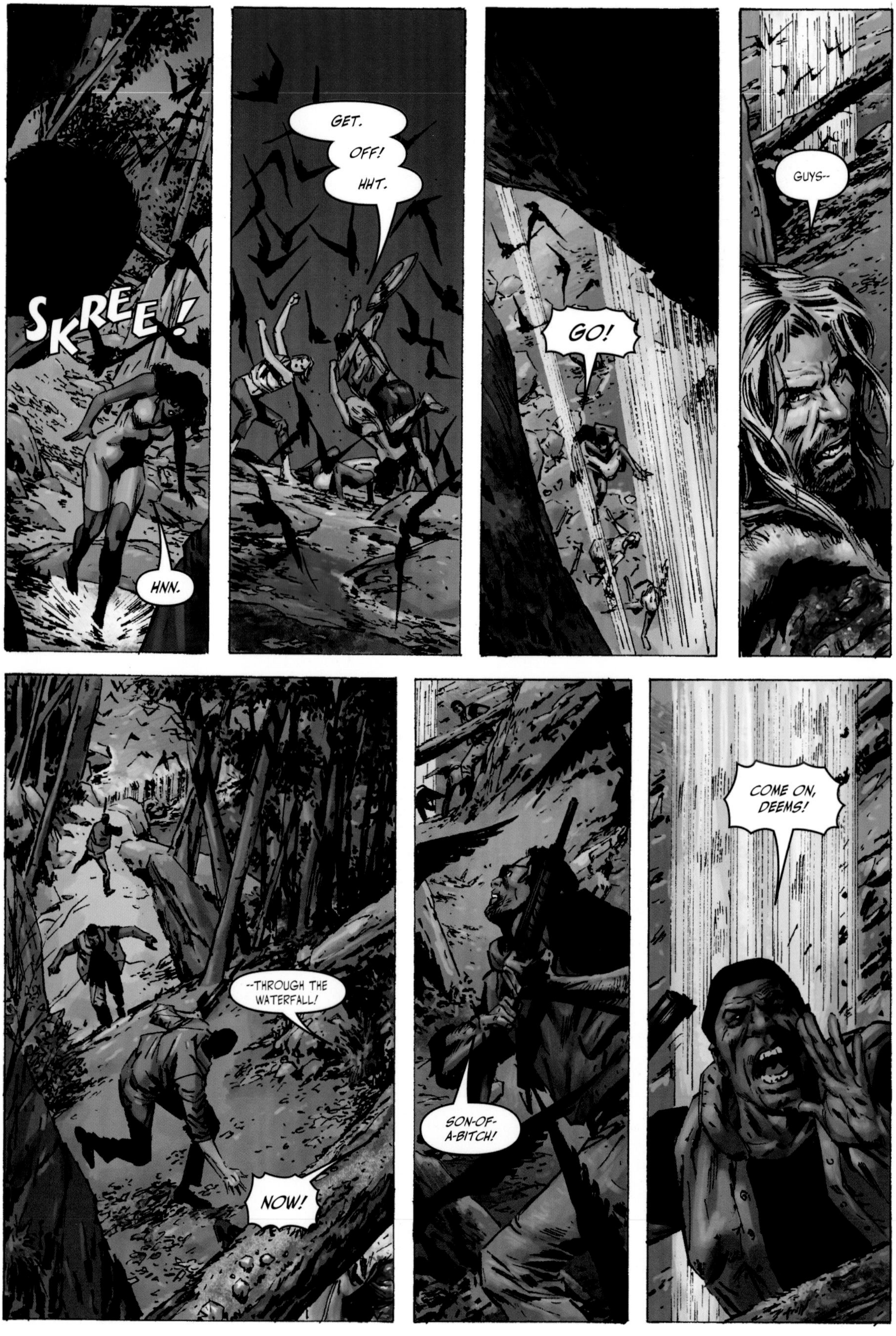
SKREE!
HNN.
GET.
OFF!
HHT.
GO!
GUYS--
--THROUGH THE WATERFALL!
NOW!
SON-OF-A-BITCH!
COME ON, DEEMS!

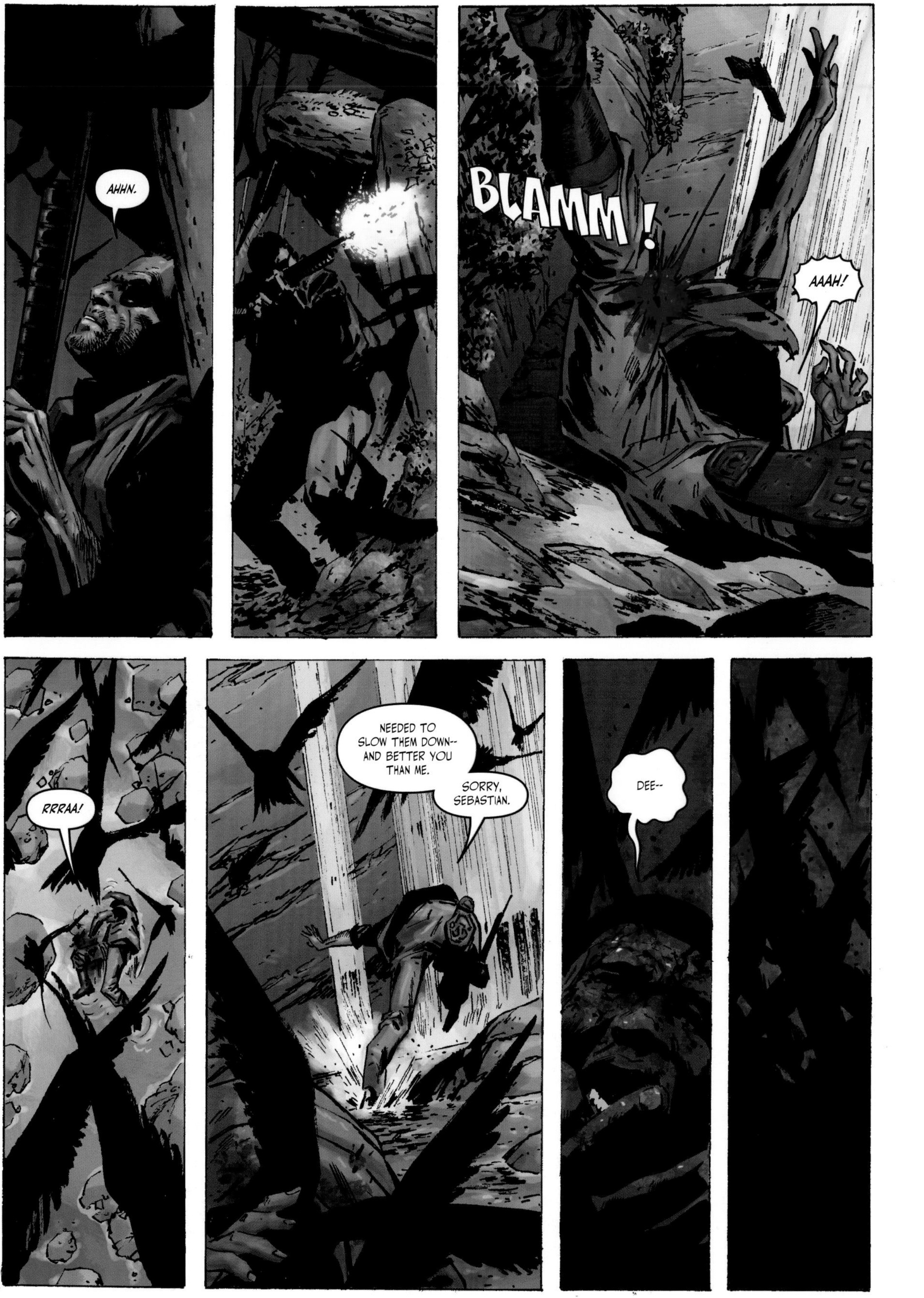
AHHN.
BLAMM!
AAAH!
RRRAA!
NEEDED TO SLOW THEM DOWN-- AND BETTER YOU THAN ME.
SORRY, SEBASTIAN.
DEE--

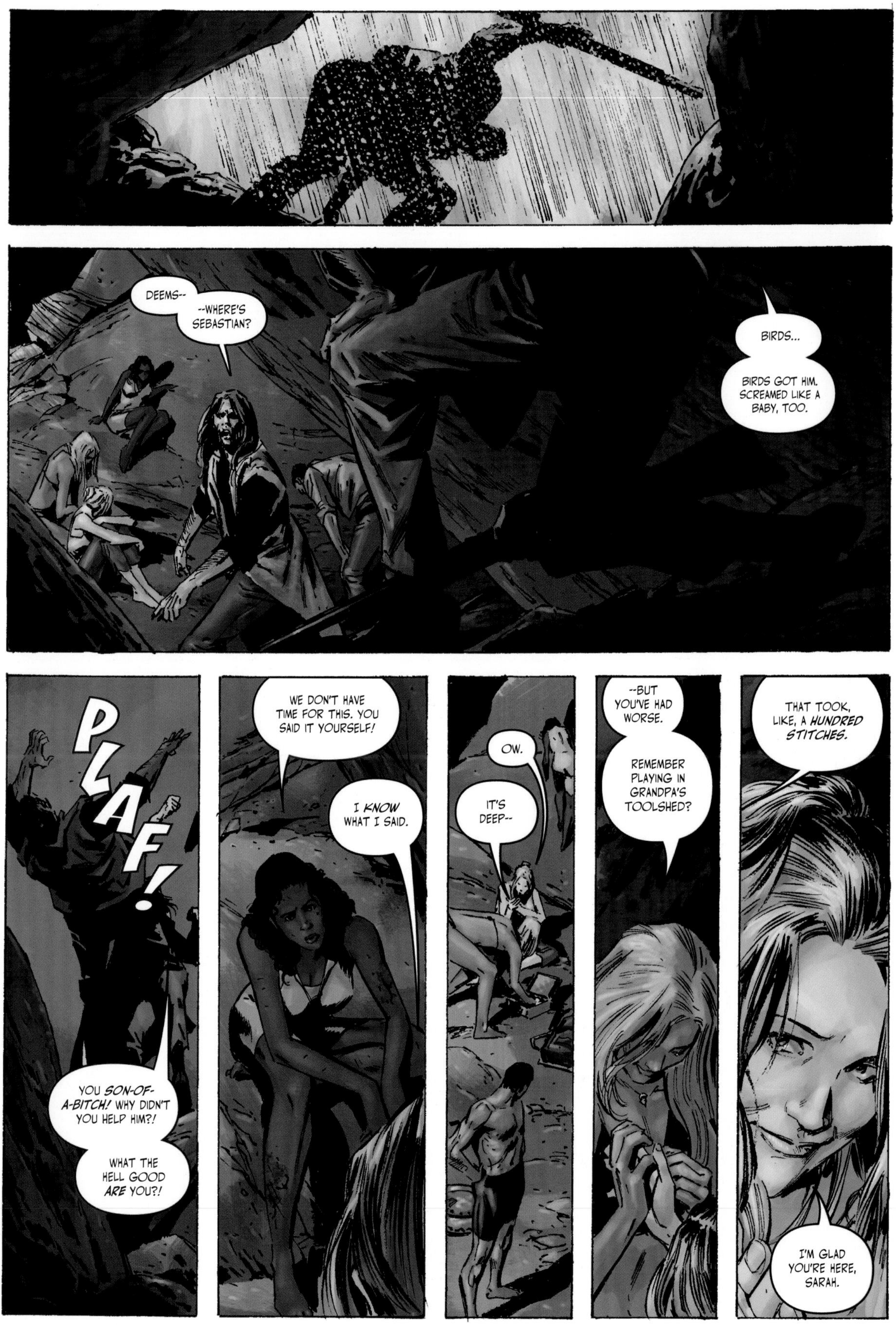
DEEMS--
--WHERE'S SEBASTIAN?
BIRDS...
BIRDS GOT HIM. SCREAMED LIKE A BABY, TOO.
PLAF!
YOU SON-OF-A-BITCH! WHY DIDN'T YOU HELP HIM?!
WHAT THE HELL GOOD ARE YOU?!
WE DON'T HAVE TIME FOR THIS. YOU SAID IT YOURSELF!
I KNOW WHAT I SAID.
OW.
IT'S DEEP--
--BUT YOU'VE HAD WORSE.
REMEMBER PLAYING IN GRANDPA'S TOOLSHED?
THAT TOOK, LIKE, A HUNDRED STITCHES.
I'M GLAD YOU'RE HERE, SARAH.

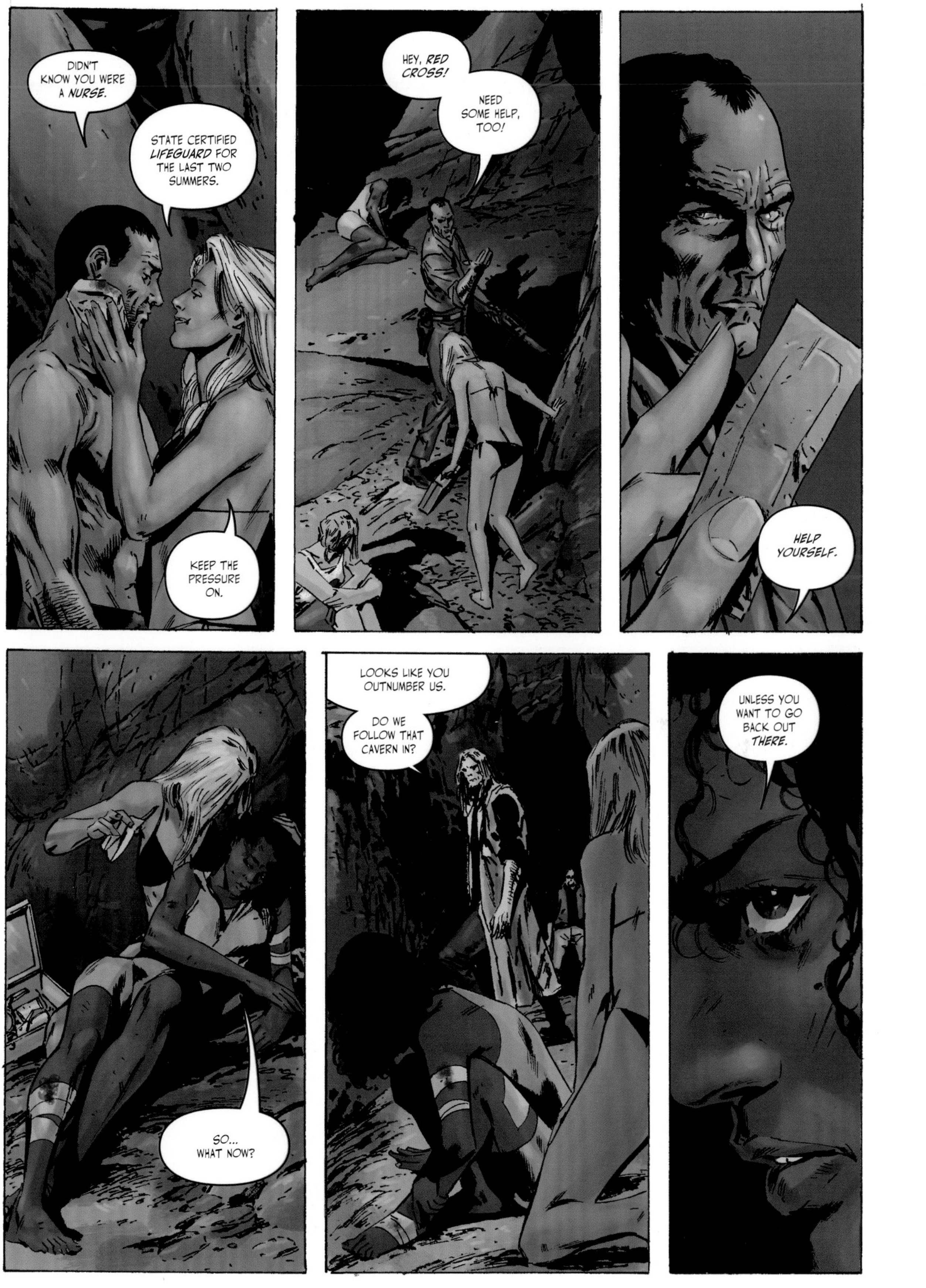
DIDN'T KNOW YOU WERE A NURSE.
STATE CERTIFIED LIFEGUARD FOR THE LAST TWO SUMMERS.
KEEP THE PRESSURE ON.
HEY, RED CROSS!
NEED SOME HELP, TOO!
HELP YOURSELF.
SO... WHAT NOW?
LOOKS LIKE YOU OUTNUMBER US.
DO WE FOLLOW THAT CAVERN IN?
UNLESS YOU WANT TO GO BACK OUT THERE.

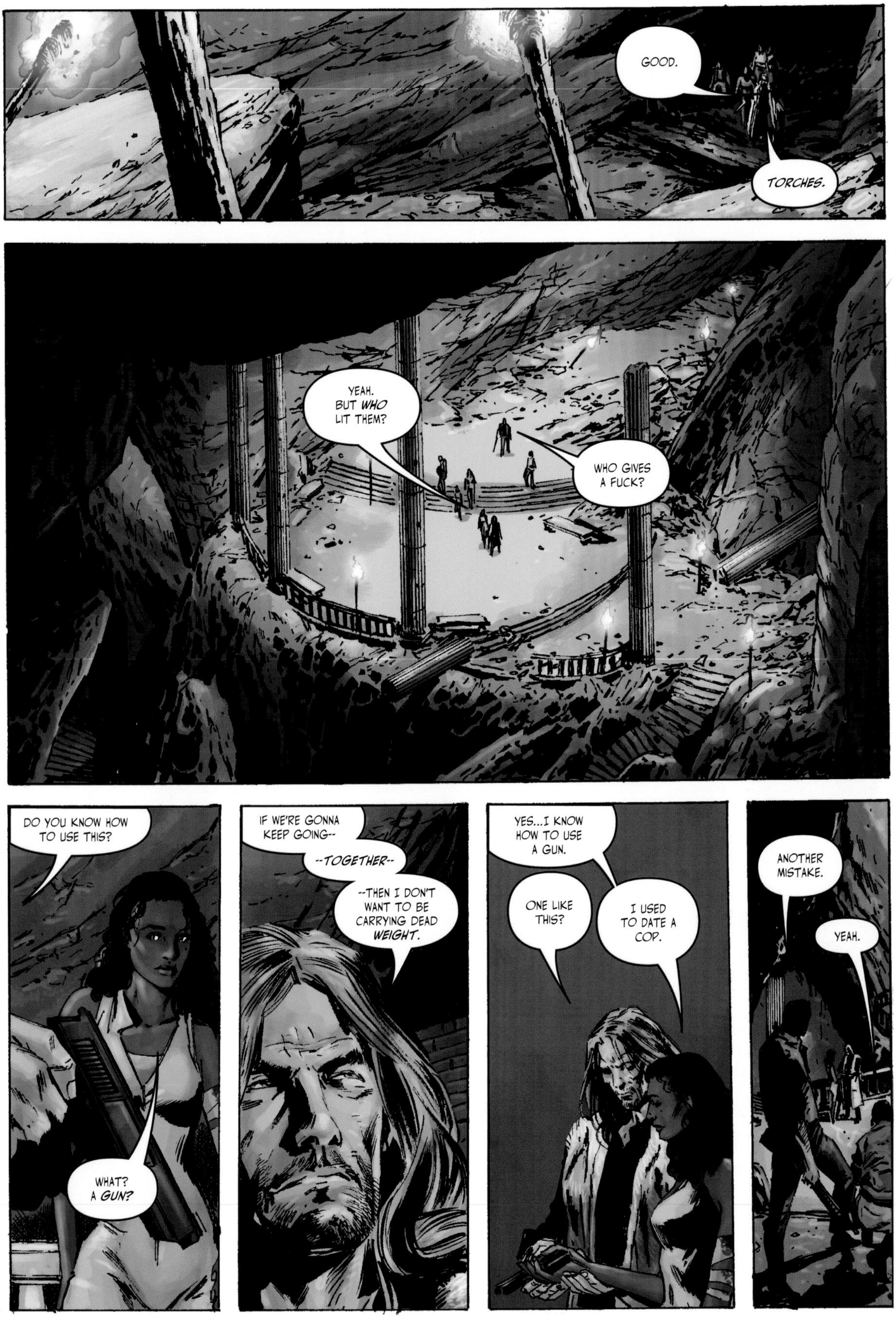
GOOD.
TORCHES.
YEAH. BUT WHO LIT THEM?
WHO GIVES A FUCK?
DO YOU KNOW HOW TO USE THIS?
WHAT? A GUN?
IF WE'RE GONNA KEEP GOING--
--TOGETHER--
--THEN I DON'T WANT TO BE CARRYING DEAD WEIGHT.
YES...I KNOW HOW TO USE A GUN.
ONE LIKE THIS?
I USED TO DATE A COP.
ANOTHER MISTAKE.
YEAH.

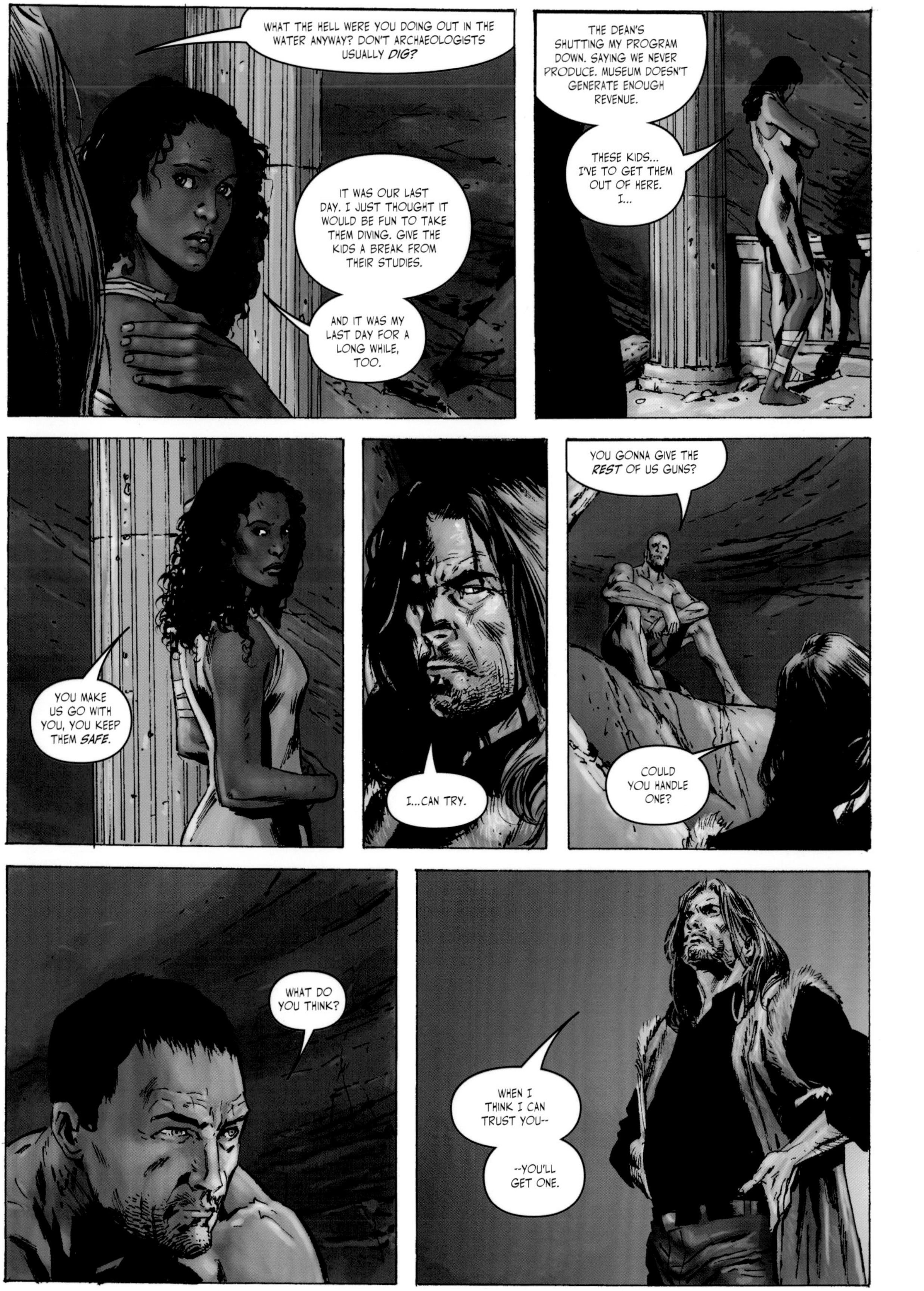

WHAT THE HELL WERE YOU DOING OUT IN THE WATER ANYWAY? DON'T ARCHAEOLOGISTS USUALLY *DIG?*
IT WAS OUR LAST DAY. I JUST THOUGHT IT WOULD BE FUN TO TAKE THEM DIVING. GIVE THE KIDS A BREAK FROM THEIR STUDIES.
AND IT WAS MY LAST DAY FOR A LONG WHILE, TOO.
THE DEAN'S SHUTTING MY PROGRAM DOWN. SAYING WE NEVER PRODUCE. MUSEUM DOESN'T GENERATE ENOUGH REVENUE.
THESE KIDS... I'VE TO GET THEM OUT OF HERE. I...
YOU MAKE US GO WITH YOU, YOU KEEP THEM *SAFE*.
I...CAN TRY.
YOU GONNA GIVE THE *REST* OF US GUNS?
COULD YOU HANDLE ONE?
WHAT DO YOU THINK?
WHEN I THINK I CAN TRUST YOU--
--YOU'LL GET ONE.

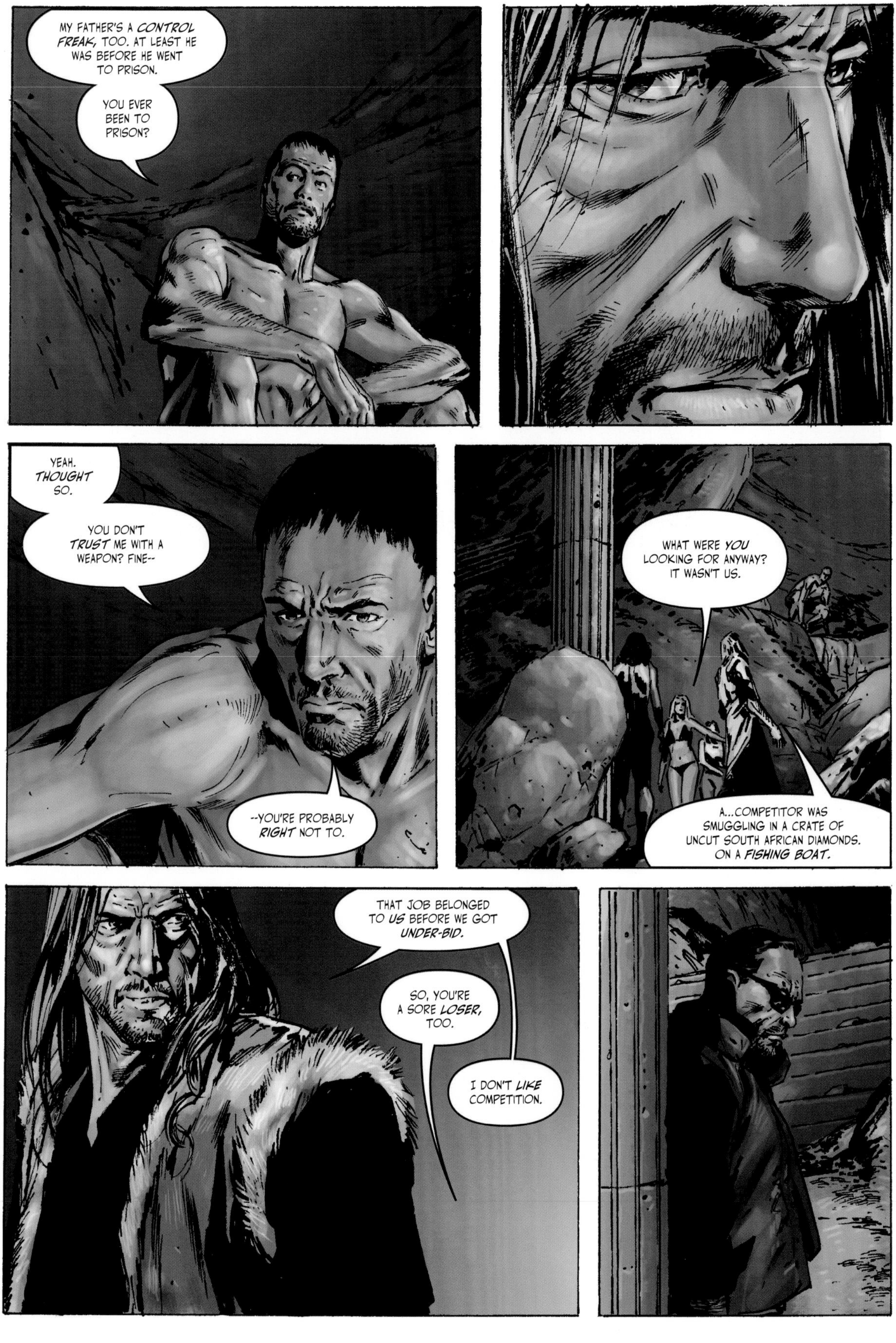
MY FATHER'S A CONTROL FREAK, TOO. AT LEAST HE WAS BEFORE HE WENT TO PRISON.
YOU EVER BEEN TO PRISON?
YEAH. THOUGHT SO.
YOU DON'T TRUST ME WITH A WEAPON? FINE--
--YOU'RE PROBABLY RIGHT NOT TO.
WHAT WERE YOU LOOKING FOR ANYWAY? IT WASN'T US.
A...COMPETITOR WAS SMUGGLING IN A CRATE OF UNCUT SOUTH AFRICAN DIAMONDS. ON A FISHING BOAT.
THAT JOB BELONGED TO US BEFORE WE GOT UNDER-BID.
SO, YOU'RE A SORE LOSER, TOO.
I DON'T LIKE COMPETITION.

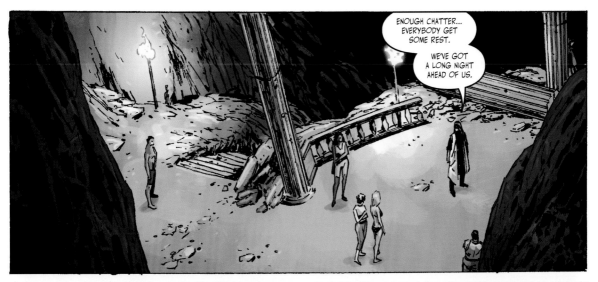

ENOUGH CHATTER...
EVERYBODY GET
SOME REST.

WE'VE GOT
A LONG NIGHT
AHEAD OF US.

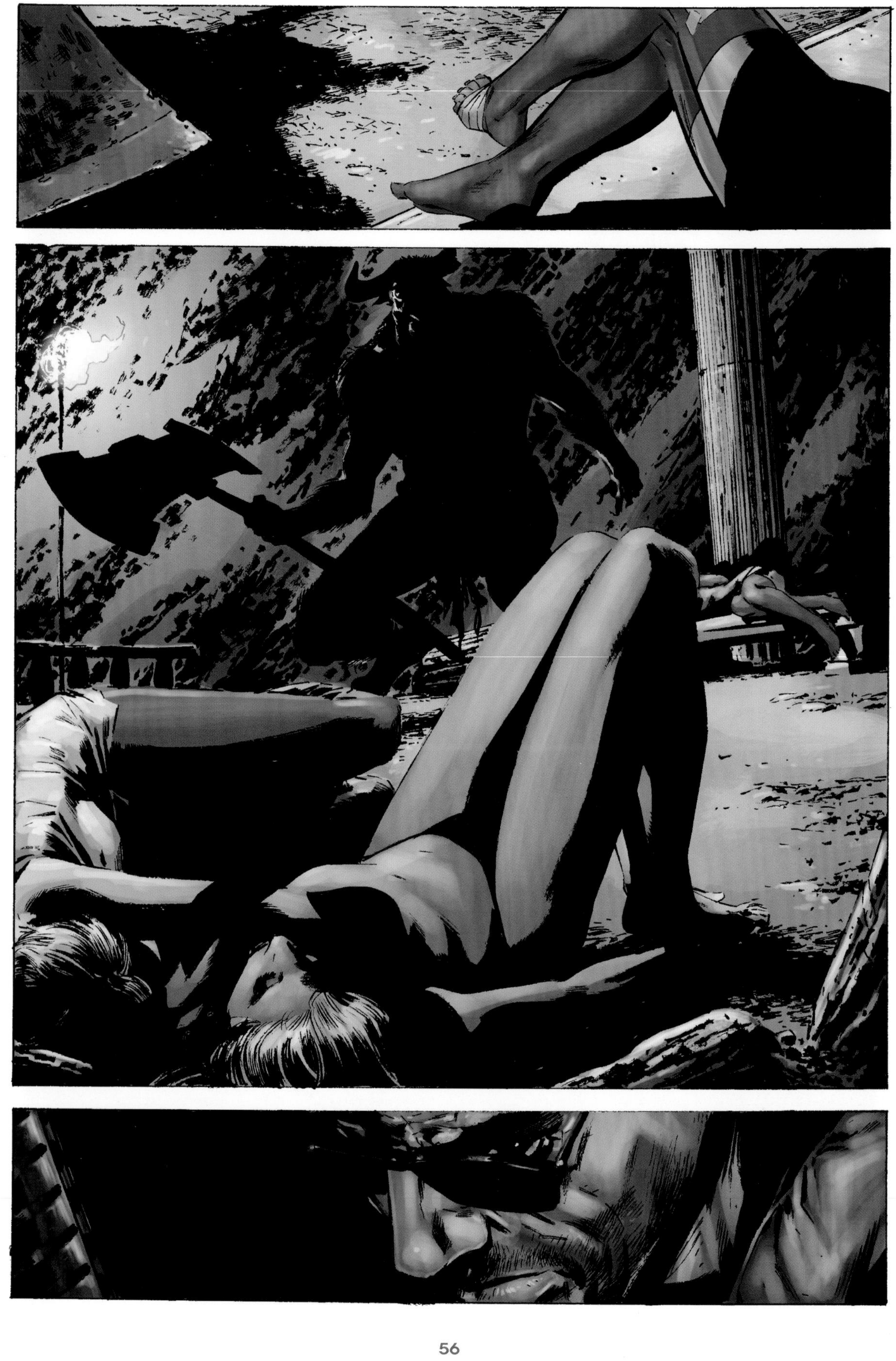

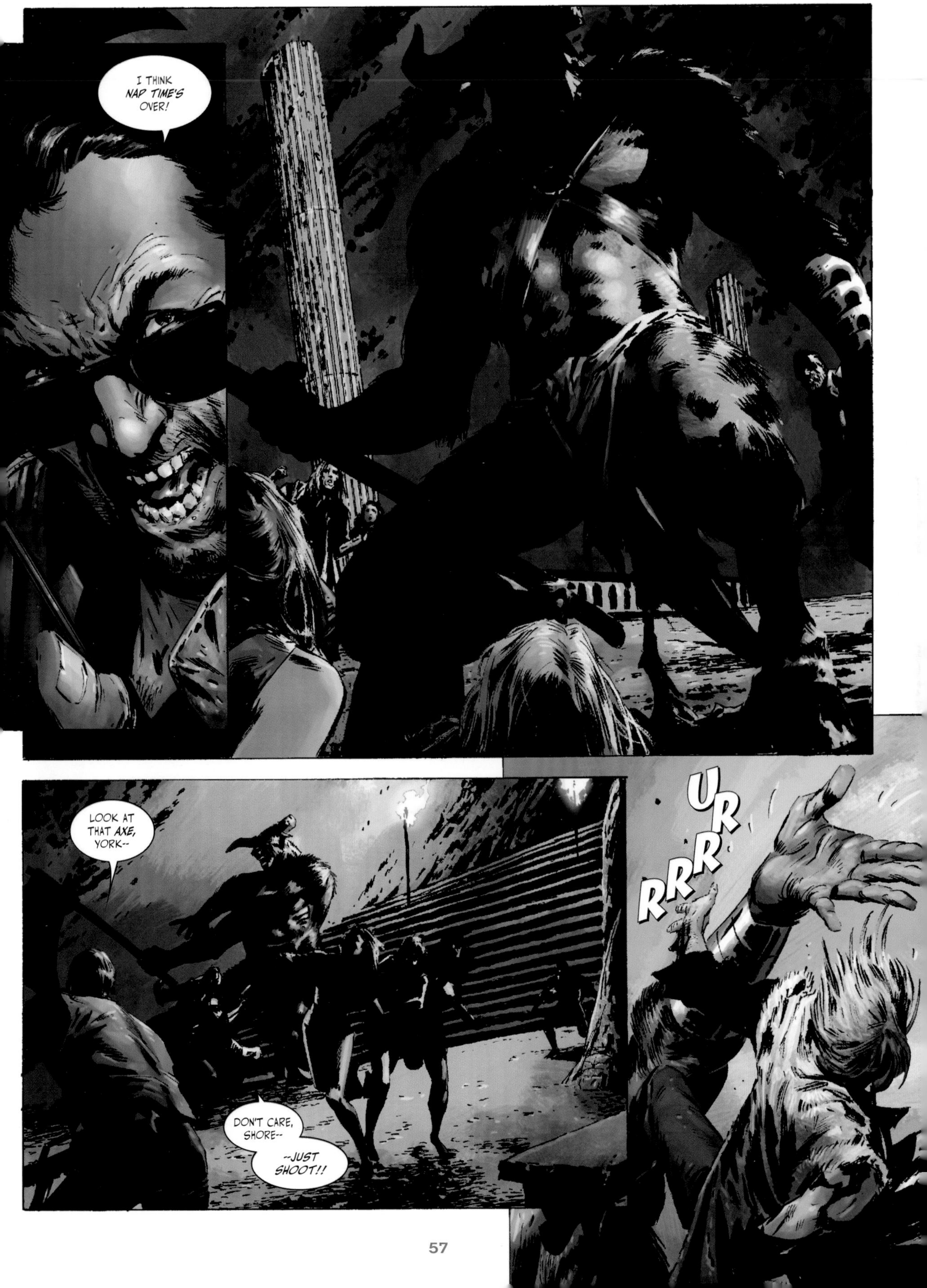
I THINK NAP TIME'S OVER!
LOOK AT THAT AXE, YORK--
DON'T CARE, SHORE--
--JUST SHOOT!!
URRRRR

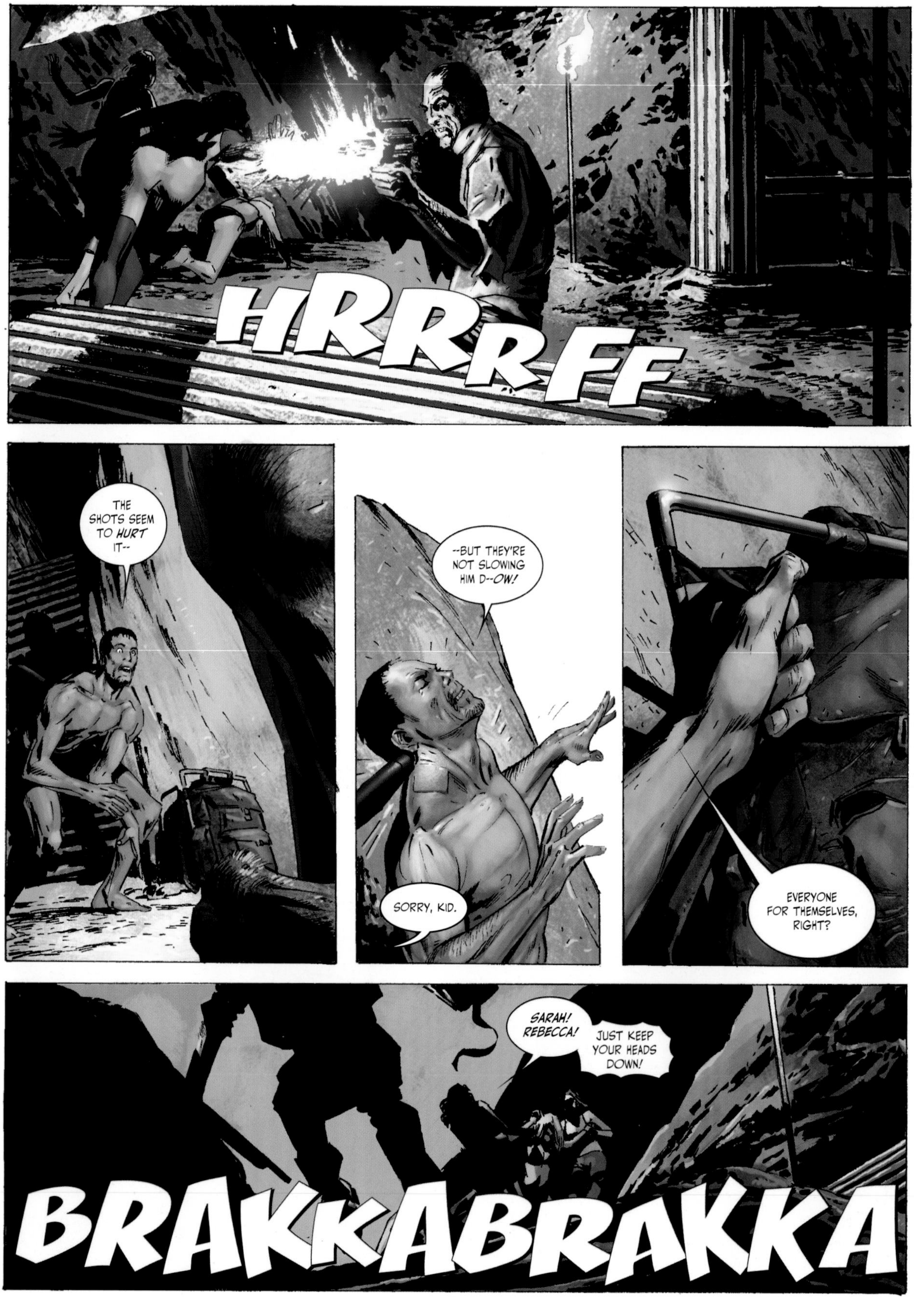
HRRRFF
THE SHOTS SEEM TO HURT IT--
--BUT THEY'RE NOT SLOWING HIM D--OW!
SORRY, KID.
EVERYONE FOR THEMSELVES, RIGHT?
SARAH! REBECCA!
JUST KEEP YOUR HEADS DOWN!
BRAKKABRAKKA

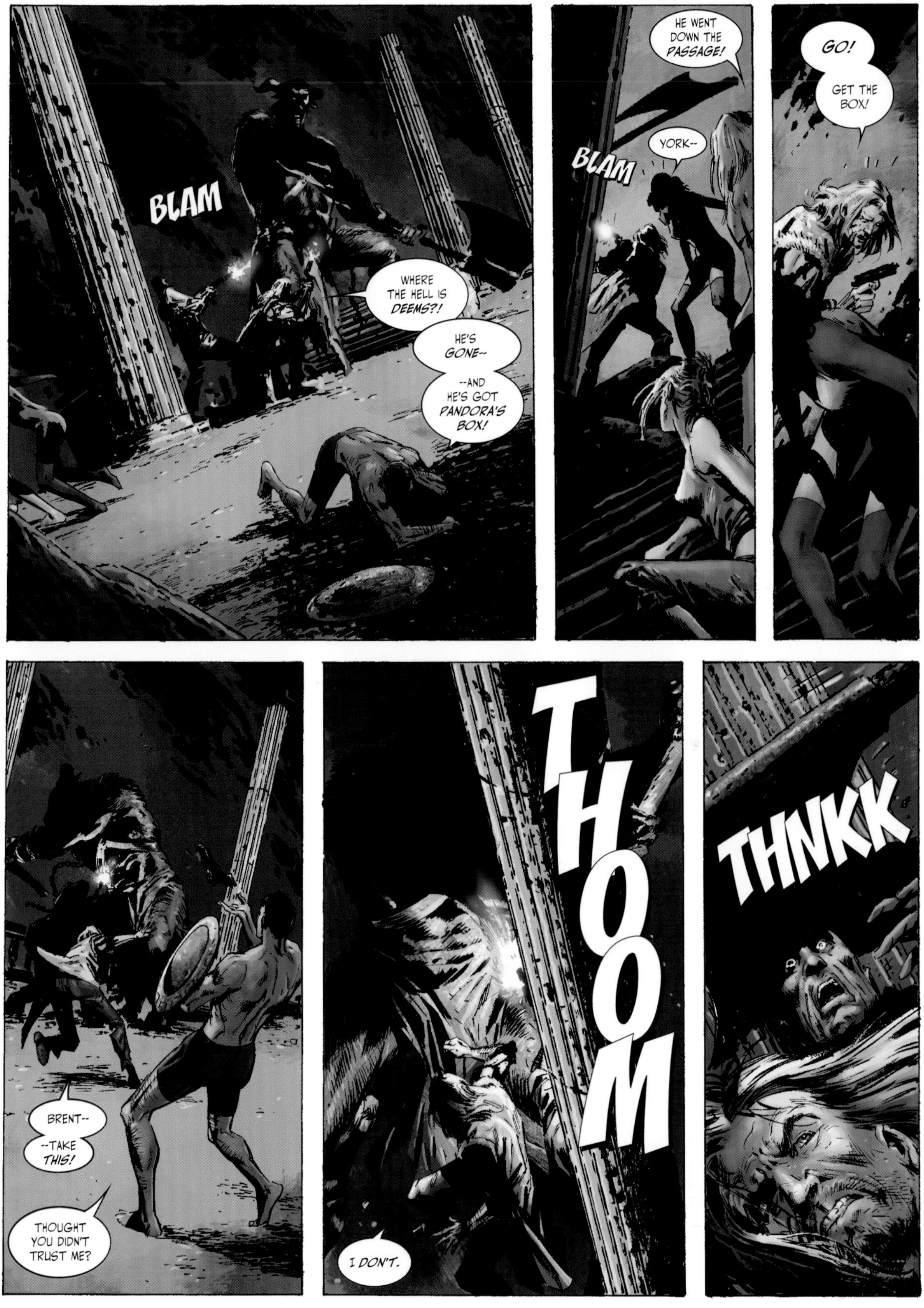
BLAM
WHERE THE HELL IS DEEMS?!
HE'S GONE--
--AND HE'S GOT PANDORA'S BOX!
HE WENT DOWN THE PASSAGE!
BLAM
YORK--
GO!
GET THE BOX!
BRENT--
--TAKE THIS!
THOUGHT YOU DIDN'T TRUST ME?
I DON'T.
THOOM
THNKK

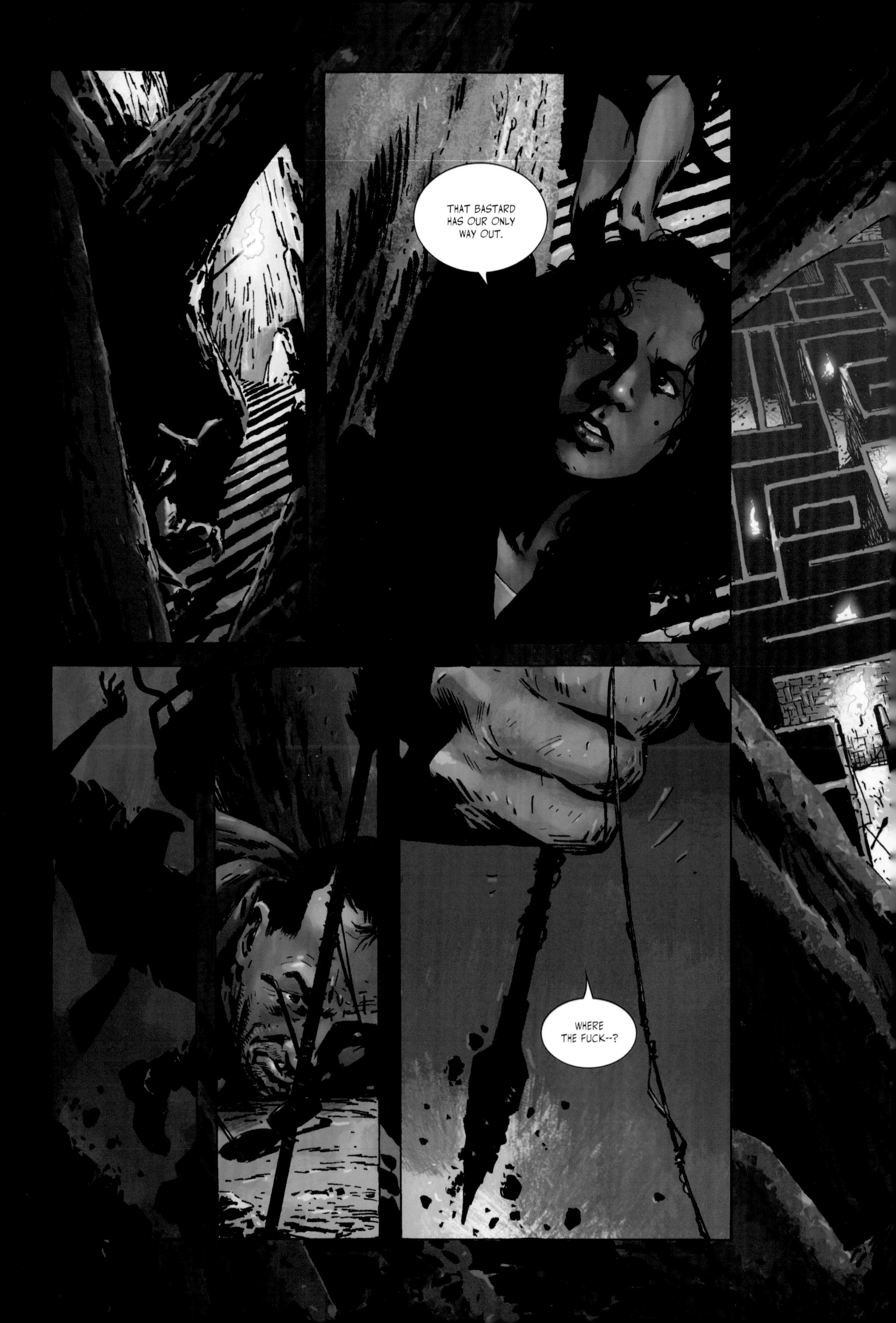
THAT BASTARD HAS OUR ONLY WAY OUT.
WHERE THE FUCK--?

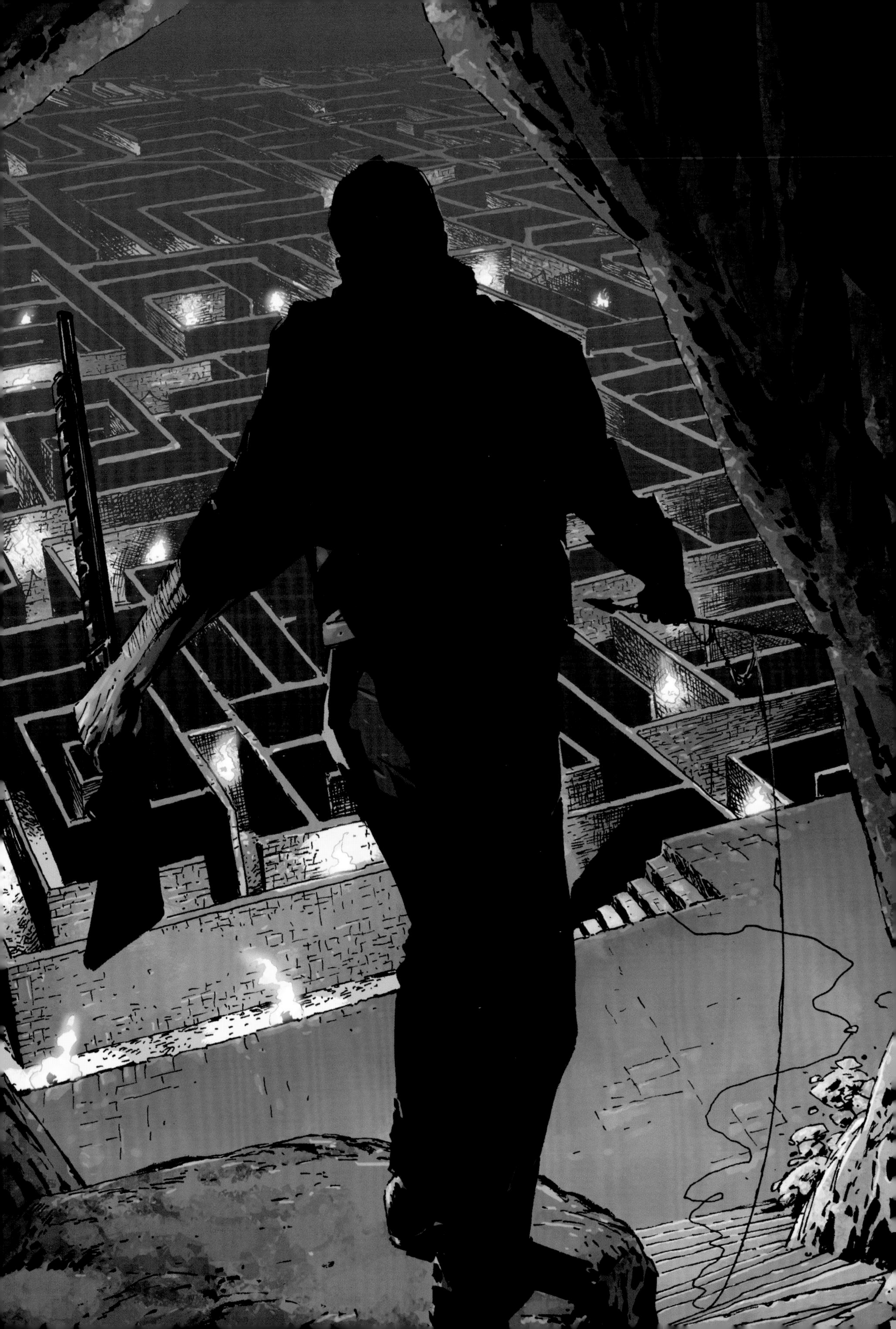

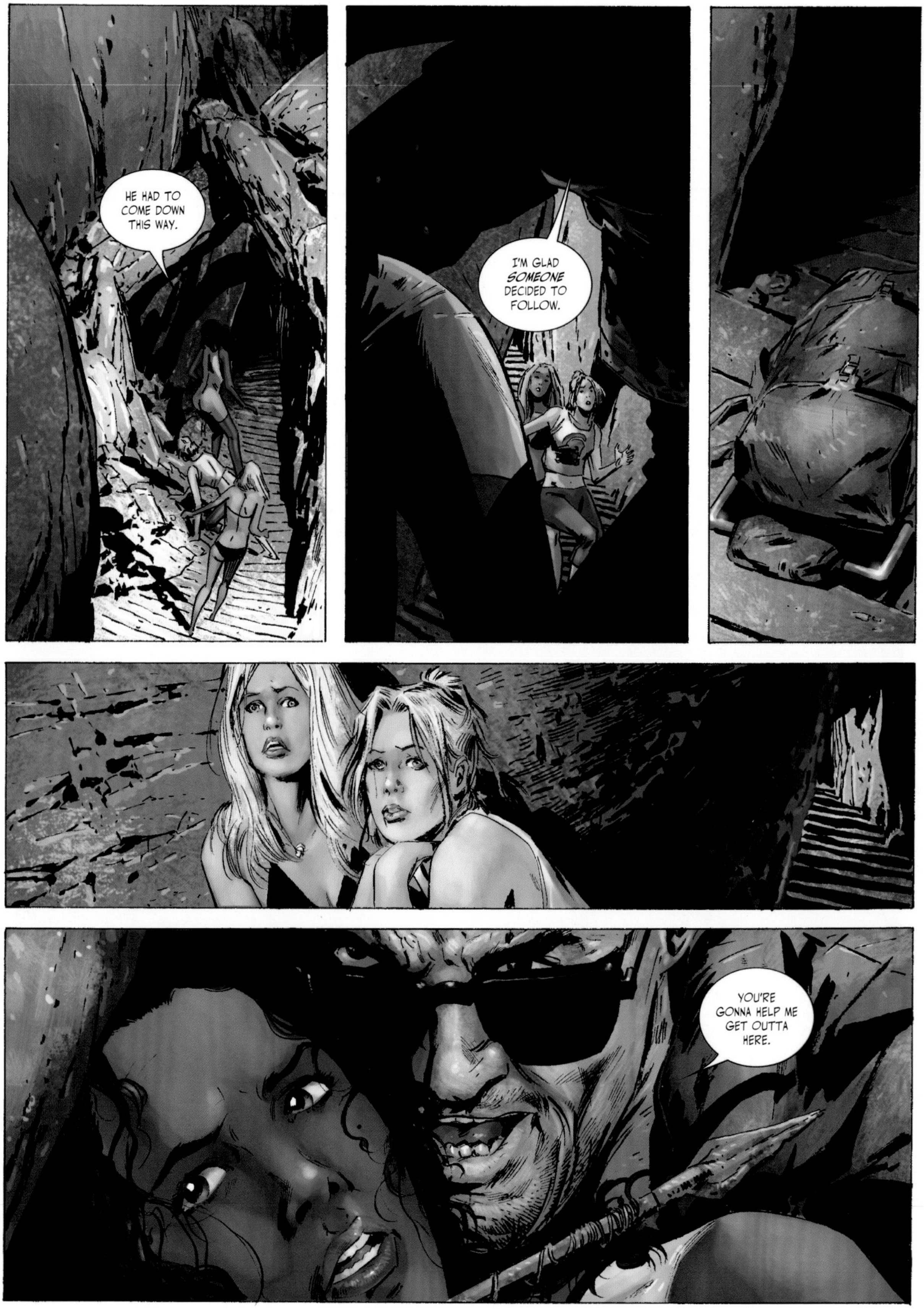
HE HAD TO COME DOWN THIS WAY.
I'M GLAD *SOMEONE* DECIDED TO FOLLOW.
YOU'RE GONNA HELP ME GET OUTTA HERE.

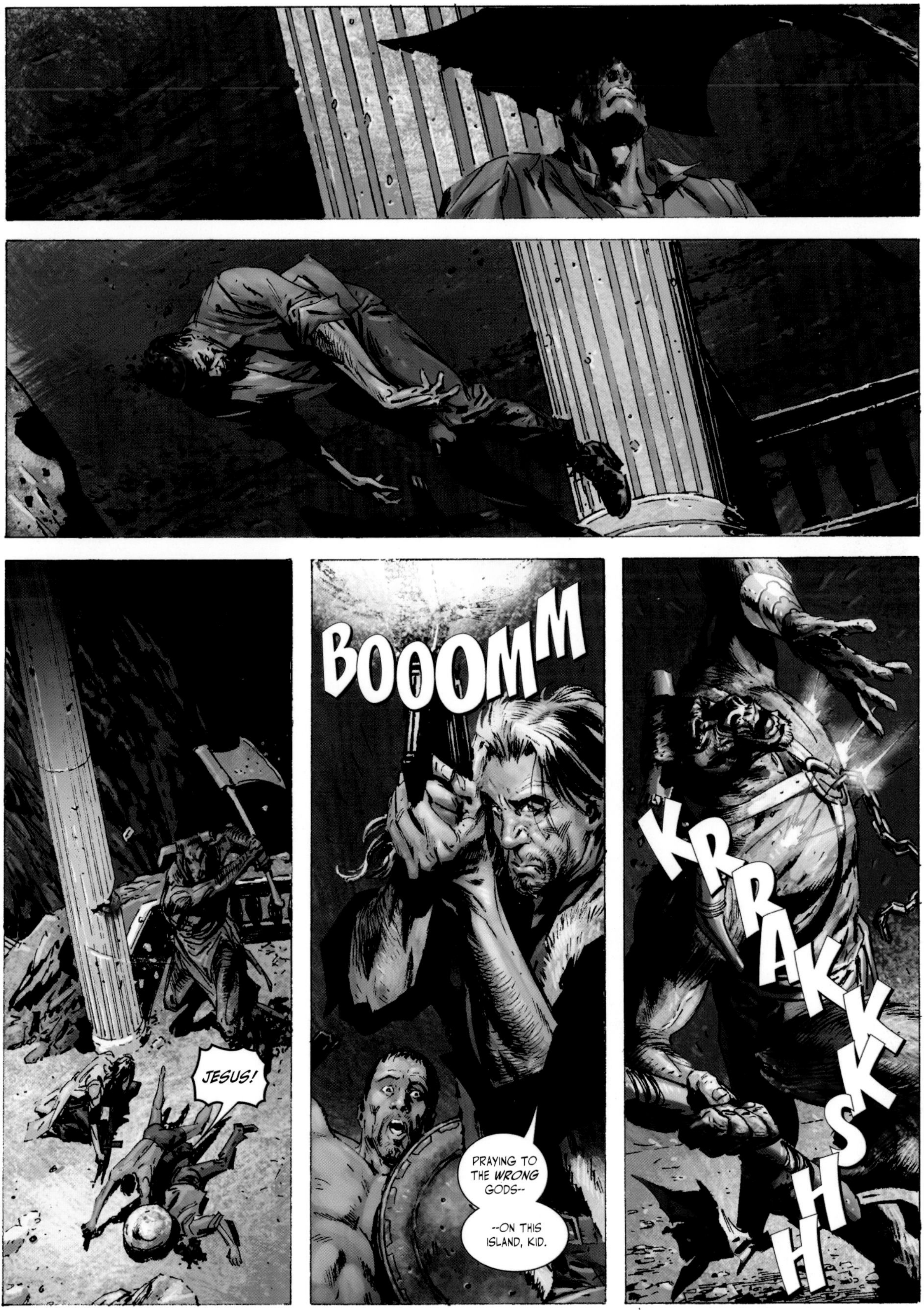
JESUS!
BOOOMM
PRAYING TO THE *WRONG* GODS--
--ON THIS ISLAND, KID.
KRRAKKKSKSHHH

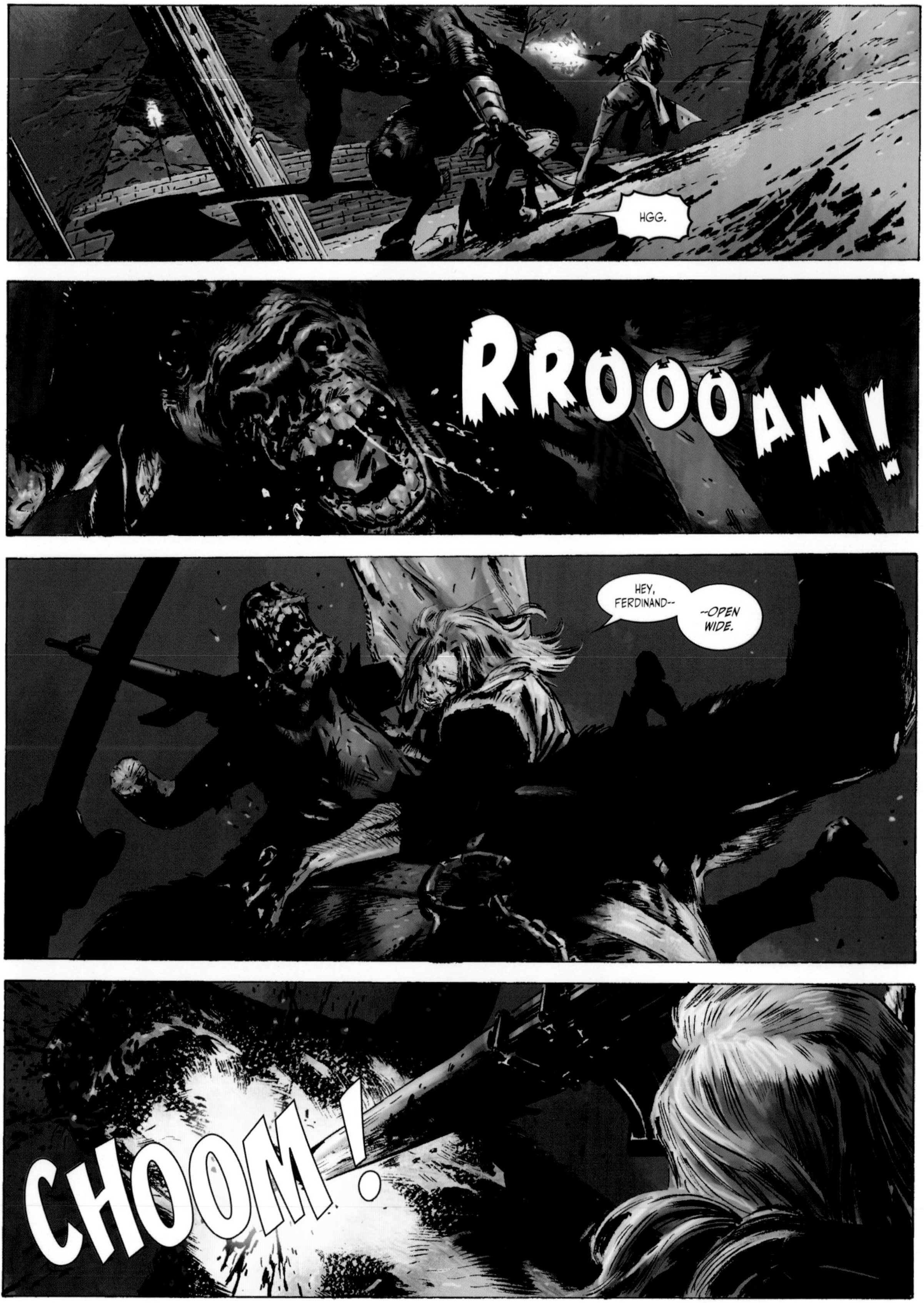
HGG.
RROOOAA!
HEY, FERDINAND--
--OPEN WIDE.
CHOOM!

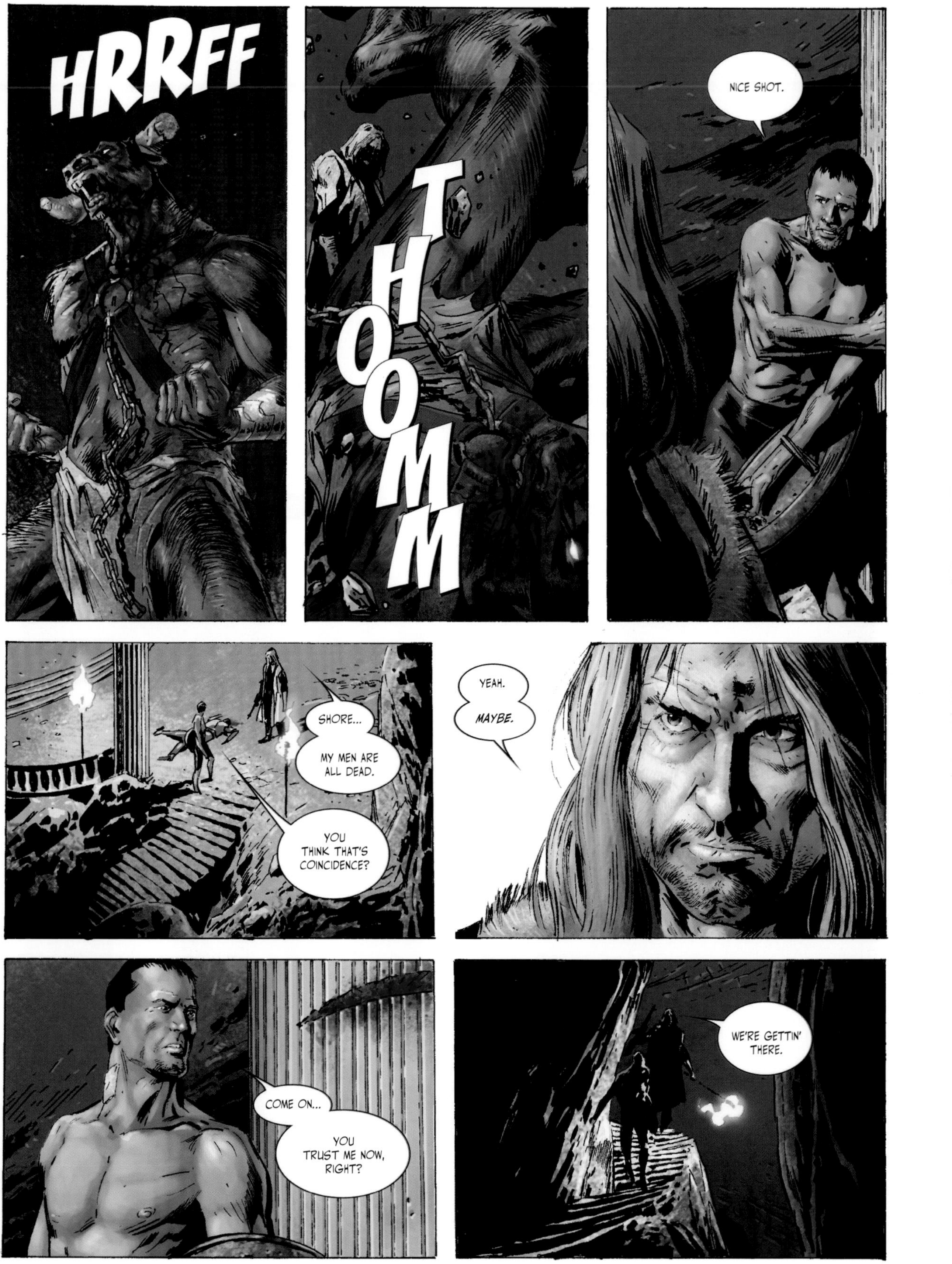
HRRFF
THOOMM
NICE SHOT.
SHORE...
MY MEN ARE ALL DEAD.
YOU THINK THAT'S COINCIDENCE?
YEAH.
MAYBE.
COME ON...
YOU TRUST ME NOW, RIGHT?
WE'RE GETTIN' THERE.

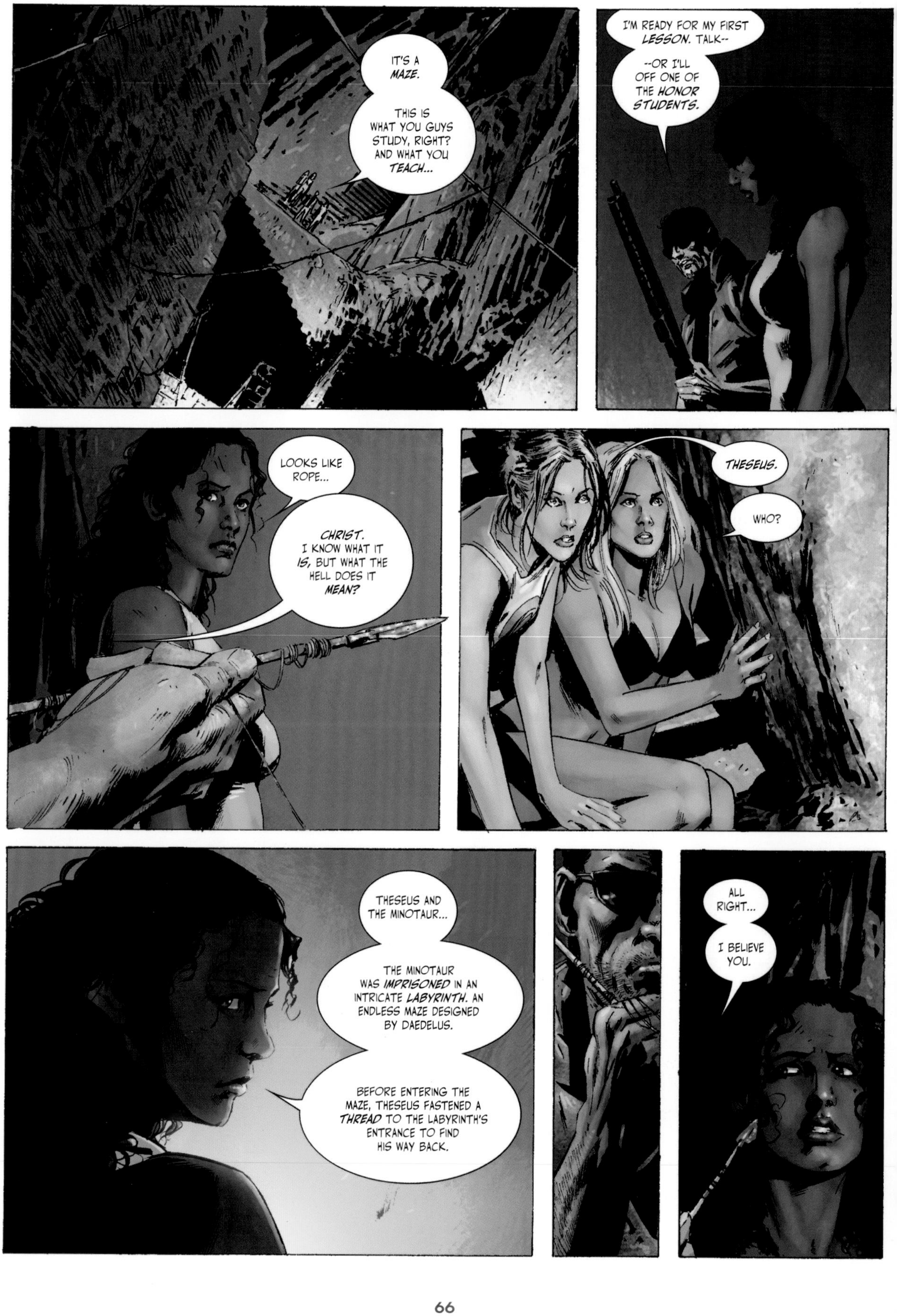
IT'S A *MAZE*.
THIS IS WHAT YOU GUYS STUDY, RIGHT? AND WHAT YOU *TEACH*...
I'M READY FOR MY FIRST *LESSON*. TALK--
--OR I'LL OFF ONE OF THE *HONOR STUDENTS*.
LOOKS LIKE ROPE...
CHRIST. I KNOW WHAT IT *IS*, BUT WHAT THE HELL DOES IT *MEAN?*
THESEUS.
WHO?
THESEUS AND THE MINOTAUR...
THE MINOTAUR WAS *IMPRISONED* IN AN INTRICATE *LABYRINTH*. AN ENDLESS MAZE DESIGNED BY DAEDELUS.
BEFORE ENTERING THE MAZE, THESEUS FASTENED A *THREAD* TO THE LABYRINTH'S ENTRANCE TO FIND HIS WAY BACK.
ALL RIGHT...
I BELIEVE YOU.

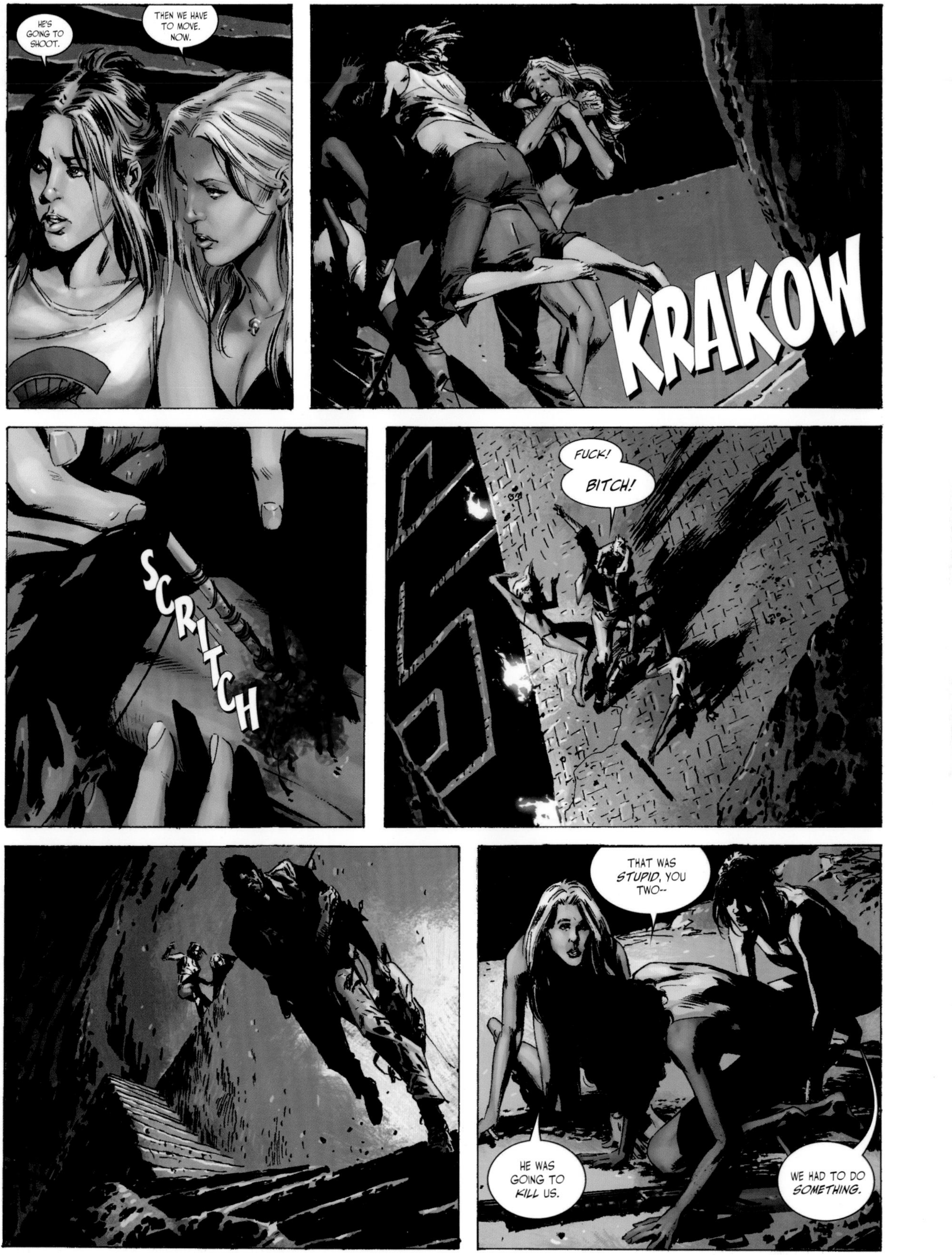
HE'S GOING TO SHOOT.
THEN WE HAVE TO MOVE. NOW.
KRAKOW
SCRITCH
FUCK!
BITCH!
THAT WAS *STUPID*, YOU TWO--
HE WAS GOING TO *KILL* US.
WE HAD TO DO *SOMETHING*.

WE'VE GOT ANOTHER PROBLEM--

--DEEMS MADE OFF WITH THE *THESEUS THREAD.*

WHAT'S A THESEUS THREAD?

I'VE ALREADY DONE THAT LECTURE. THE MINOTAUR?

DEAD. YOU FIND DEEMS?

YEAH, BUT HE MADE OFF WITH OUR ONLY WAY *THROUGH* THAT MAZE.

AND HE STILL HAS THE BOX.

HEY, YOU GUYS--

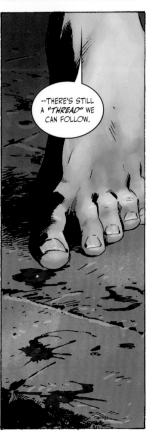

--THERE'S STILL A *"THREAD"* WE CAN FOLLOW.

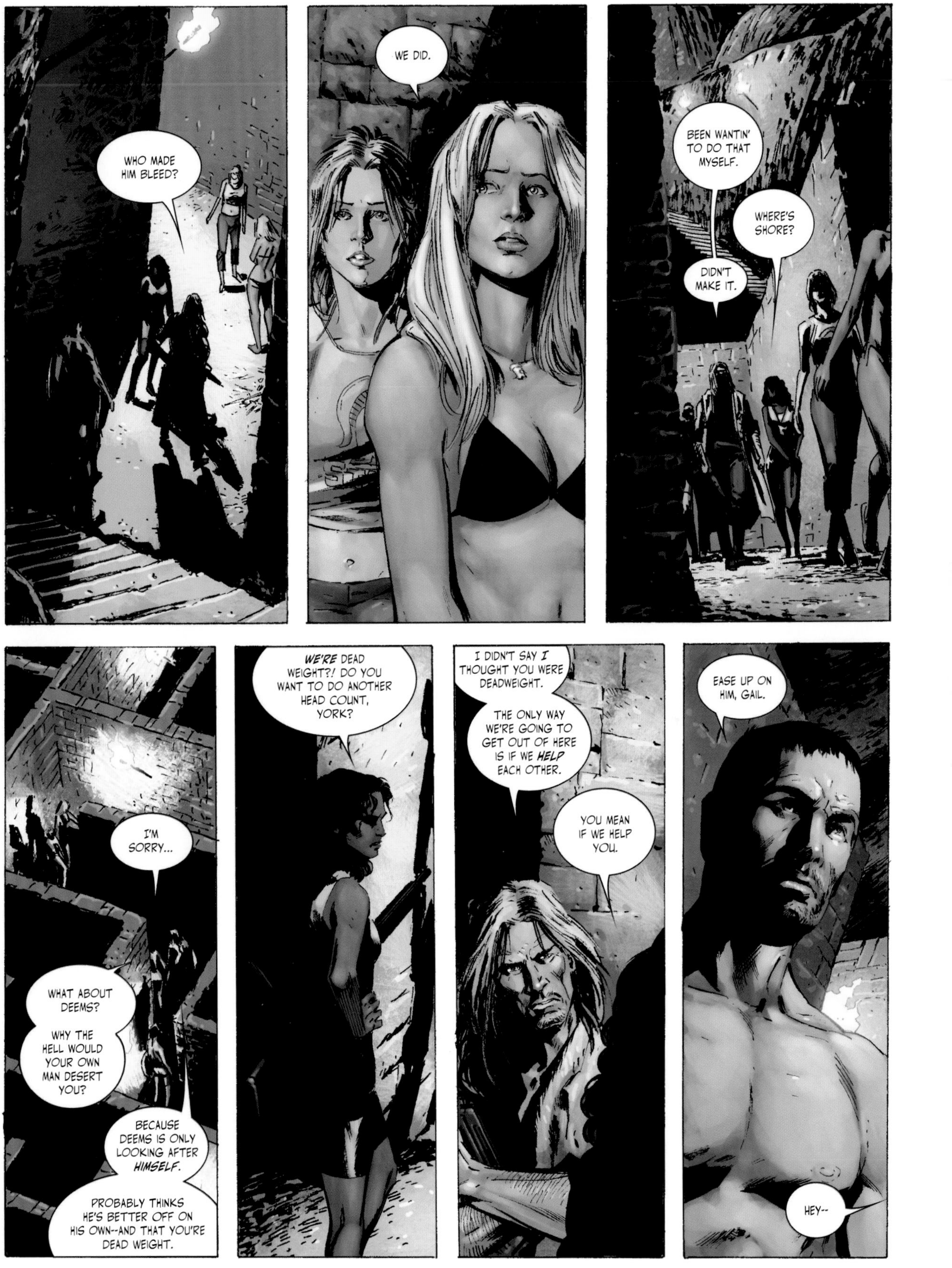
WHO MADE HIM BLEED?
WE DID.
BEEN WANTIN' TO DO THAT MYSELF.
WHERE'S SHORE?
DIDN'T MAKE IT.
I'M SORRY...
WHAT ABOUT DEEMS?
WHY THE HELL WOULD YOUR OWN MAN DESERT YOU?
BECAUSE DEEMS IS ONLY LOOKING AFTER *HIMSELF*.
PROBABLY THINKS HE'S BETTER OFF ON HIS OWN--AND THAT YOU'RE DEAD WEIGHT.
WE'RE DEAD WEIGHT?! DO YOU WANT TO DO ANOTHER HEAD COUNT, YORK?
I DIDN'T SAY *I* THOUGHT YOU WERE DEADWEIGHT.
THE ONLY WAY WE'RE GOING TO GET OUT OF HERE IS IF WE *HELP* EACH OTHER.
YOU MEAN IF WE HELP YOU.
EASE UP ON HIM, GAIL.
HEY--

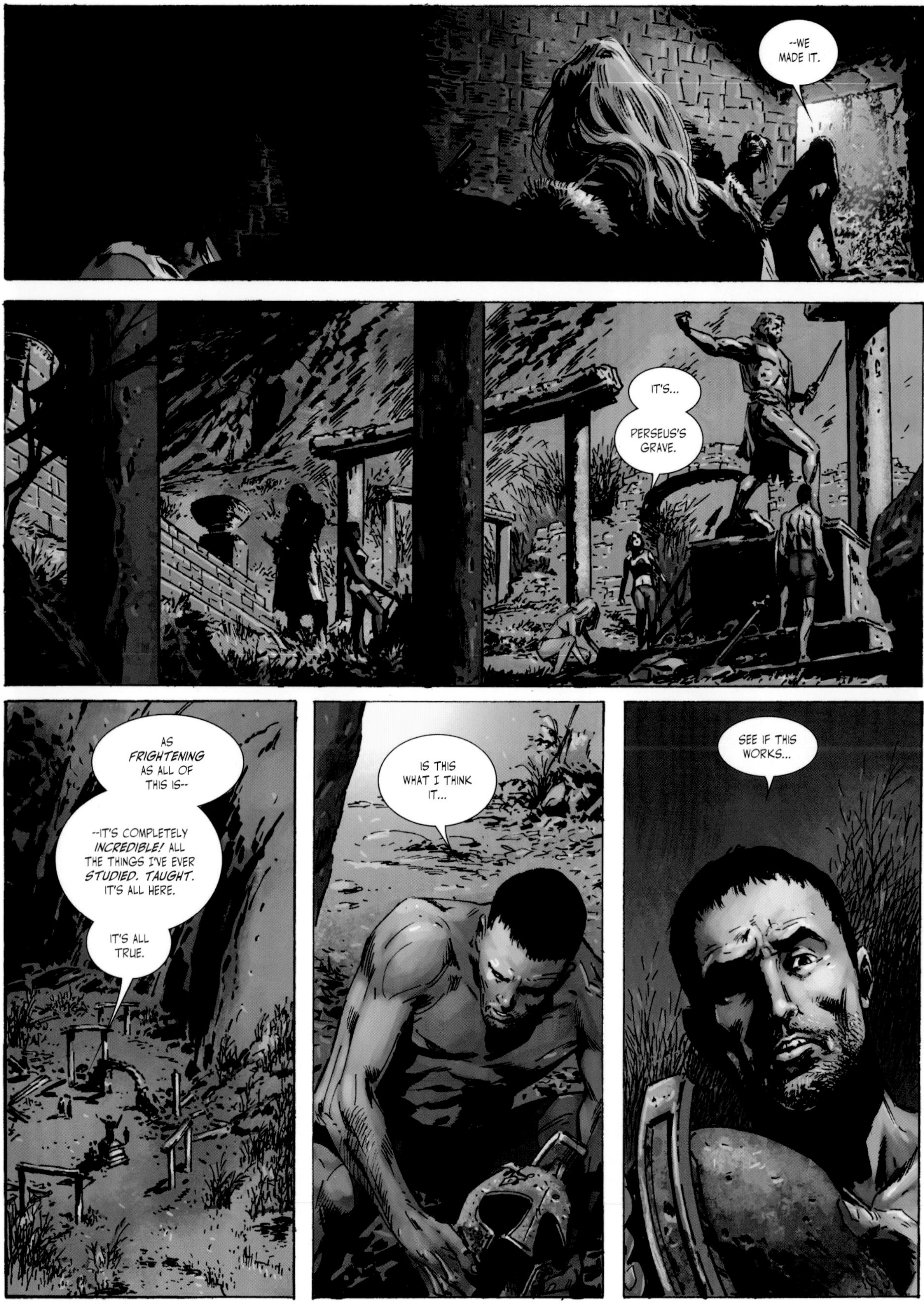
--WE MADE IT.
IT'S...
PERSEUS'S GRAVE.
AS FRIGHTENING AS ALL OF THIS IS--
--IT'S COMPLETELY INCREDIBLE! ALL THE THINGS I'VE EVER STUDIED. TAUGHT. IT'S ALL HERE.
IT'S ALL TRUE.
IS THIS WHAT I THINK IT...
SEE IF THIS WORKS...

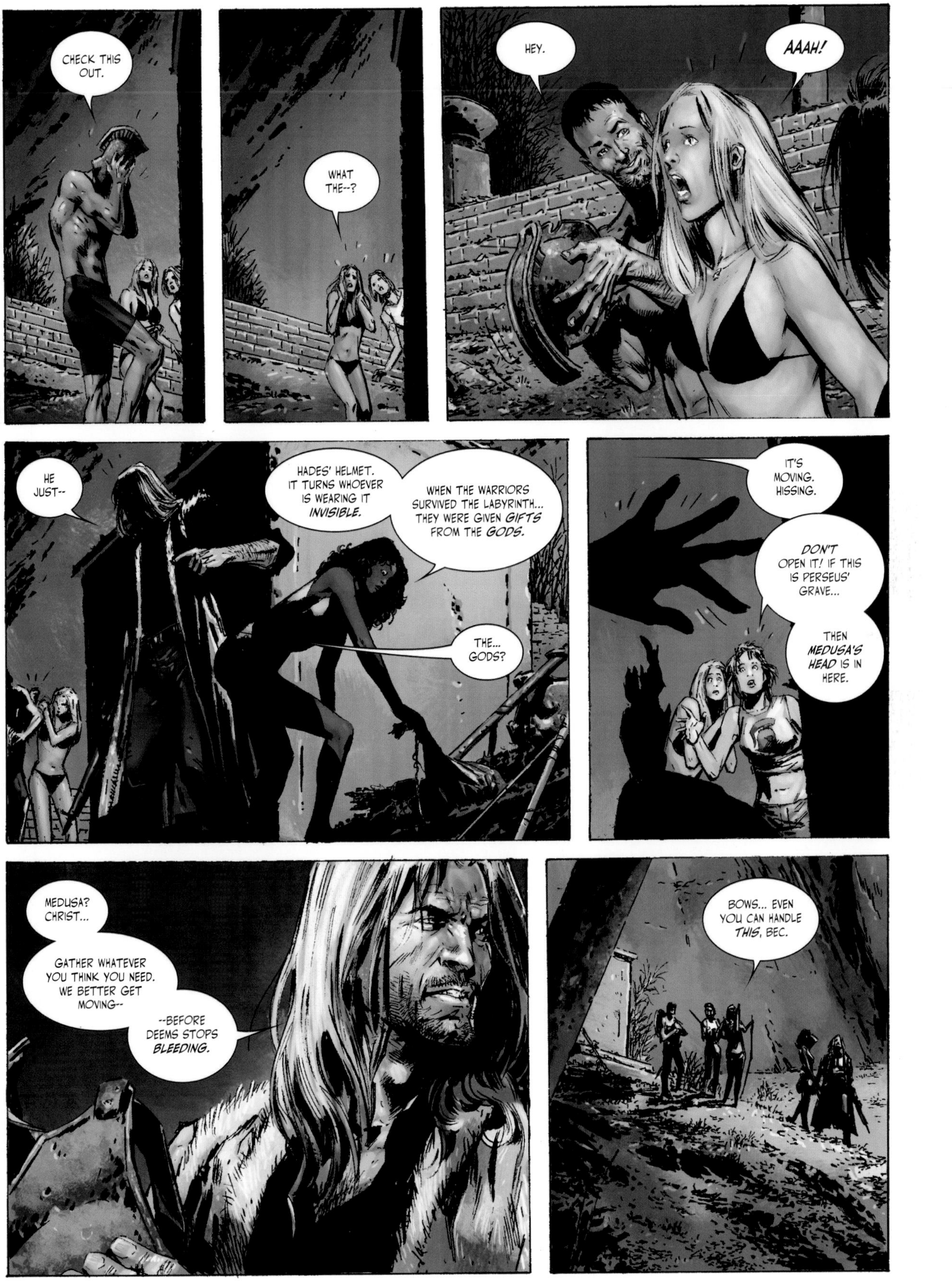
CHECK THIS OUT.
WHAT THE--?
HEY.
AAAH!
HE JUST--
HADES' HELMET. IT TURNS WHOEVER IS WEARING IT INVISIBLE.
WHEN THE WARRIORS SURVIVED THE LABYRINTH... THEY WERE GIVEN GIFTS FROM THE GODS.
THE... GODS?
IT'S MOVING. HISSING.
DON'T OPEN IT! IF THIS IS PERSEUS' GRAVE...
THEN MEDUSA'S HEAD IS IN HERE.
MEDUSA? CHRIST...
GATHER WHATEVER YOU THINK YOU NEED. WE BETTER GET MOVING--
--BEFORE DEEMS STOPS BLEEDING.
BOWS... EVEN YOU CAN HANDLE THIS, BEC.

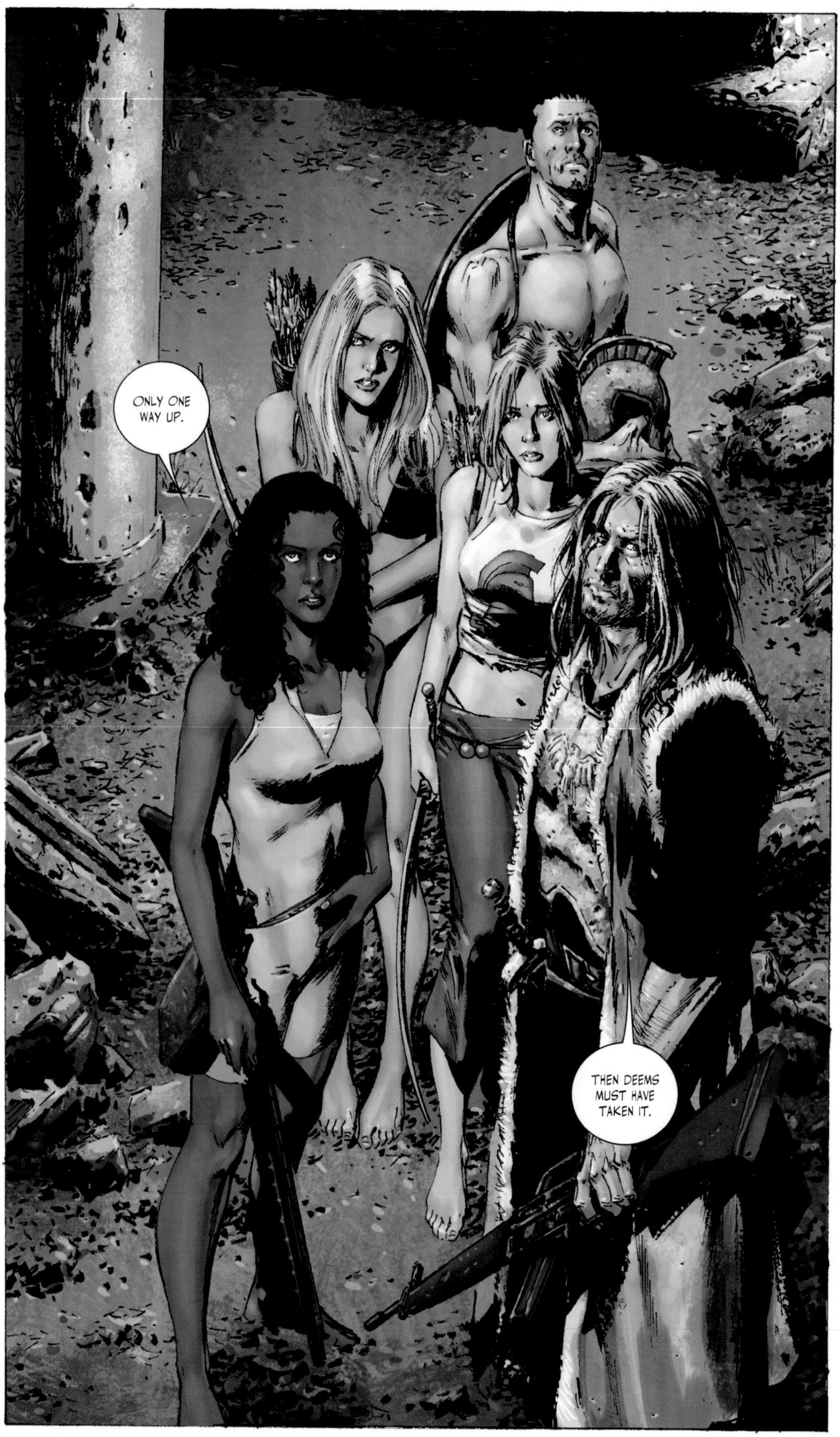
ONLY ONE WAY UP.
THEN DEEMS MUST HAVE TAKEN IT.

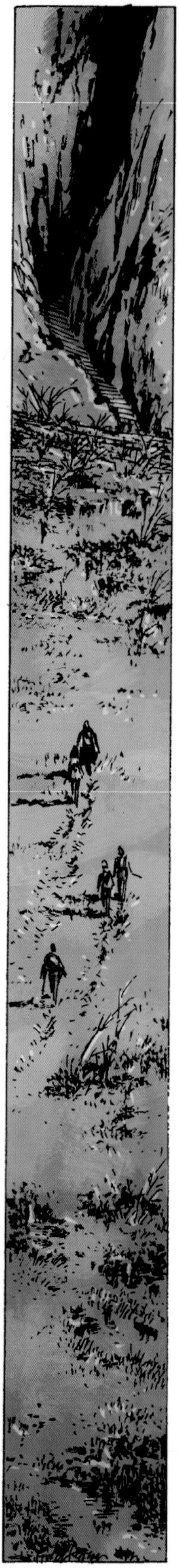

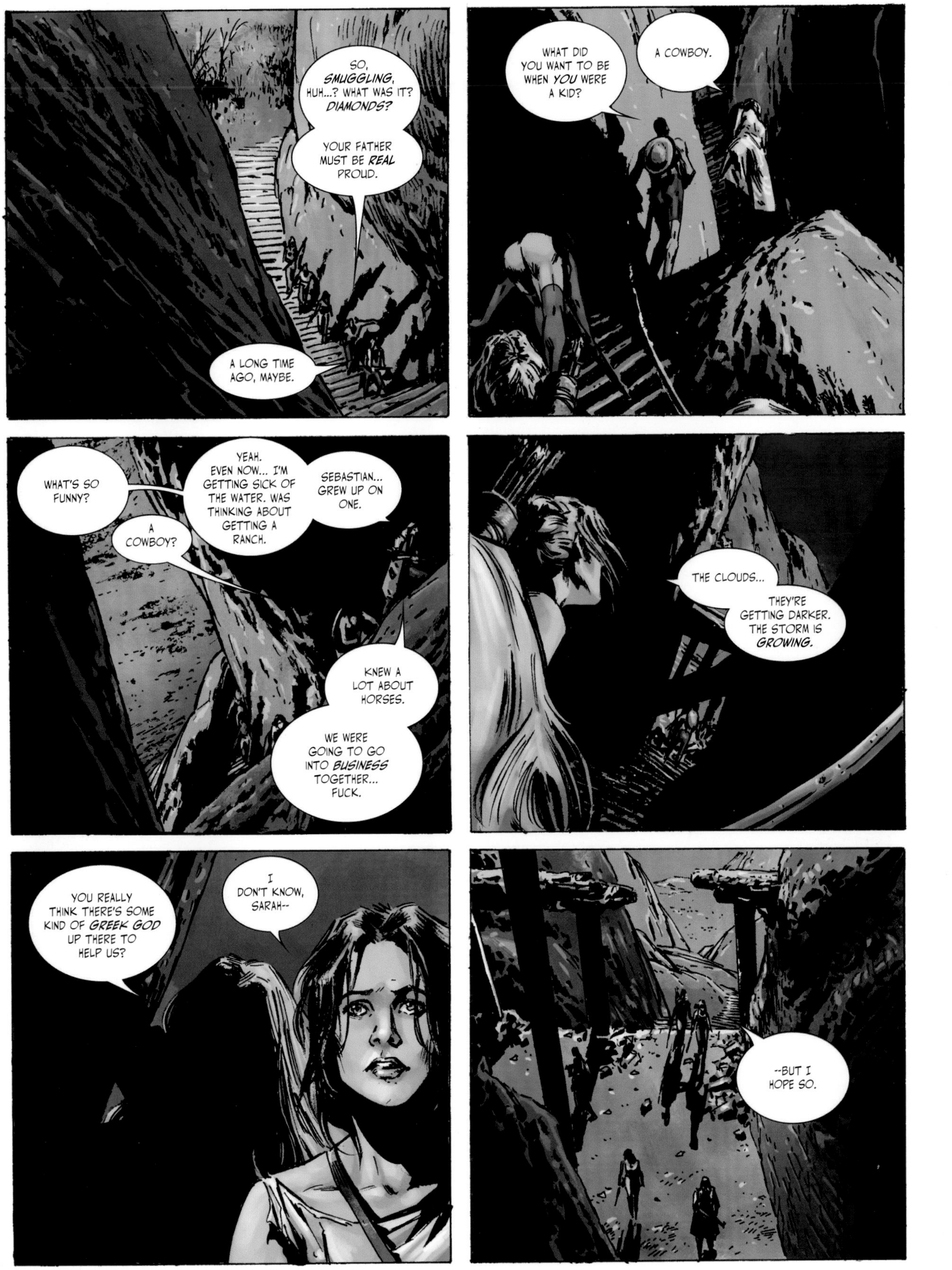
SO, SMUGGLING, HUH...? WHAT WAS IT? DIAMONDS?
YOUR FATHER MUST BE REAL PROUD.
A LONG TIME AGO, MAYBE.
WHAT DID YOU WANT TO BE WHEN YOU WERE A KID?
A COWBOY.
WHAT'S SO FUNNY?
A COWBOY?
YEAH. EVEN NOW... I'M GETTING SICK OF THE WATER. WAS THINKING ABOUT GETTING A RANCH.
SEBASTIAN... GREW UP ON ONE.
KNEW A LOT ABOUT HORSES.
WE WERE GOING TO GO INTO BUSINESS TOGETHER... FUCK.
THE CLOUDS...
THEY'RE GETTING DARKER. THE STORM IS GROWING.
YOU REALLY THINK THERE'S SOME KIND OF GREEK GOD UP THERE TO HELP US?
I DON'T KNOW, SARAH--
--BUT I HOPE SO.

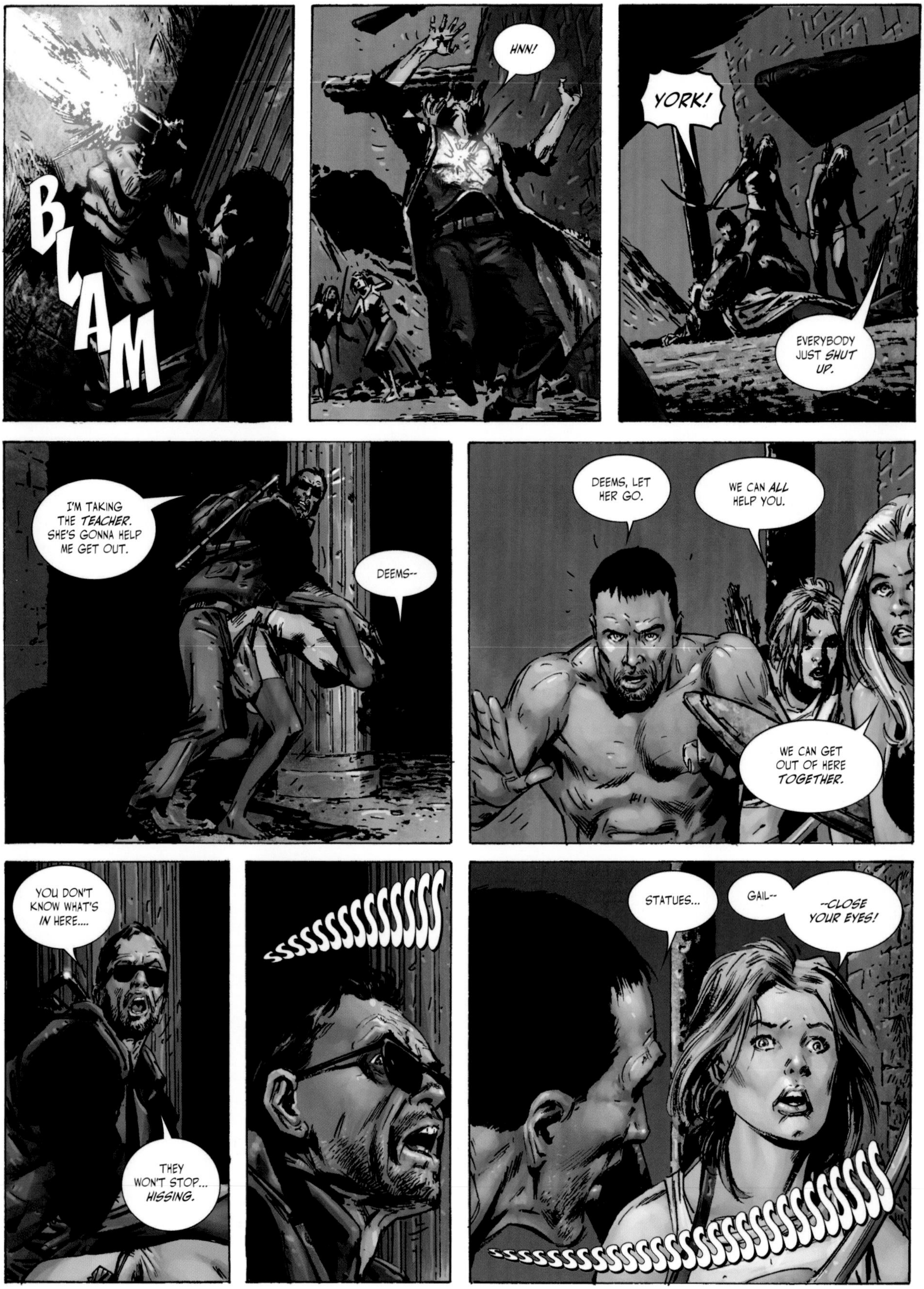
BLAM
HNN!
YORK!
EVERYBODY JUST SHUT UP.
I'M TAKING THE TEACHER. SHE'S GONNA HELP ME GET OUT.
DEEMS--
DEEMS, LET HER GO.
WE CAN ALL HELP YOU.
WE CAN GET OUT OF HERE TOGETHER.
YOU DON'T KNOW WHAT'S IN HERE....
THEY WON'T STOP... HISSING.
SSSSSSSSSSSSSSSS
STATUES...
GAIL--
--CLOSE YOUR EYES!
SSSSSSSSSSSSSSSSSSSSSSSSSSSSSSSSSSSSSS

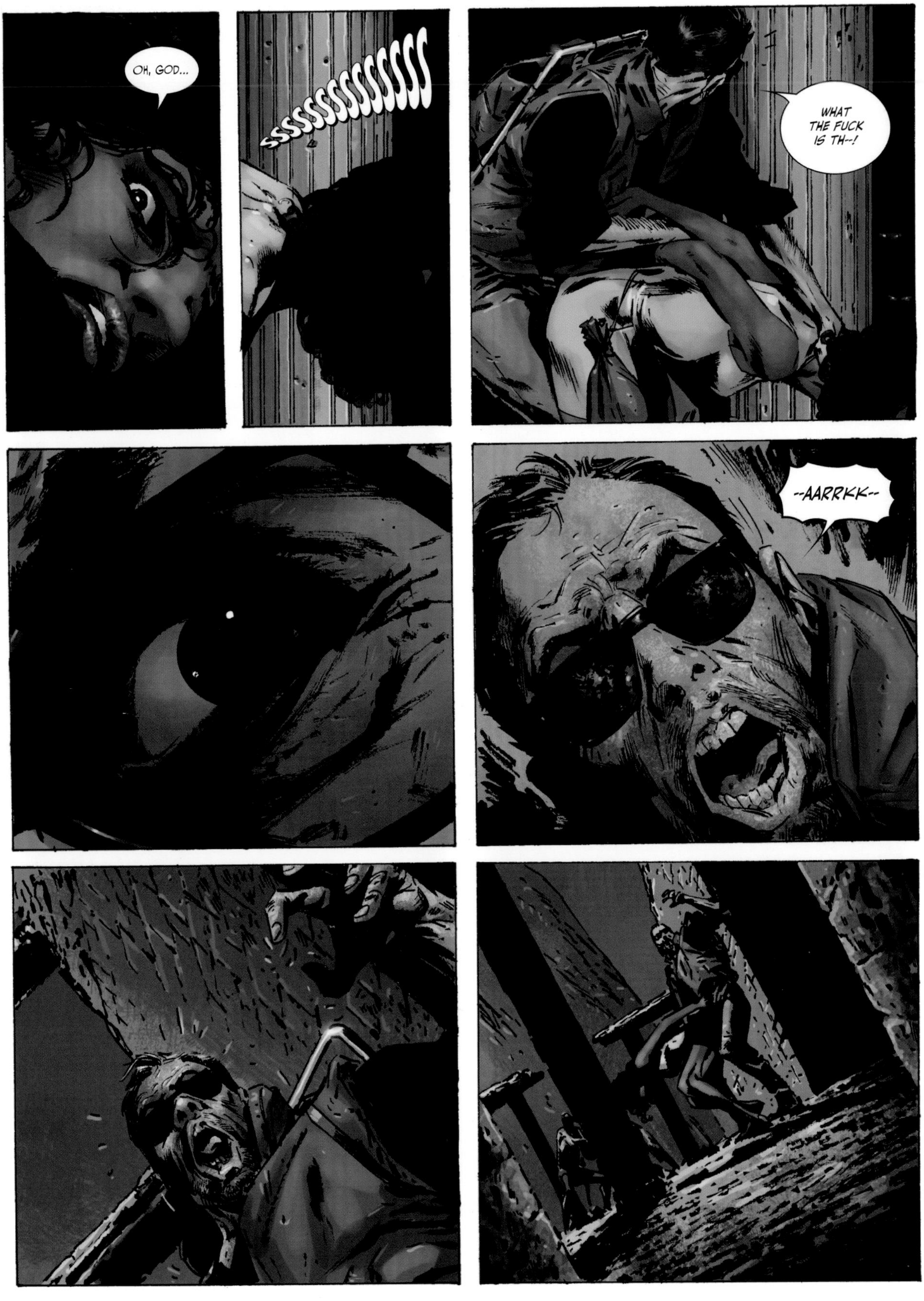
OH, GOD...
SSSSSSSSSSSSSSSS
WHAT THE FUCK IS TH--!
--AARRKK--

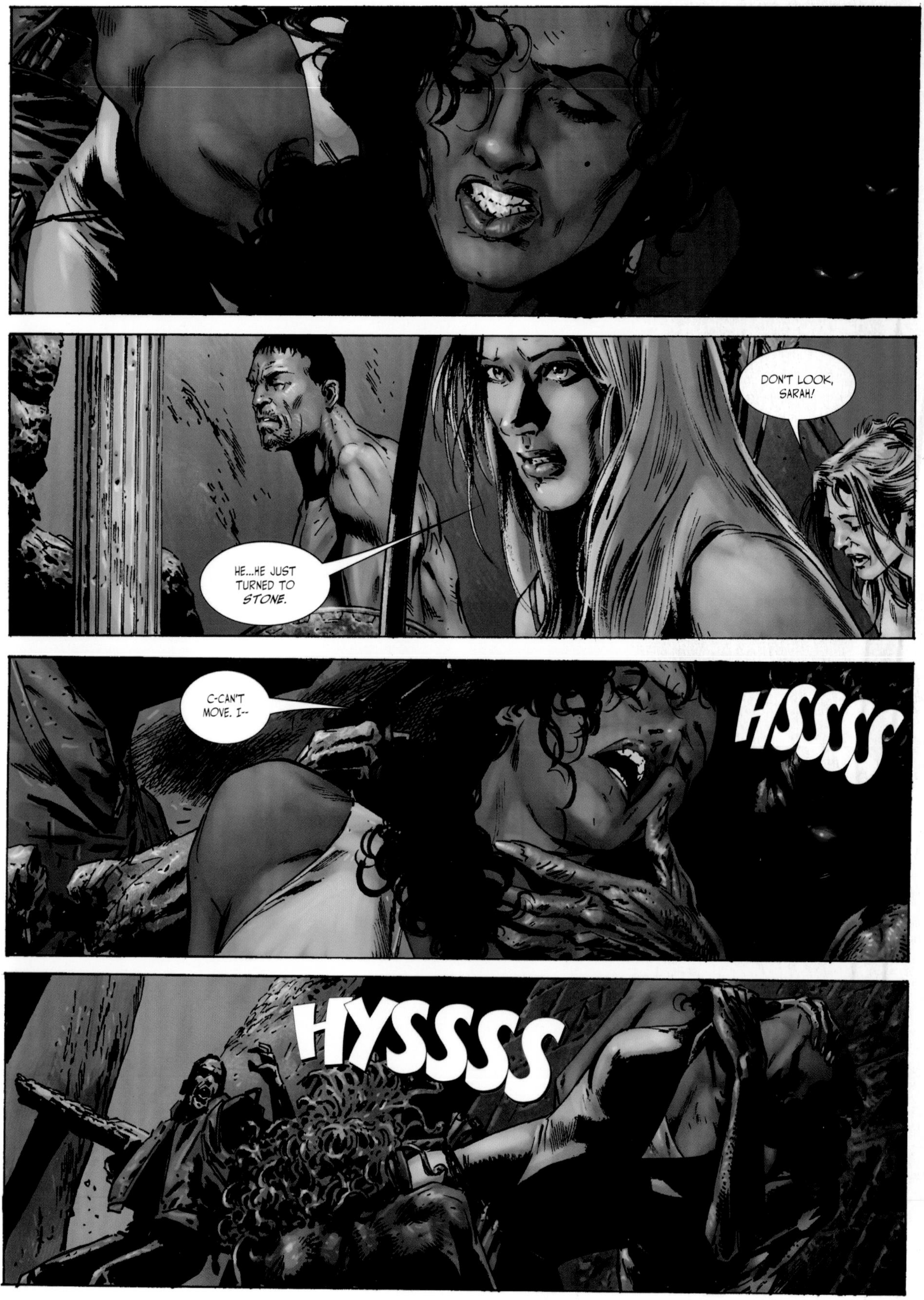
DON'T LOOK, SARAH!
HE...HE JUST TURNED TO STONE.
C-CAN'T MOVE. I--
HSSSS
HYSSSS

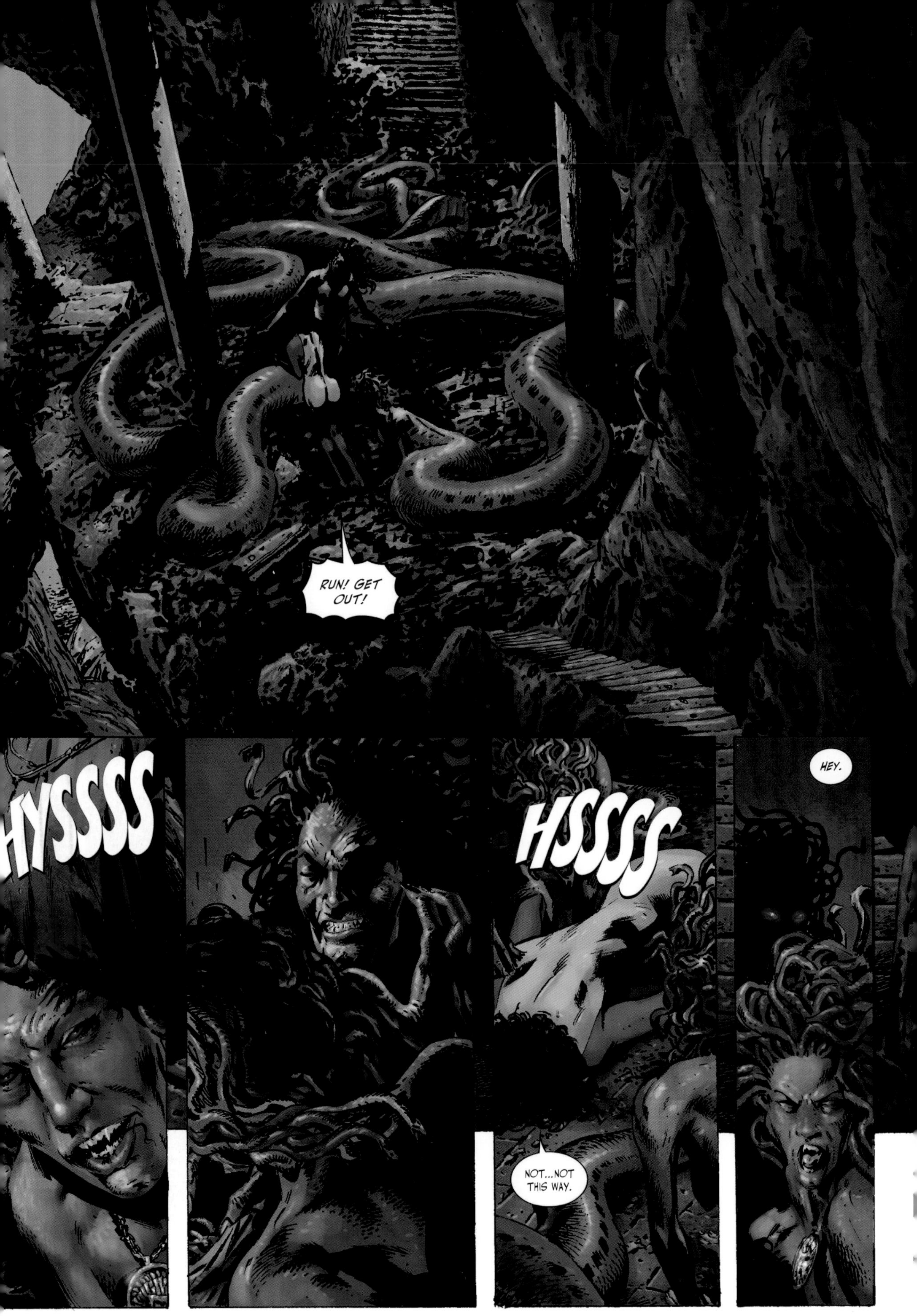
RUN! GET OUT!
HYSSSS
HSSSS
NOT...NOT THIS WAY.
HEY.

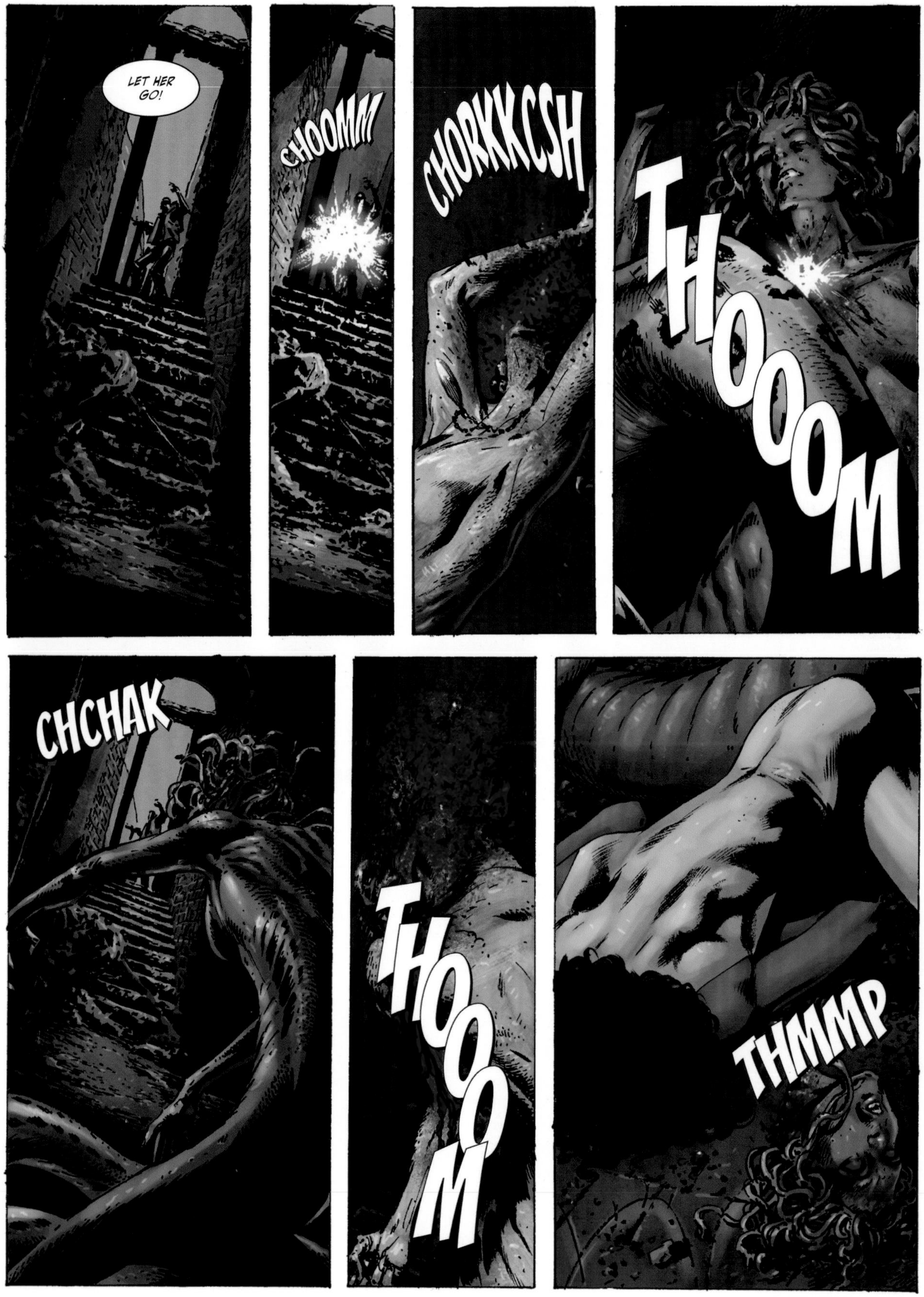
LET HER GO!
CHOOMM
CHORKKCSH
THOOOOM
CHCHAK
THOOOOM
THMMP

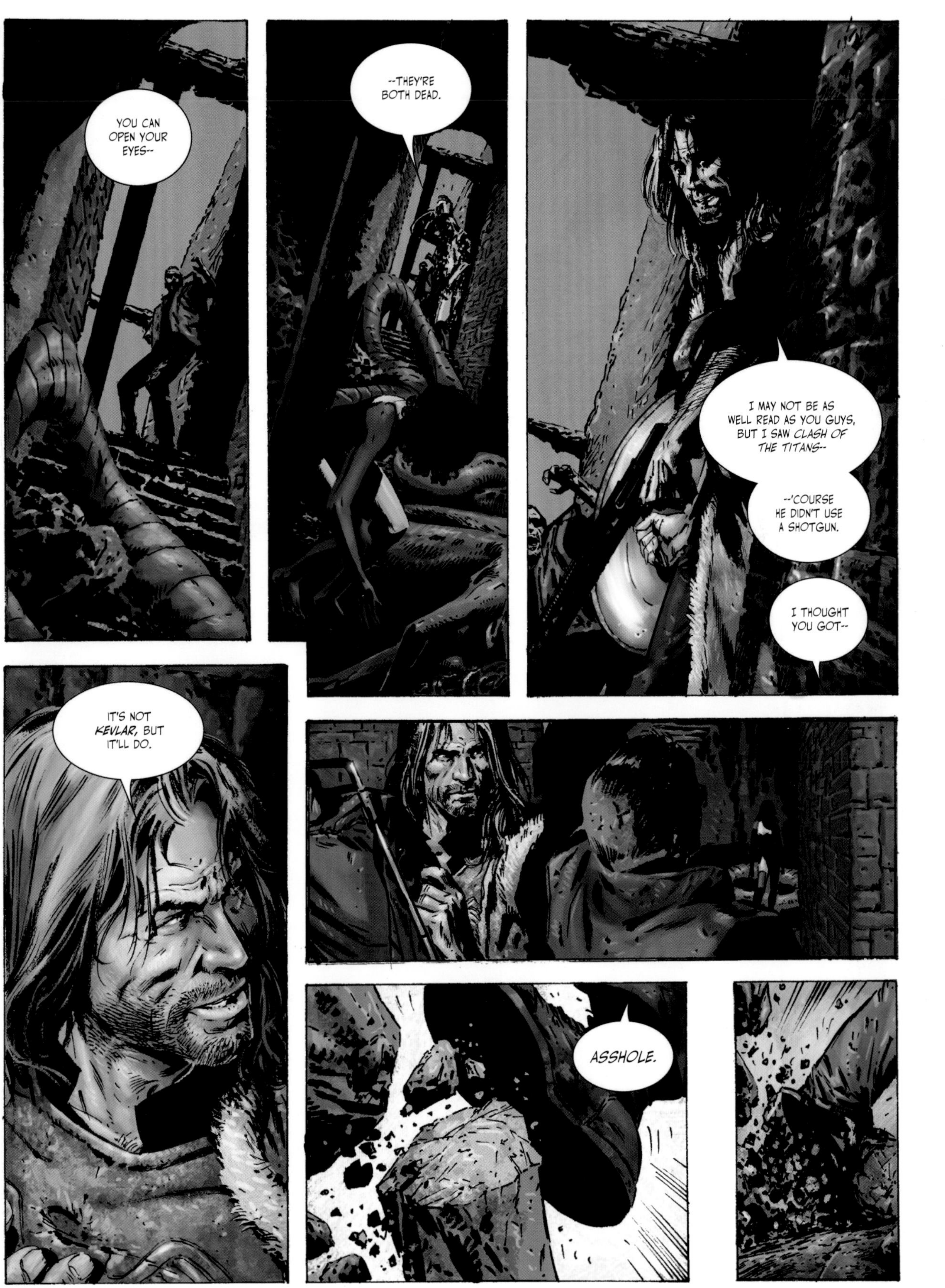
YOU CAN OPEN YOUR EYES--
--THEY'RE BOTH DEAD.
I MAY NOT BE AS WELL READ AS YOU GUYS, BUT I SAW CLASH OF THE TITANS--
--'COURSE HE DIDN'T USE A SHOTGUN.
I THOUGHT YOU GOT--
IT'S NOT KEVLAR, BUT IT'LL DO.
ASSHOLE.

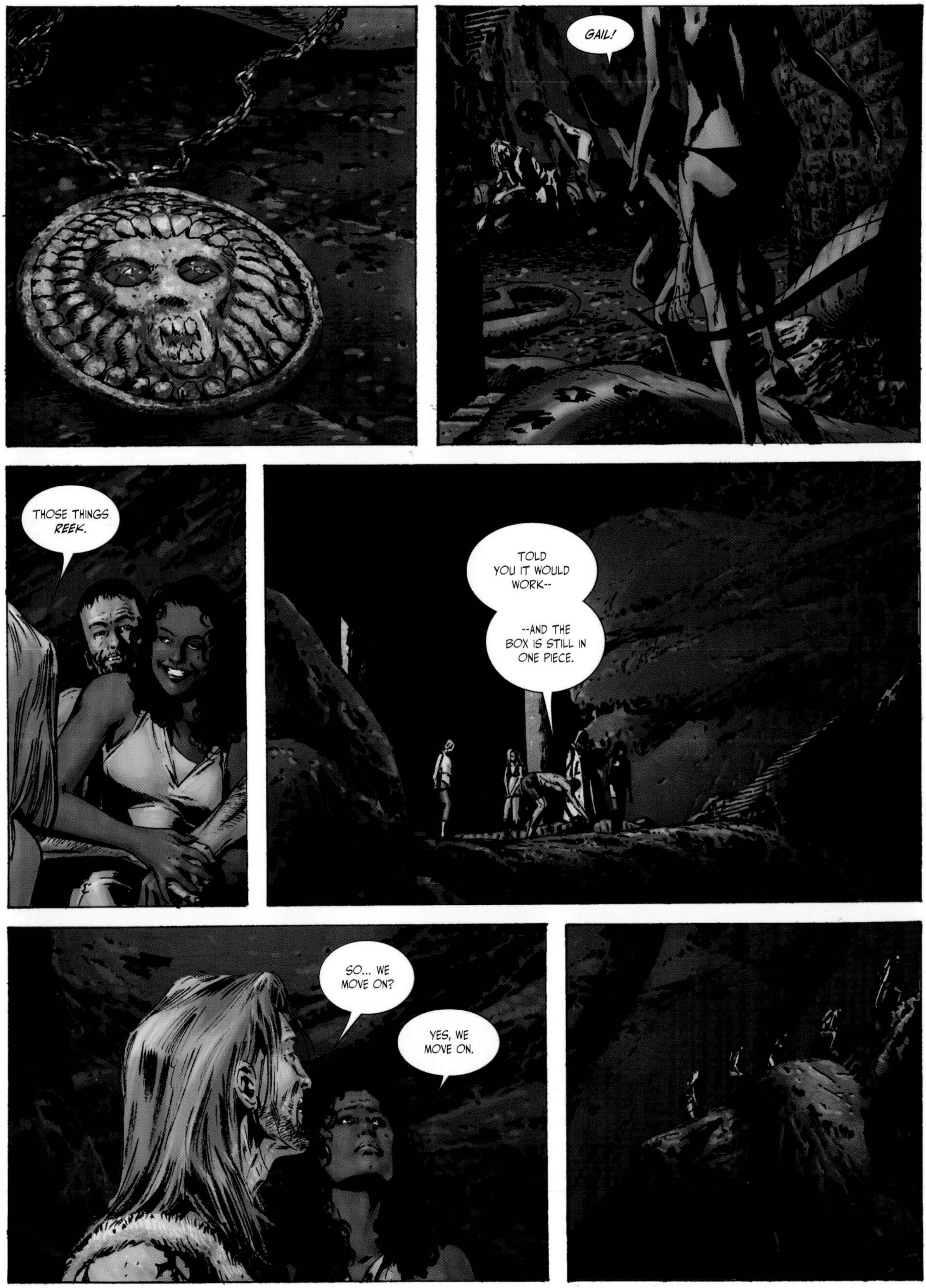
GAIL!
THOSE THINGS REEK.
TOLD YOU IT WOULD WORK--
--AND THE BOX IS STILL IN ONE PIECE.
SO... WE MOVE ON?
YES, WE MOVE ON.

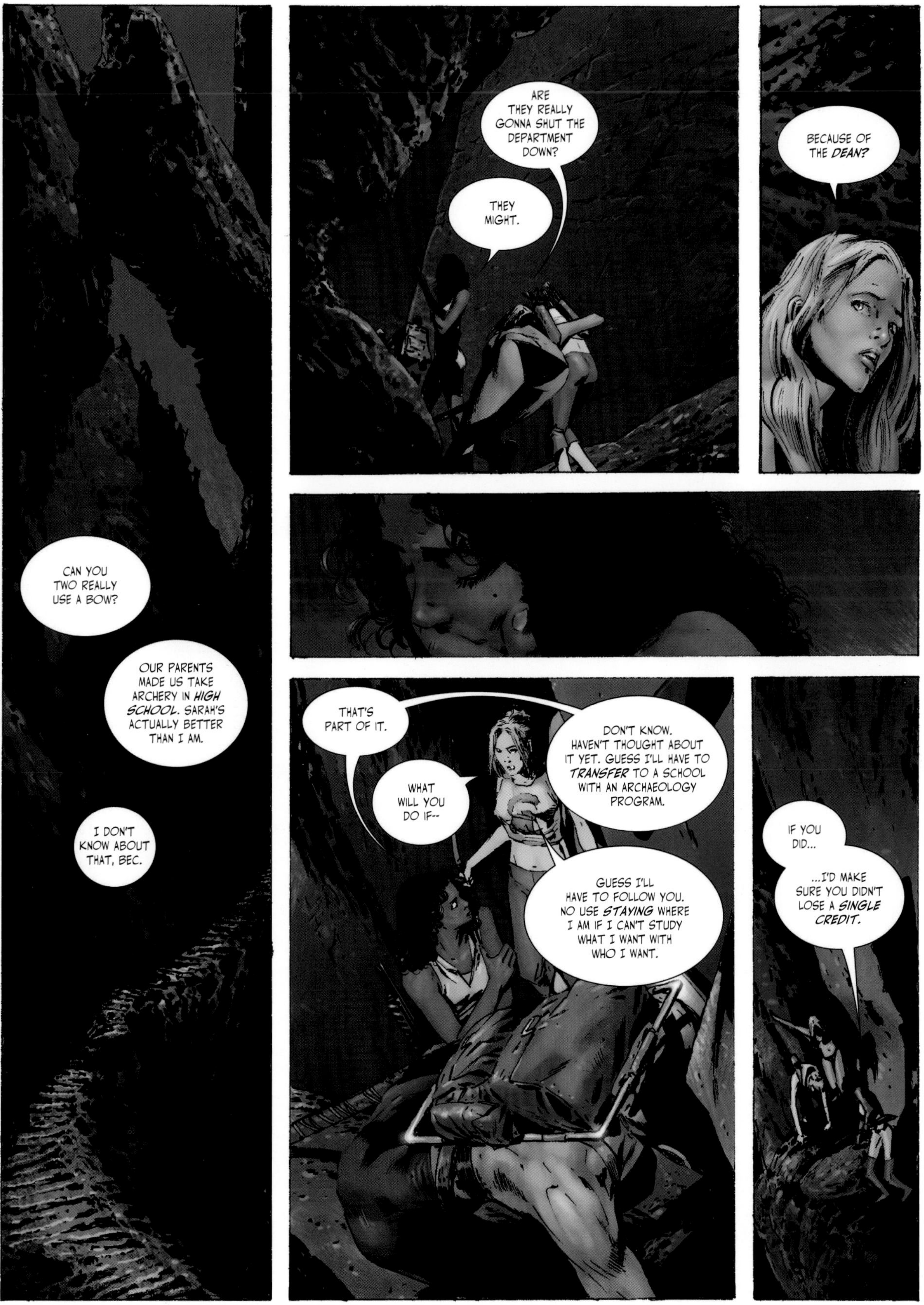
CAN YOU TWO REALLY USE A BOW?
OUR PARENTS MADE US TAKE ARCHERY IN HIGH SCHOOL. SARAH'S ACTUALLY BETTER THAN I AM.
I DON'T KNOW ABOUT THAT, BEC.
ARE THEY REALLY GONNA SHUT THE DEPARTMENT DOWN?
THEY MIGHT.
BECAUSE OF THE DEAN?
THAT'S PART OF IT.
WHAT WILL YOU DO IF--
DON'T KNOW. HAVEN'T THOUGHT ABOUT IT YET. GUESS I'LL HAVE TO TRANSFER TO A SCHOOL WITH AN ARCHAEOLOGY PROGRAM.
GUESS I'LL HAVE TO FOLLOW YOU. NO USE STAYING WHERE I AM IF I CAN'T STUDY WHAT I WANT WITH WHO I WANT.
IF YOU DID...
...I'D MAKE SURE YOU DIDN'T LOSE A SINGLE CREDIT.

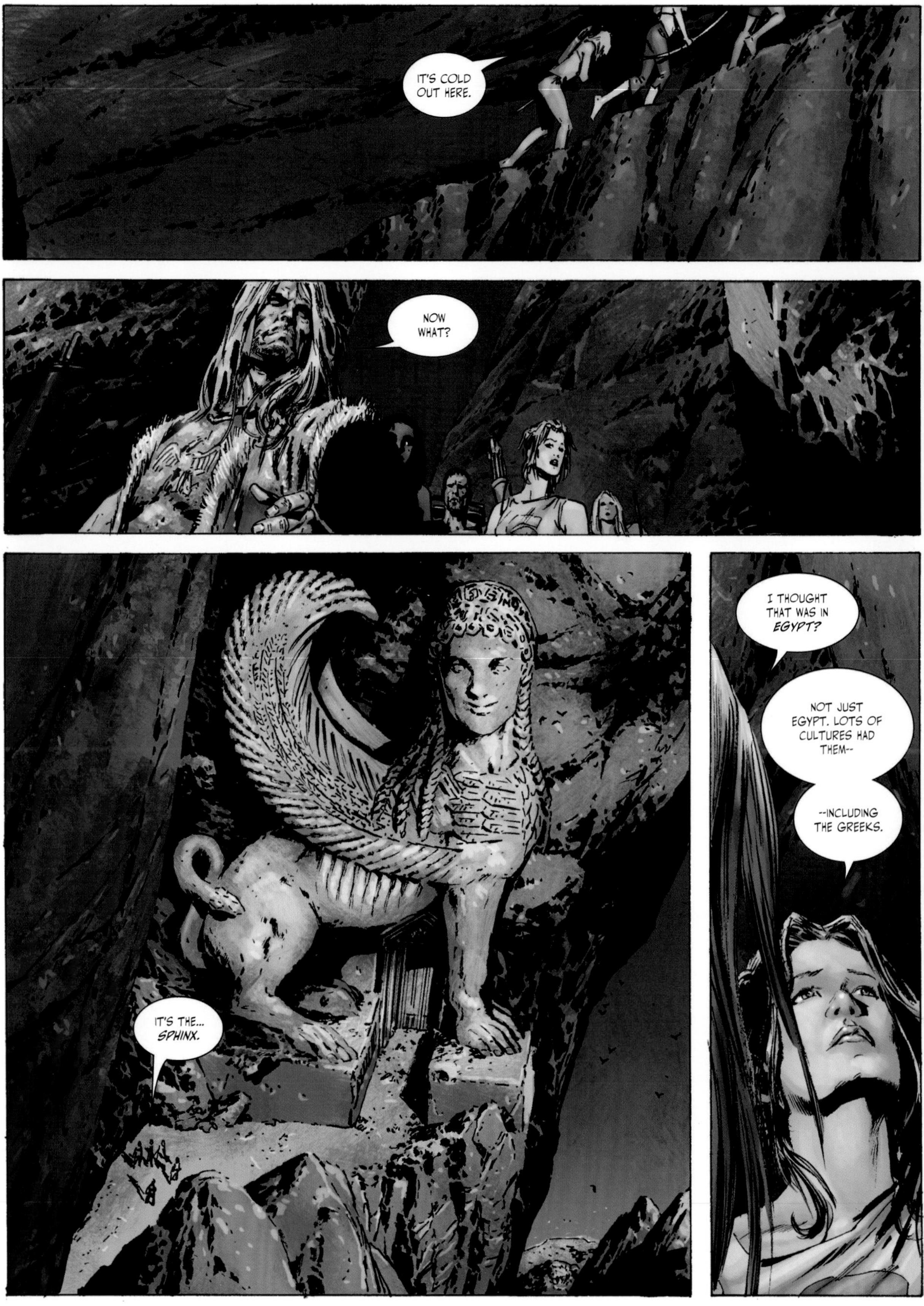
IT'S COLD OUT HERE.
NOW WHAT?
IT'S THE... SPHINX.
I THOUGHT THAT WAS IN EGYPT?
NOT JUST EGYPT. LOTS OF CULTURES HAD THEM--
--INCLUDING THE GREEKS.

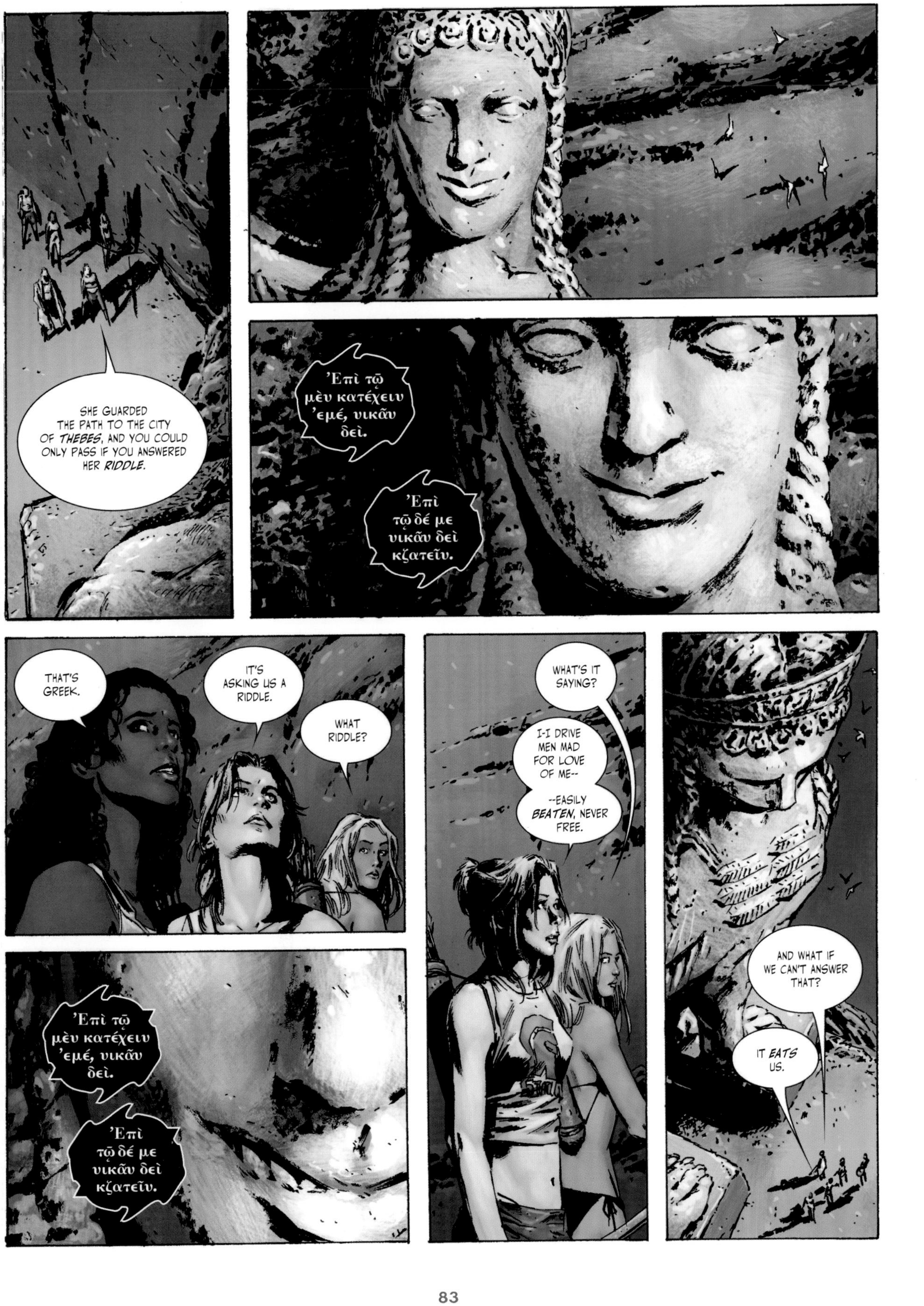
SHE GUARDED THE PATH TO THE CITY OF *THEBES*, AND YOU COULD ONLY PASS IF YOU ANSWERED HER *RIDDLE*.
’Επὶ τῷ μὲν κατέχειυ ’εμέ, νικᾶυ δεὶ.
’Επὶ τῷ δέ με νικᾶυ δεὶ κζατεῖυ.
THAT'S GREEK.
IT'S ASKING US A RIDDLE.
WHAT RIDDLE?
’Επὶ τῷ μὲν κατέχειυ ’εμέ, νικᾶυ δεὶ.
’Επὶ τῷ δέ με νικᾶυ δεὶ κζατεῖυ.
WHAT'S IT SAYING?
I-I DRIVE MEN MAD FOR LOVE OF ME--
--EASILY *BEATEN*, NEVER FREE.
AND WHAT IF WE CAN'T ANSWER THAT?
IT *EATS* US.

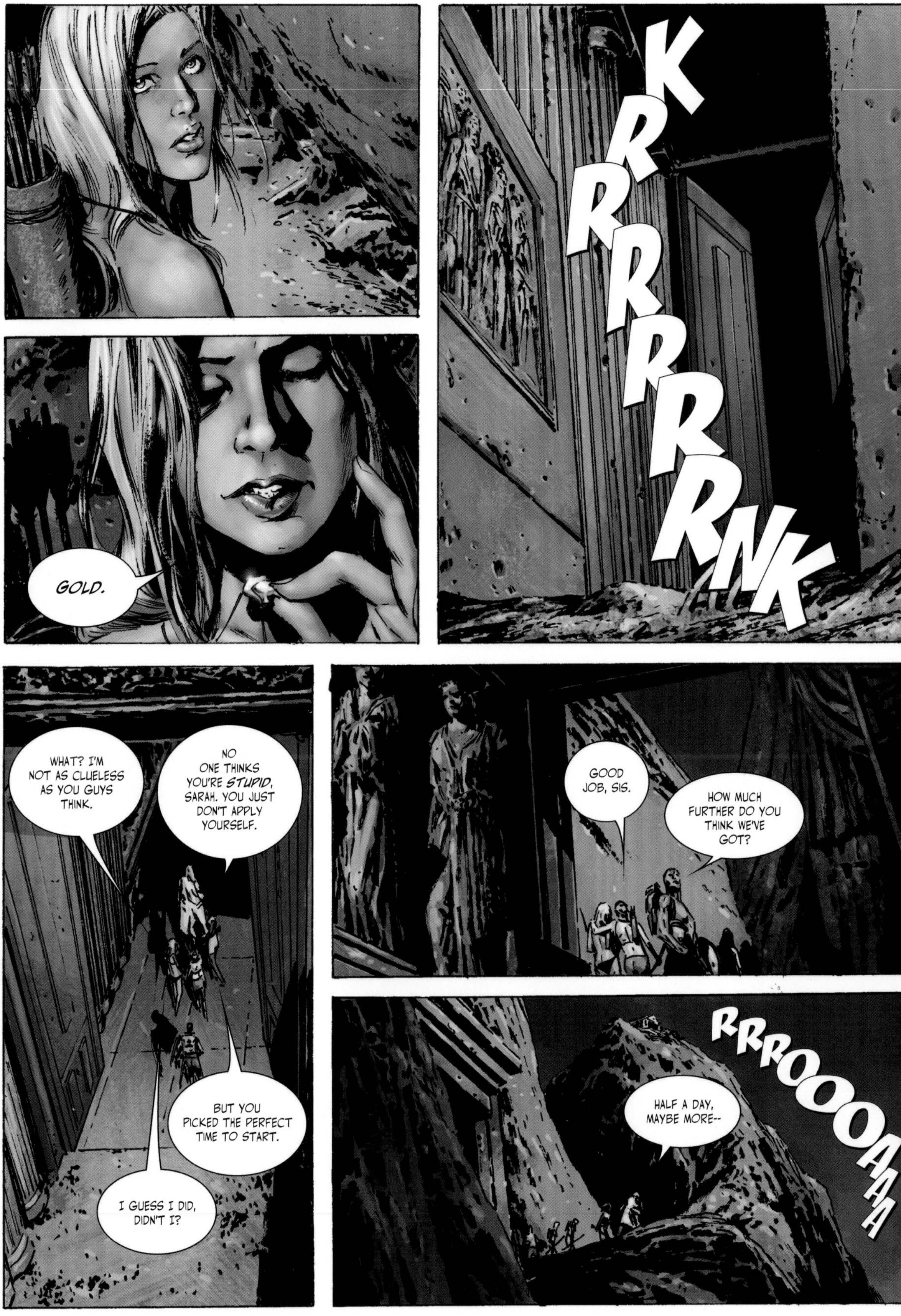
GOLD.
KRRRRRRRRNK
WHAT? I'M NOT AS CLUELESS AS YOU GUYS THINK.
NO ONE THINKS YOU'RE *STUPID*, SARAH. YOU JUST DON'T APPLY YOURSELF.
BUT YOU PICKED THE PERFECT TIME TO START.
I GUESS I DID, DIDN'T I?
GOOD JOB, SIS.
HOW MUCH FURTHER DO YOU THINK WE'VE GOT?
RRROOOOAAA
HALF A DAY, MAYBE MORE--

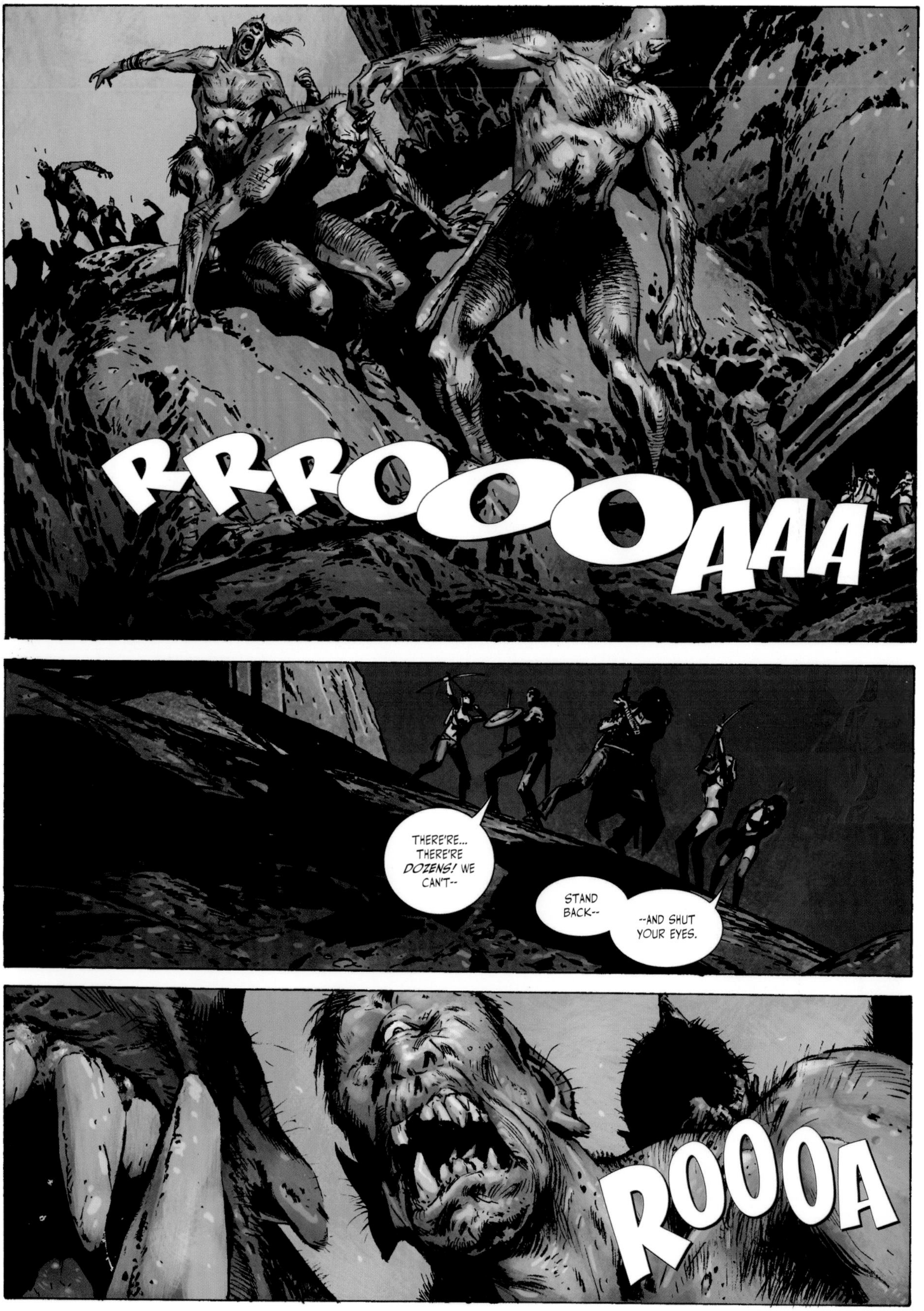
RRROOOOAAA
THERE'RE... THERE'RE DOZENS! WE CAN'T--
STAND BACK--
--AND SHUT YOUR EYES.
ROOOA

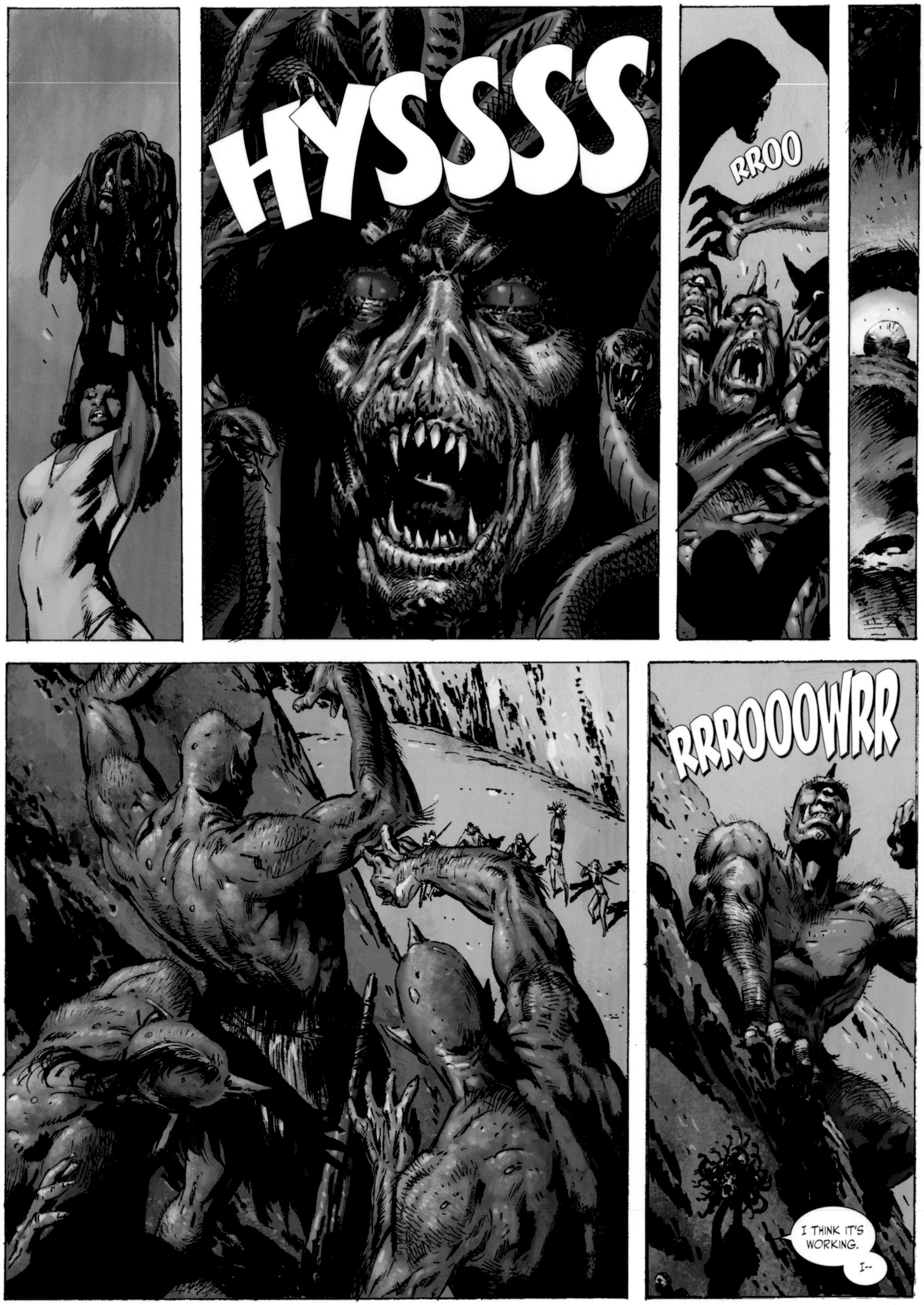
HYSSSS
RROO
RRROOOWRR
I THINK IT'S WORKING.
I--

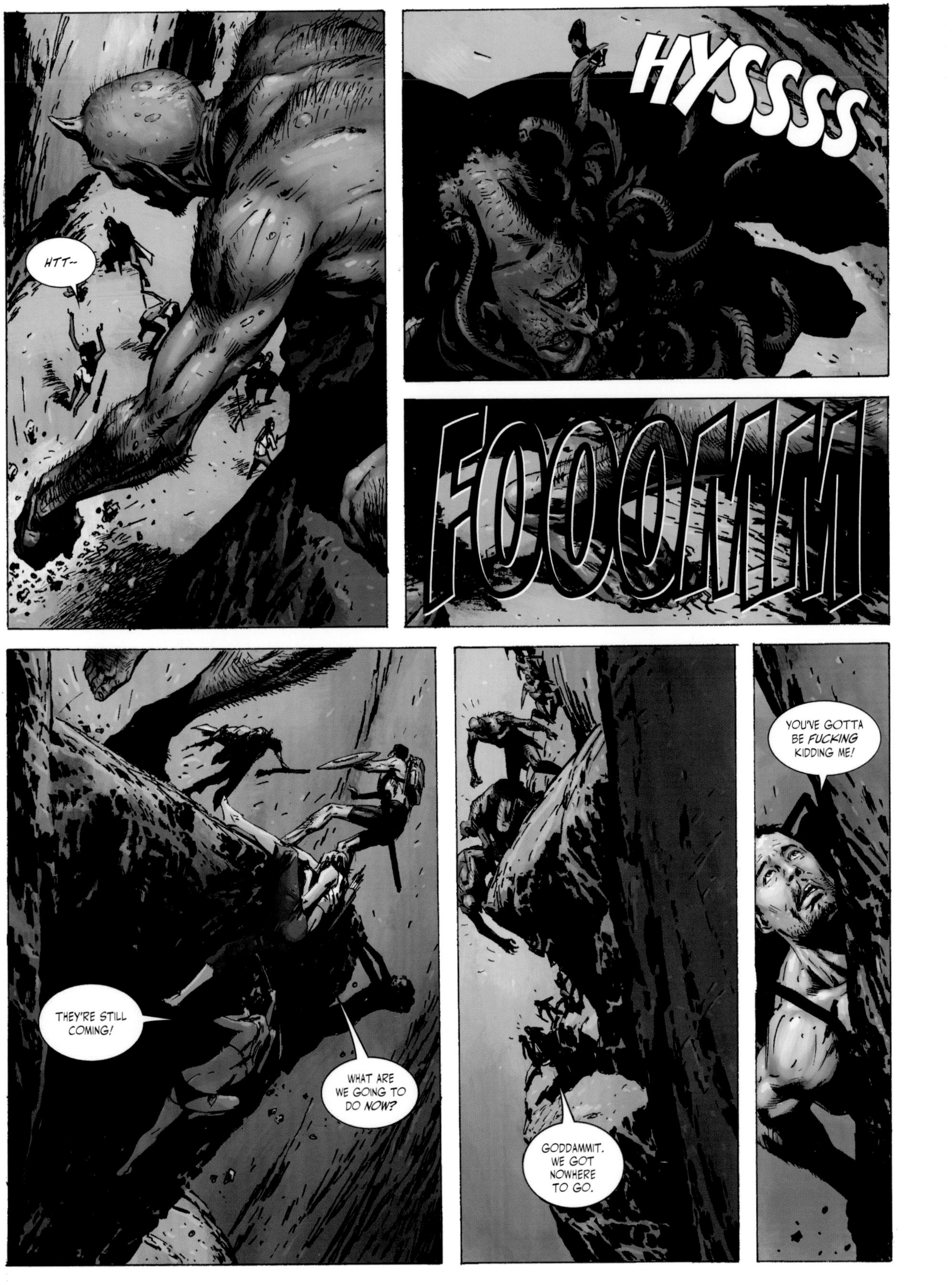
HTT--
HYSSSS
FOOOMM
THEY'RE STILL COMING!
WHAT ARE WE GOING TO DO NOW?
GODDAMMIT. WE GOT NOWHERE TO GO.
YOU'VE GOTTA BE FUCKING KIDDING ME!

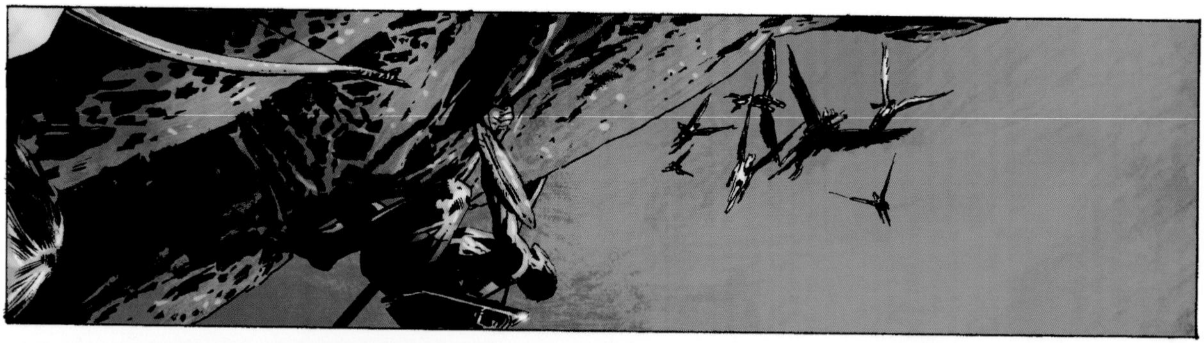

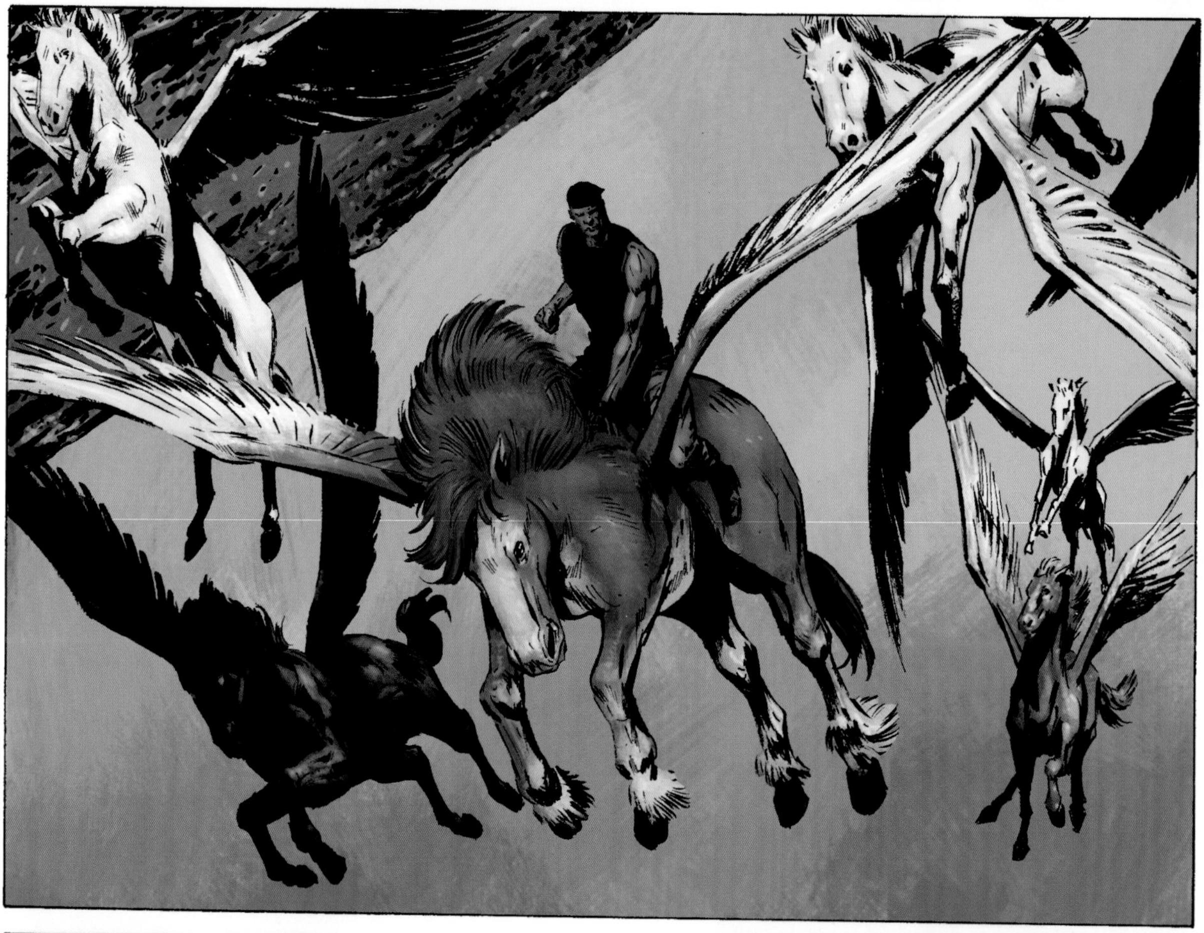

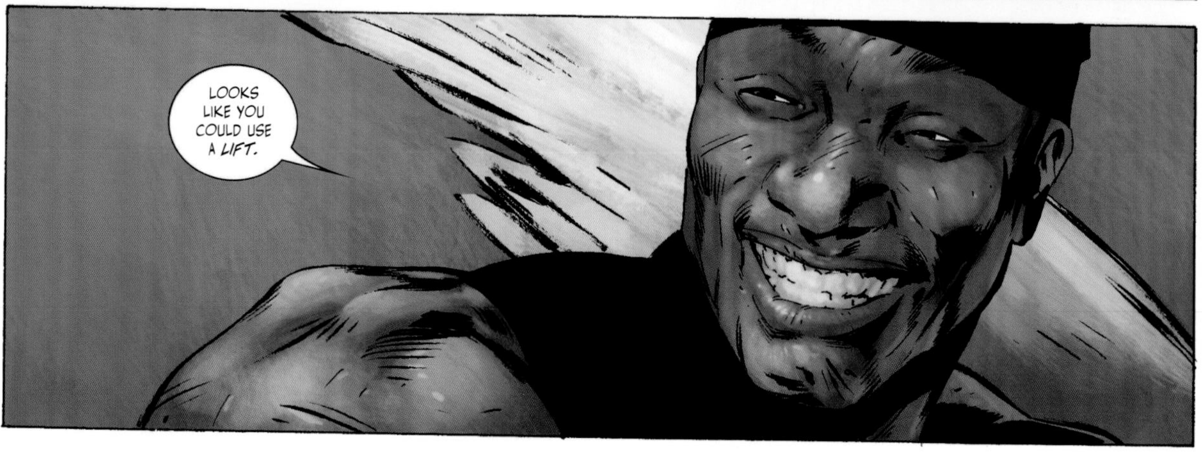
LOOKS LIKE YOU COULD USE A *LIFT*.

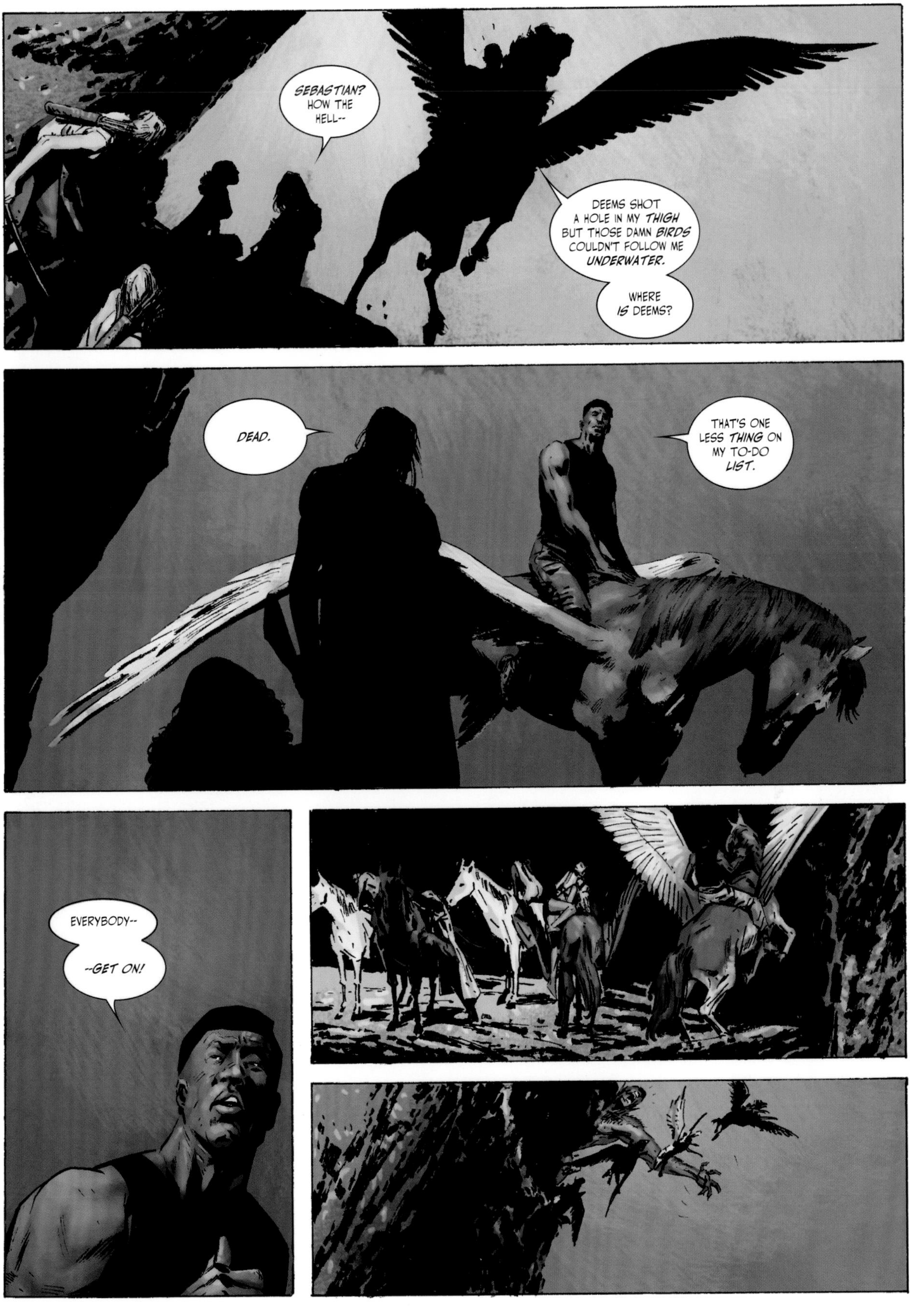
SEBASTIAN? HOW THE HELL--
DEEMS SHOT A HOLE IN MY THIGH BUT THOSE DAMN BIRDS COULDN'T FOLLOW ME UNDERWATER.
WHERE IS DEEMS?
DEAD.
THAT'S ONE LESS THING ON MY TO-DO LIST.
EVERYBODY--
--GET ON!

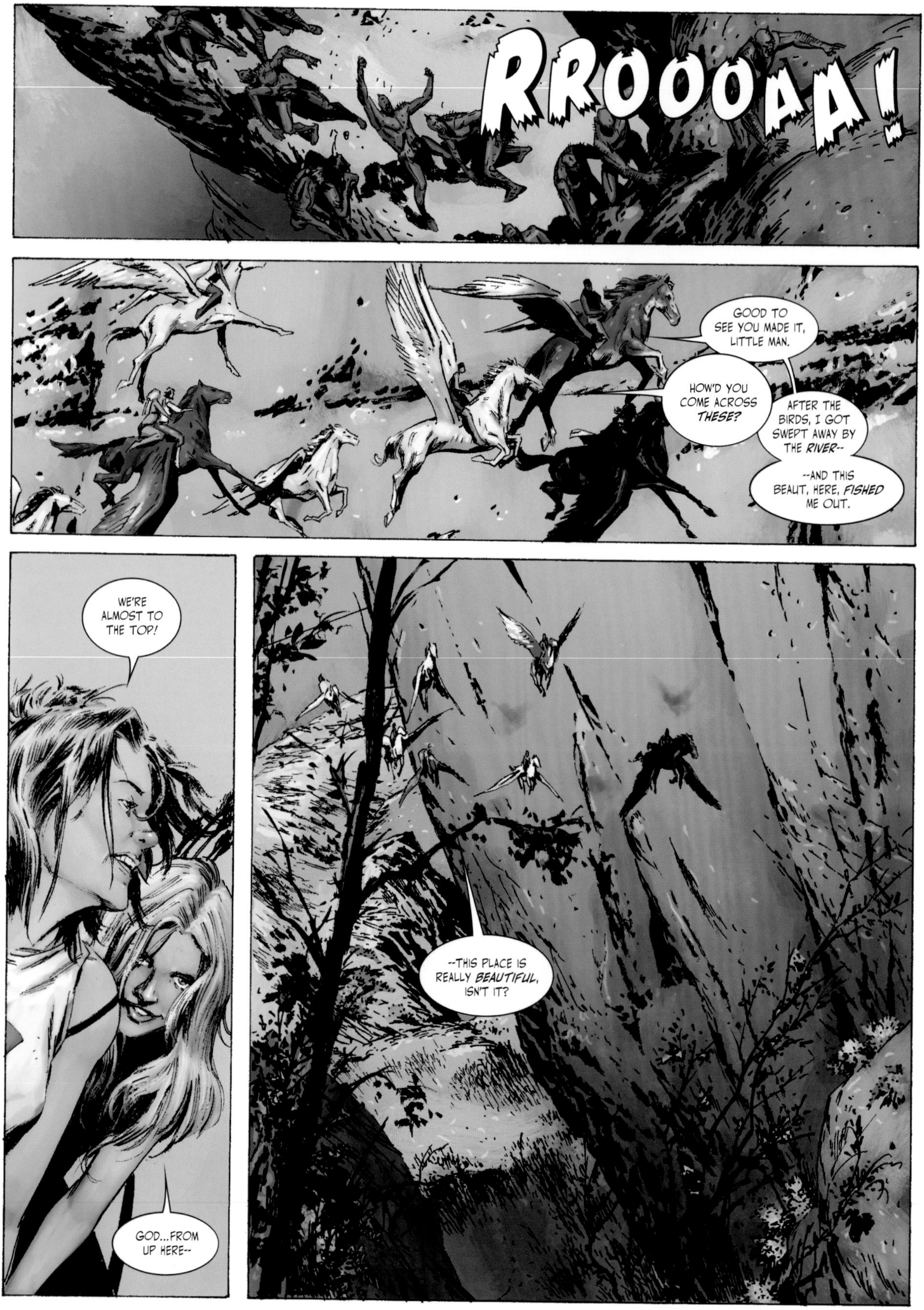
RROOOAA!
GOOD TO SEE YOU MADE IT, LITTLE MAN.
HOW'D YOU COME ACROSS *THESE?*
AFTER THE BIRDS, I GOT SWEPT AWAY BY THE *RIVER*--
--AND THIS BEAUT, HERE, *FISHED* ME OUT.
WE'RE ALMOST TO THE TOP!
GOD...FROM UP HERE--
--THIS PLACE IS REALLY *BEAUTIFUL*, ISN'T IT?

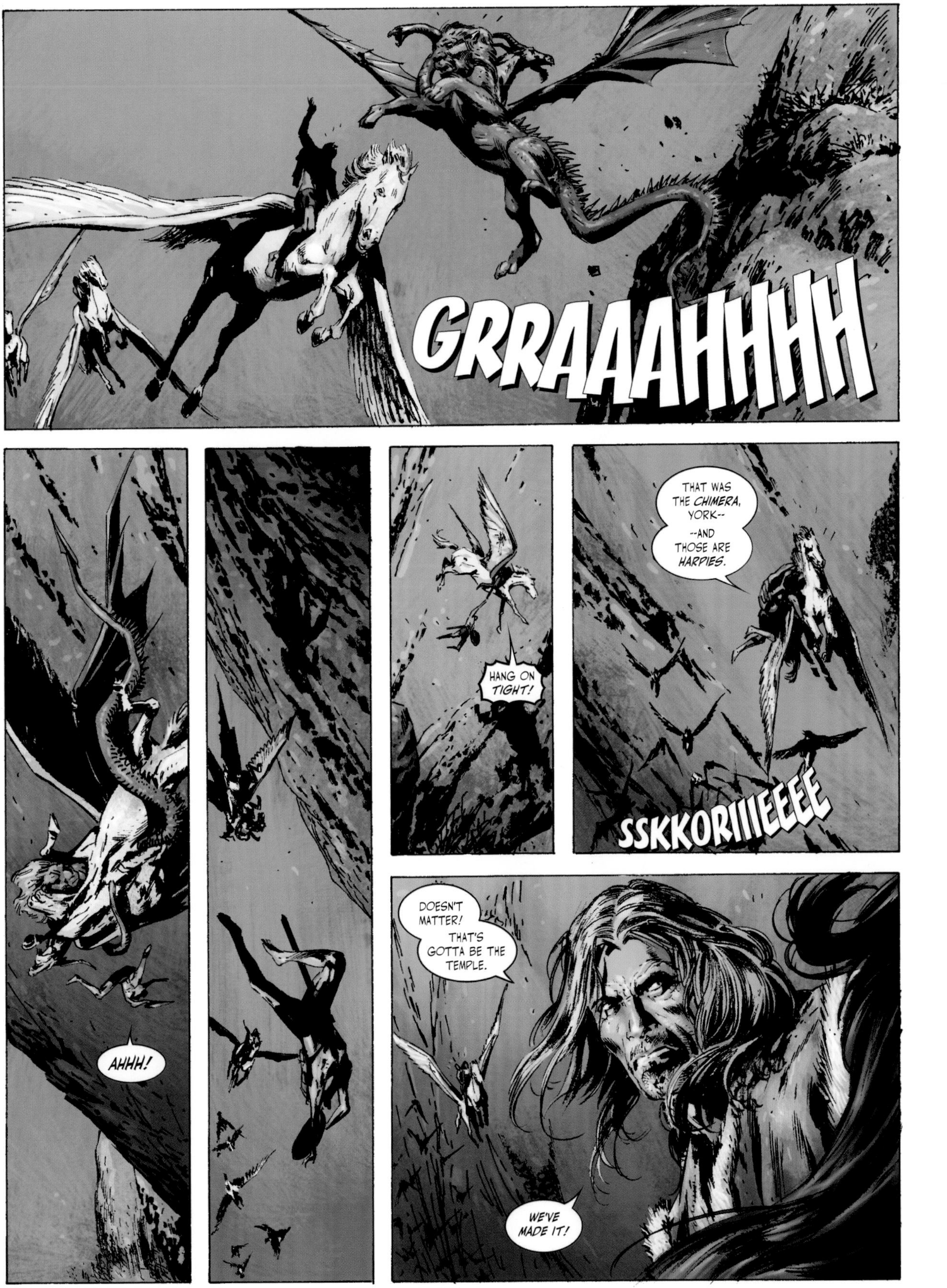
GRRAAAHHHH
THAT WAS THE CHIMERA, YORK--
--AND THOSE ARE HARPIES.
HANG ON TIGHT!
SSKKORIIIEEEE
AHHH!
DOESN'T MATTER! THAT'S GOTTA BE THE TEMPLE.
WE'VE MADE IT!

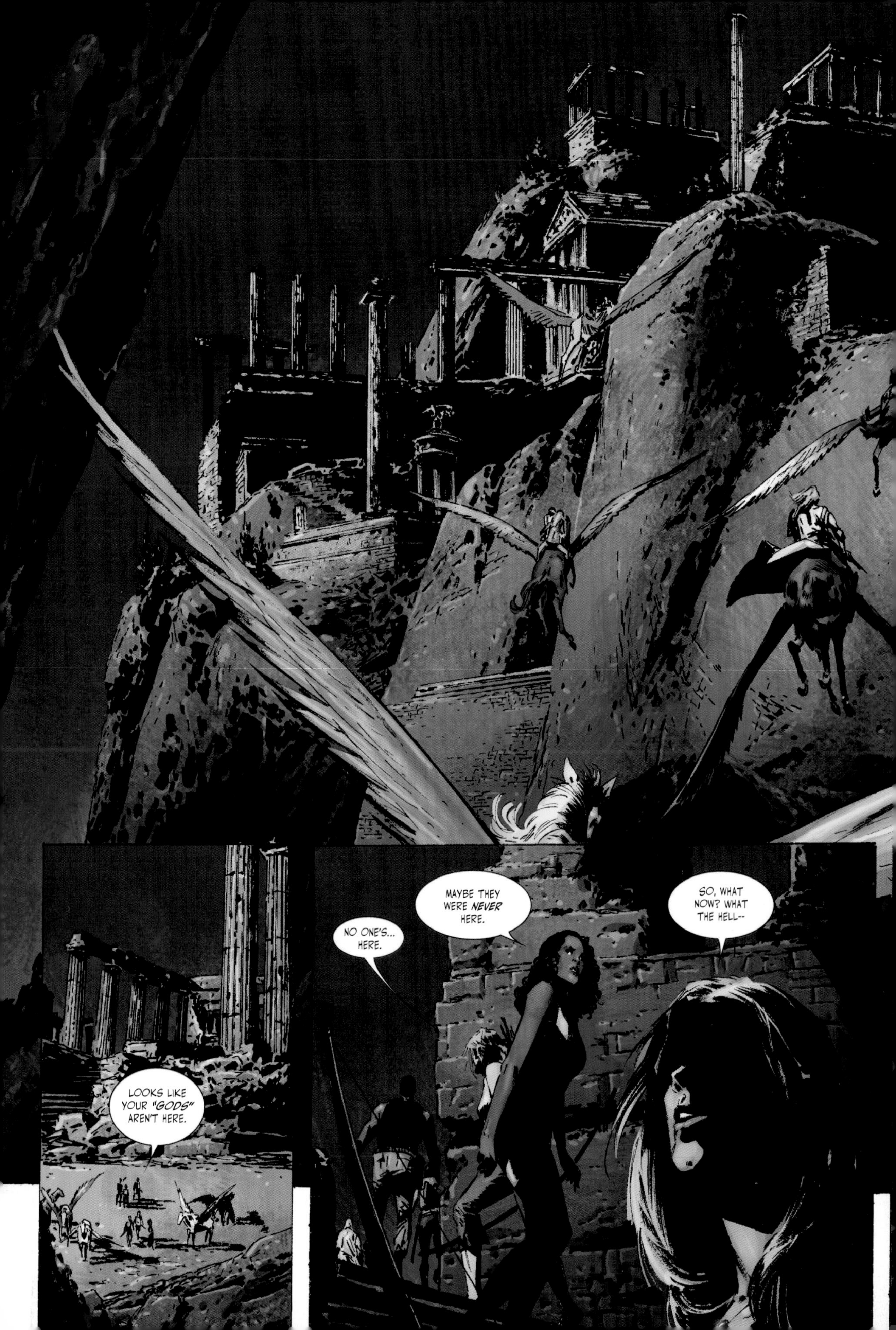
LOOKS LIKE YOUR "GODS" AREN'T HERE.
NO ONE'S... HERE.
MAYBE THEY WERE NEVER HERE.
SO, WHAT NOW? WHAT THE HELL--

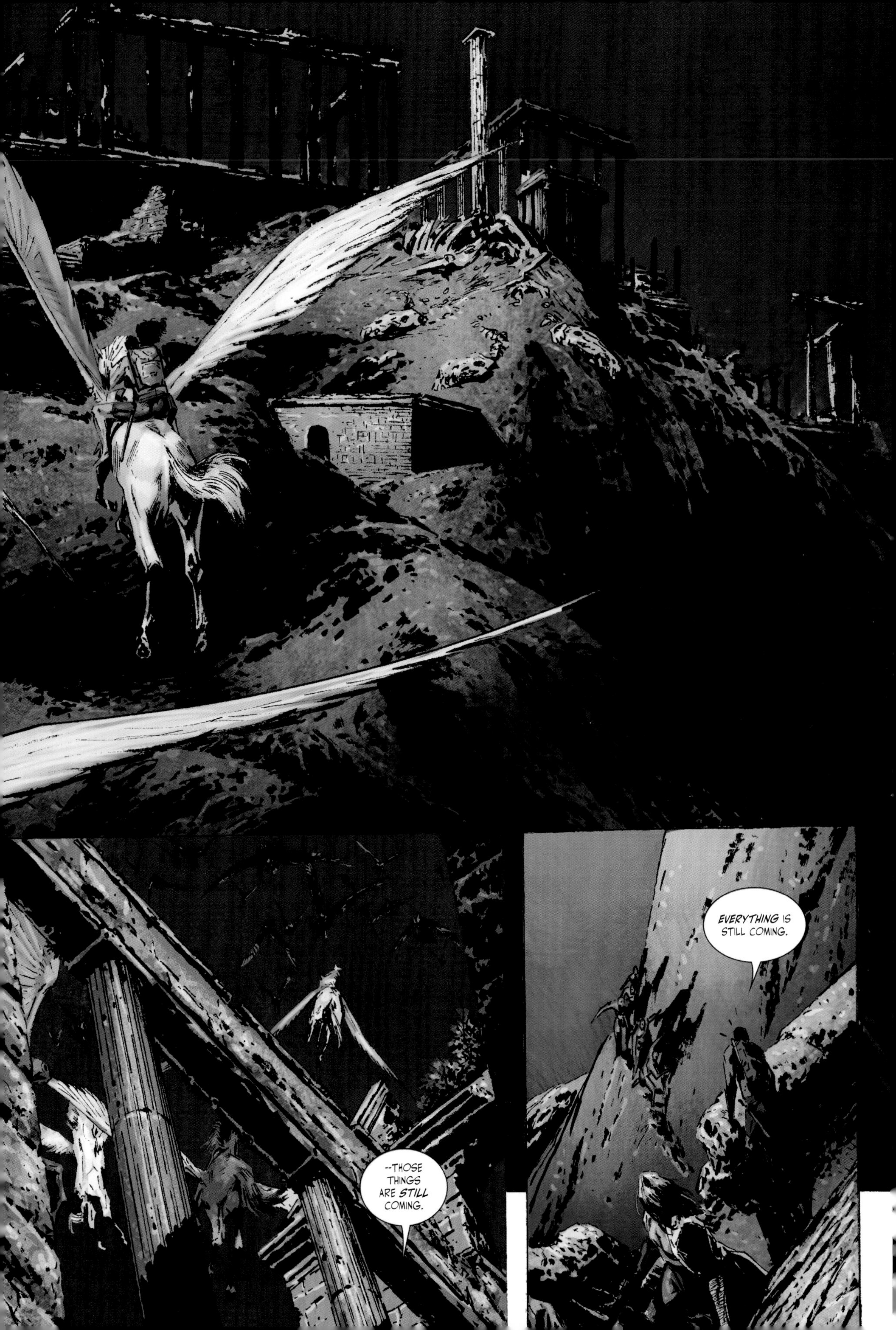
--THOSE THINGS ARE STILL COMING.
EVERYTHING IS STILL COMING.

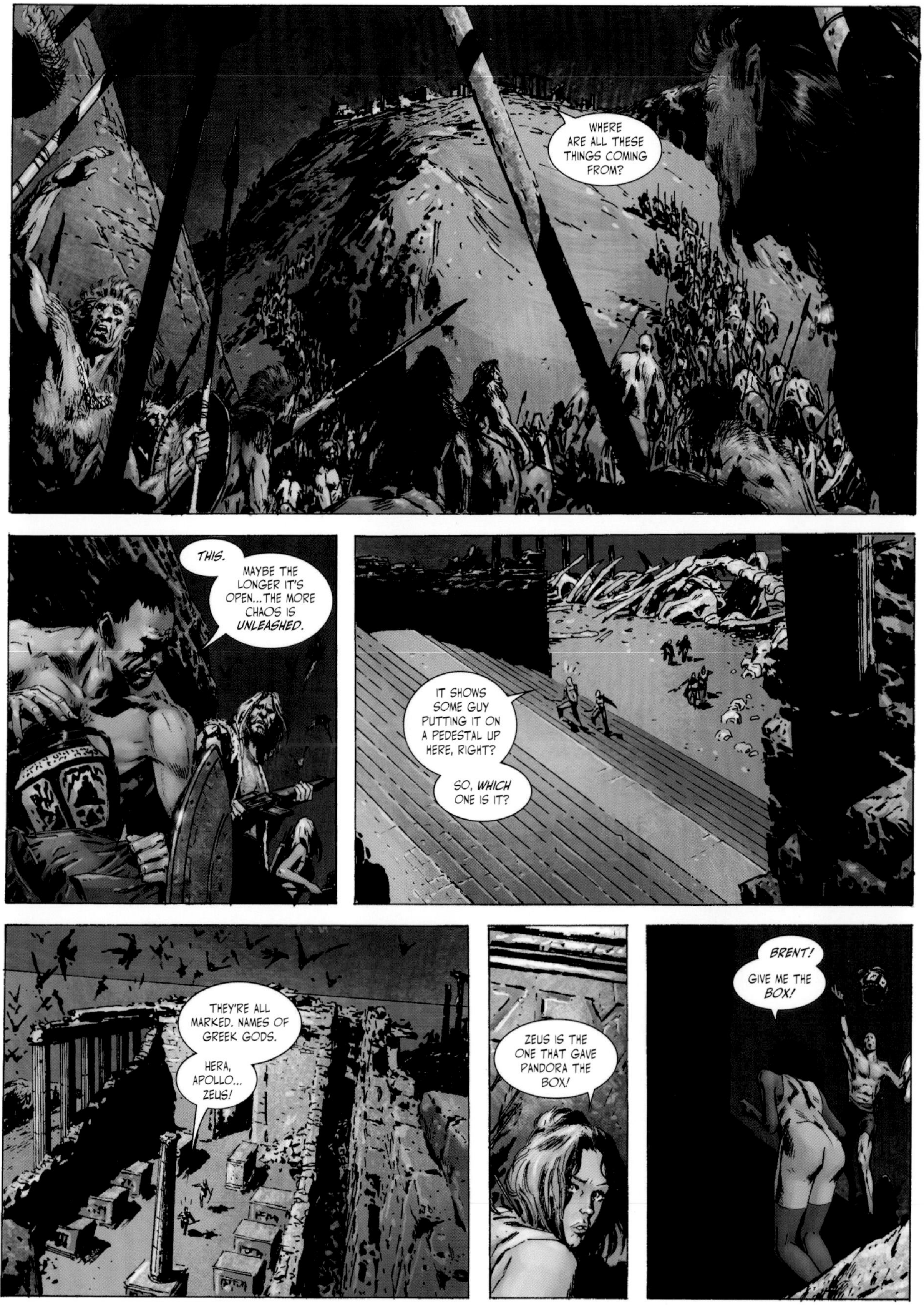
WHERE ARE ALL THESE THINGS COMING FROM?
THIS.
MAYBE THE LONGER IT'S OPEN...THE MORE CHAOS IS UNLEASHED.
IT SHOWS SOME GUY PUTTING IT ON A PEDESTAL UP HERE, RIGHT?
SO, WHICH ONE IS IT?
THEY'RE ALL MARKED. NAMES OF GREEK GODS.
HERA, APOLLO... ZEUS!
ZEUS IS THE ONE THAT GAVE PANDORA THE BOX!
BRENT!
GIVE ME THE BOX!

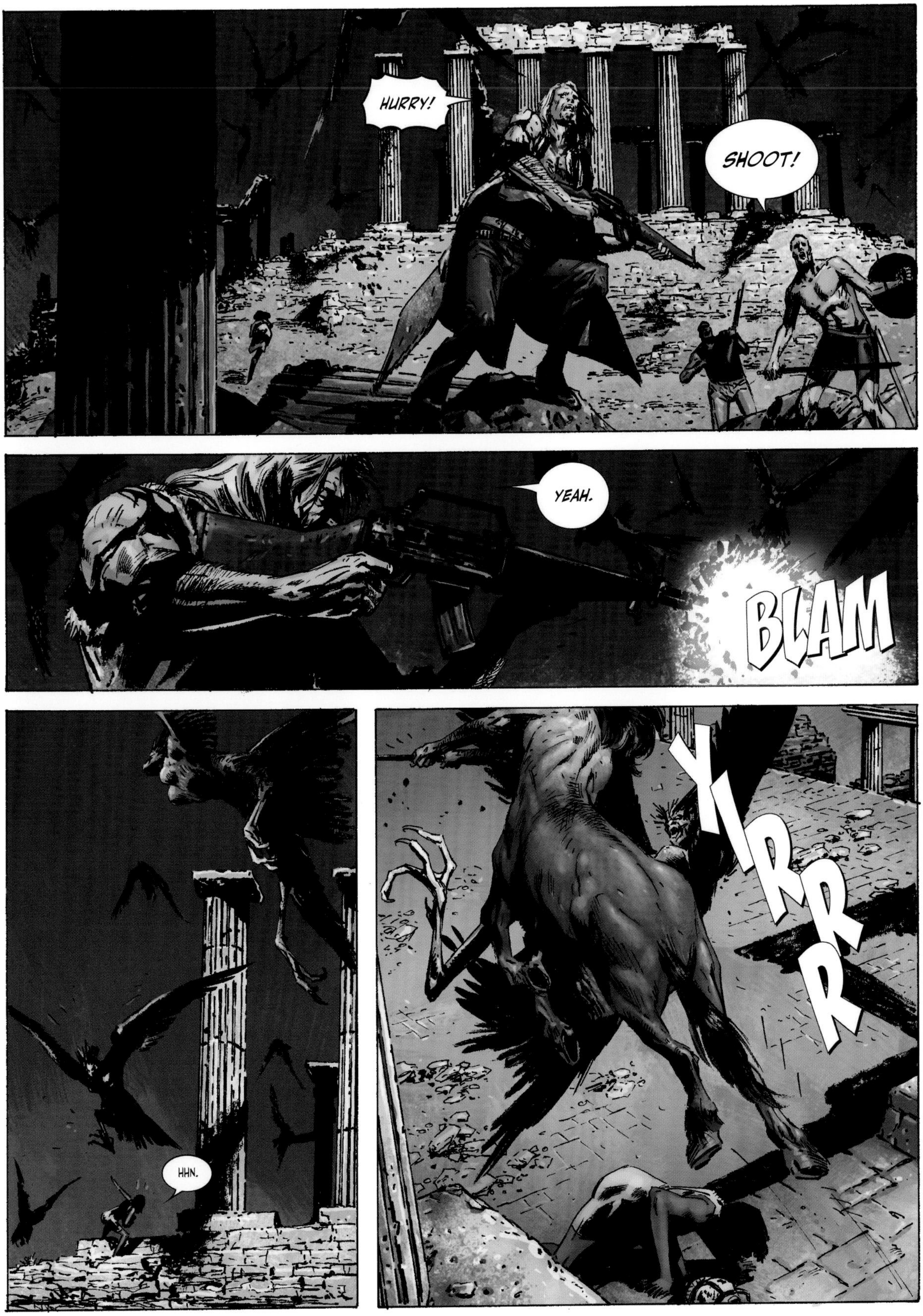
HURRY!
SHOOT!
YEAH.
BLAM
HHN.
YIRRR

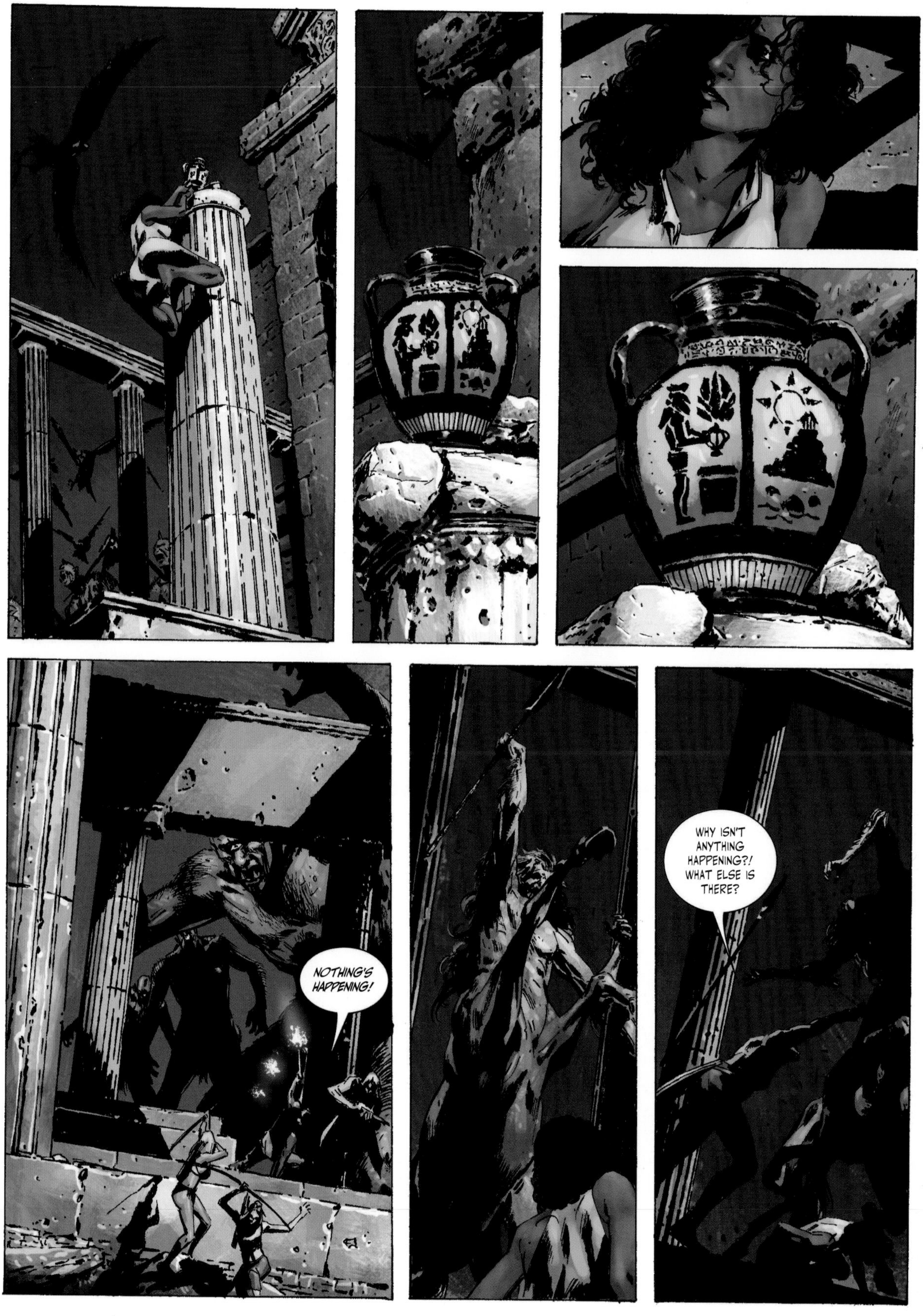
NOTHING'S HAPPENING!
WHY ISN'T ANYTHING HAPPENING?! WHAT ELSE IS THERE?

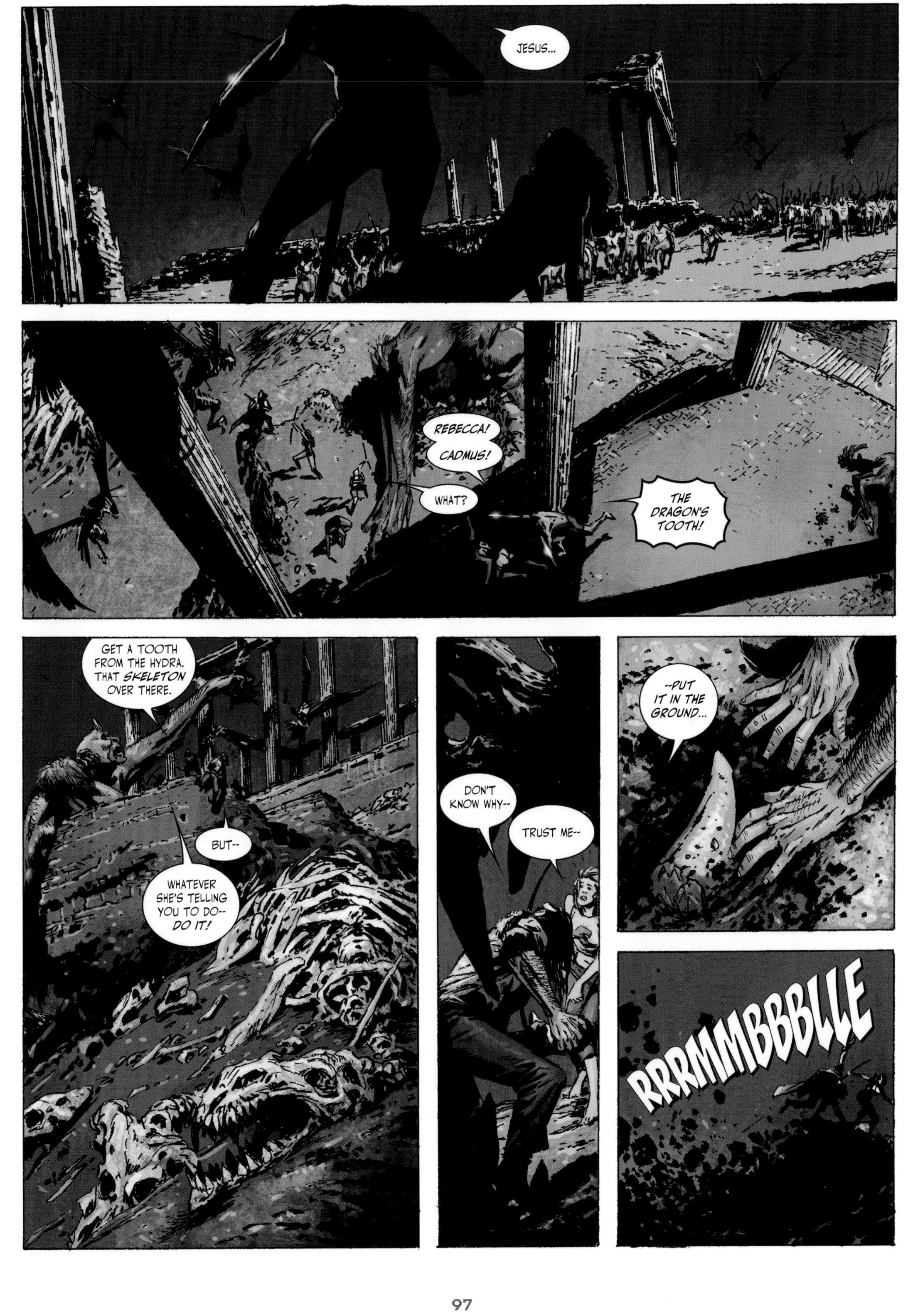
JESUS...
REBECCA!
CADMUS!
WHAT?
THE DRAGON'S TOOTH!
GET A TOOTH FROM THE HYDRA. THAT SKELETON OVER THERE.
BUT--
WHATEVER SHE'S TELLING YOU TO DO-- DO IT!
DON'T KNOW WHY--
TRUST ME--
--PUT IT IN THE GROUND...
RRRMMBBBLLE

WHAT DID I JUST *DO?*

"IN ORDER TO DEFEAT HIS ENEMIES, CADMUS KILLED A DRAGON AND PLANTED ITS TEETH IN THE GROUND--"

"--THE PRODUCT OF WHICH WERE CALLED *SPARTI*--"

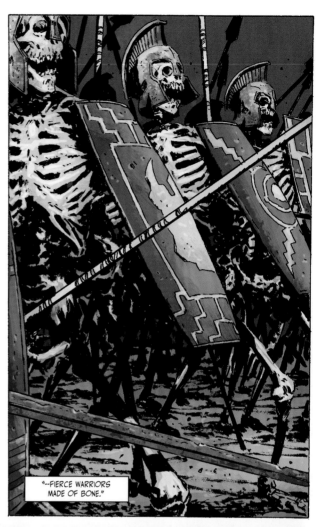

"--FIERCE WARRIORS MADE OF BONE."

"THEY'RE VICIOUS--"

"--AND THEY'LL FIGHT UNTIL THERE'S NOTHING LEFT."

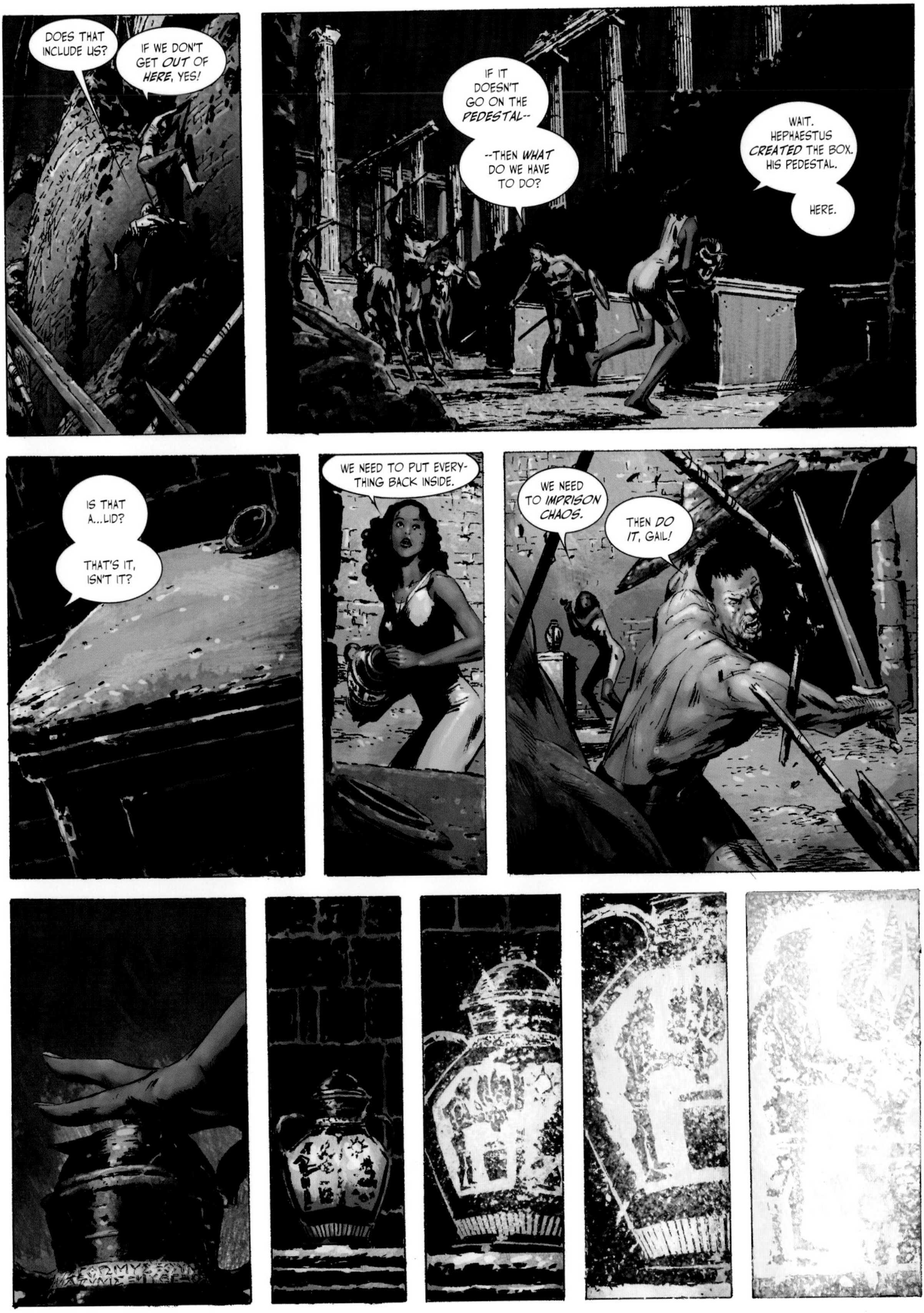
DOES THAT INCLUDE US?
IF WE DON'T GET OUT OF HERE, YES!
IF IT DOESN'T GO ON THE PEDESTAL--
--THEN WHAT DO WE HAVE TO DO?
WAIT. HEPHAESTUS CREATED THE BOX. HIS PEDESTAL.
HERE.
IS THAT A...LID?
THAT'S IT, ISN'T IT?
WE NEED TO PUT EVERYTHING BACK INSIDE.
WE NEED TO IMPRISON CHAOS.
THEN DO IT, GAIL!

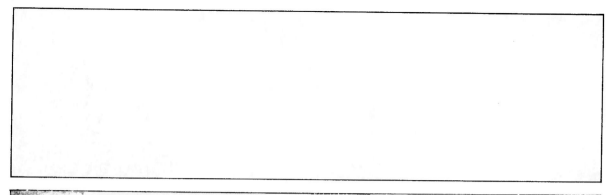

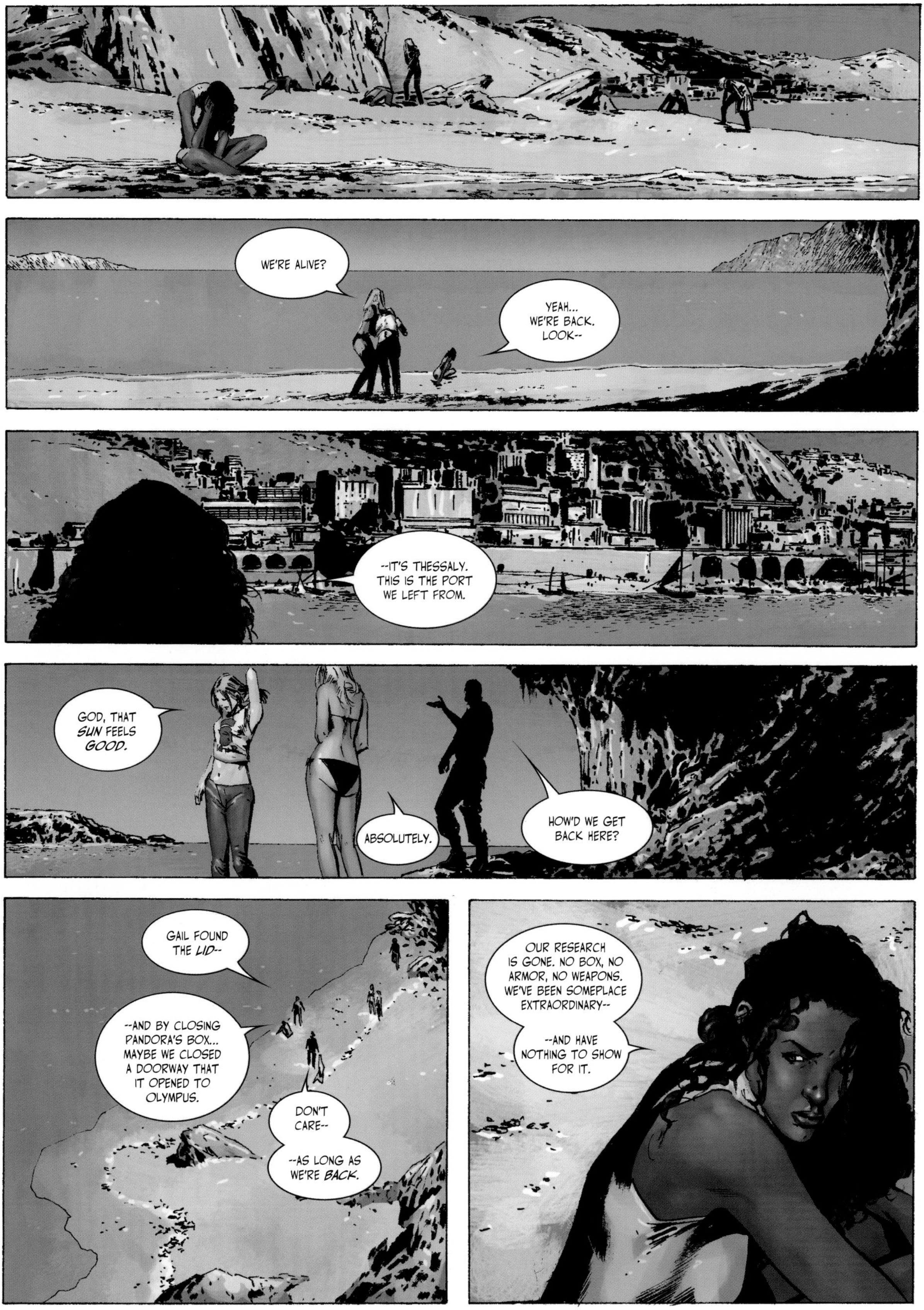
WE'RE ALIVE?
YEAH... WE'RE BACK. LOOK--
--IT'S THESSALY. THIS IS THE PORT WE LEFT FROM.
GOD, THAT *SUN* FEELS *GOOD.*
ABSOLUTELY.
HOW'D WE GET BACK HERE?
GAIL FOUND THE *LID*--
--AND BY CLOSING PANDORA'S BOX... MAYBE WE CLOSED A DOORWAY THAT IT OPENED TO OLYMPUS.
DON'T CARE--
--AS LONG AS WE'RE *BACK.*
OUR RESEARCH IS GONE. NO BOX, NO ARMOR, NO WEAPONS. WE'VE BEEN SOMEPLACE EXTRAORDINARY--
--AND HAVE NOTHING TO SHOW FOR IT.

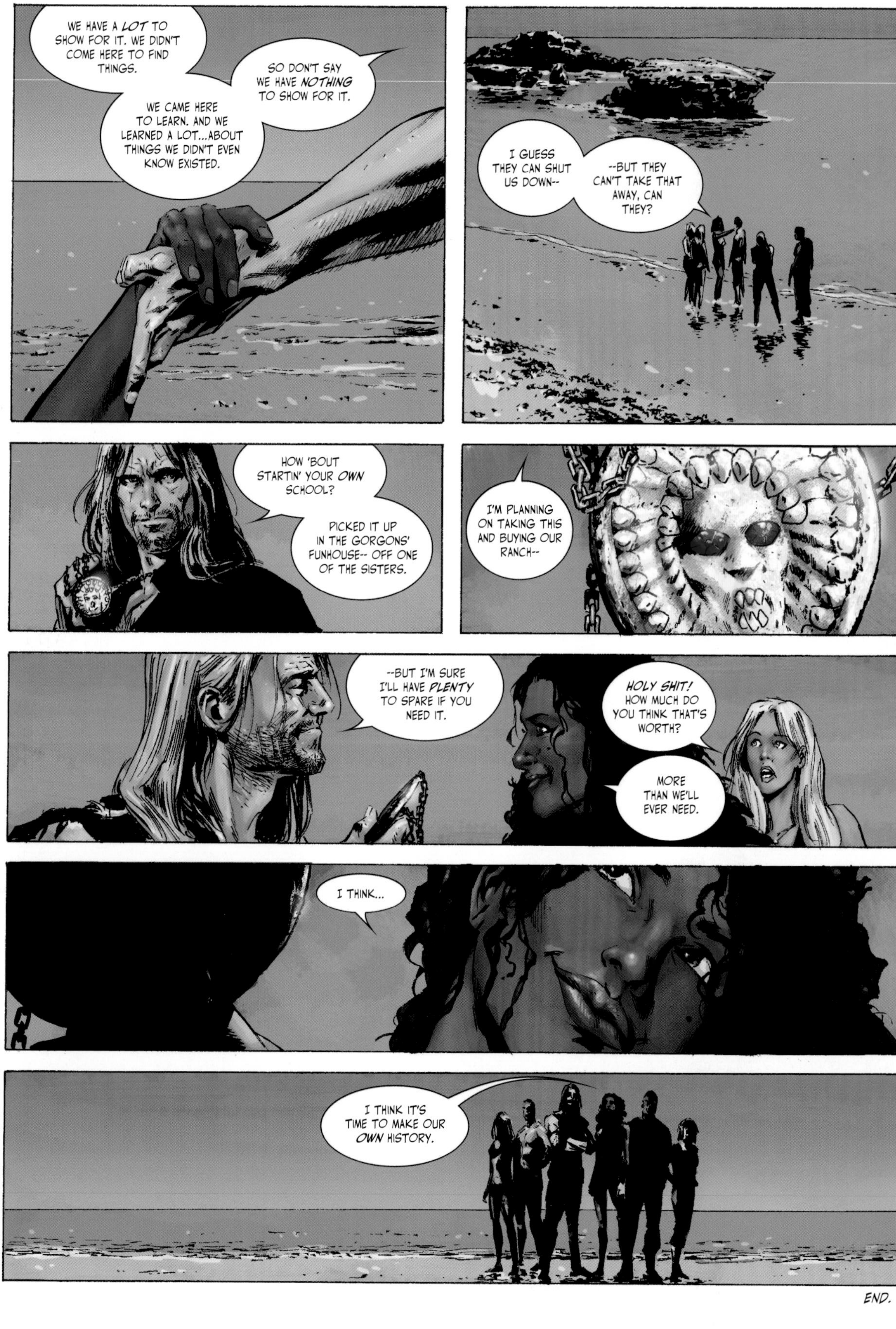
WE HAVE A LOT TO SHOW FOR IT. WE DIDN'T COME HERE TO FIND THINGS.
WE CAME HERE TO LEARN. AND WE LEARNED A LOT...ABOUT THINGS WE DIDN'T EVEN KNOW EXISTED.
SO DON'T SAY WE HAVE NOTHING TO SHOW FOR IT.
I GUESS THEY CAN SHUT US DOWN--
--BUT THEY CAN'T TAKE THAT AWAY, CAN THEY?
HOW 'BOUT STARTIN' YOUR OWN SCHOOL?
PICKED IT UP IN THE GORGONS' FUNHOUSE-- OFF ONE OF THE SISTERS.
I'M PLANNING ON TAKING THIS AND BUYING OUR RANCH--
--BUT I'M SURE I'LL HAVE PLENTY TO SPARE IF YOU NEED IT.
HOLY SHIT! HOW MUCH DO YOU THINK THAT'S WORTH?
MORE THAN WE'LL EVER NEED.
I THINK...
I THINK IT'S TIME TO MAKE OUR OWN HISTORY.

END.

BONUS
BUTCH GUICE SKETCHBOOK

EARLY CYCLOPS ILLUSTRATION

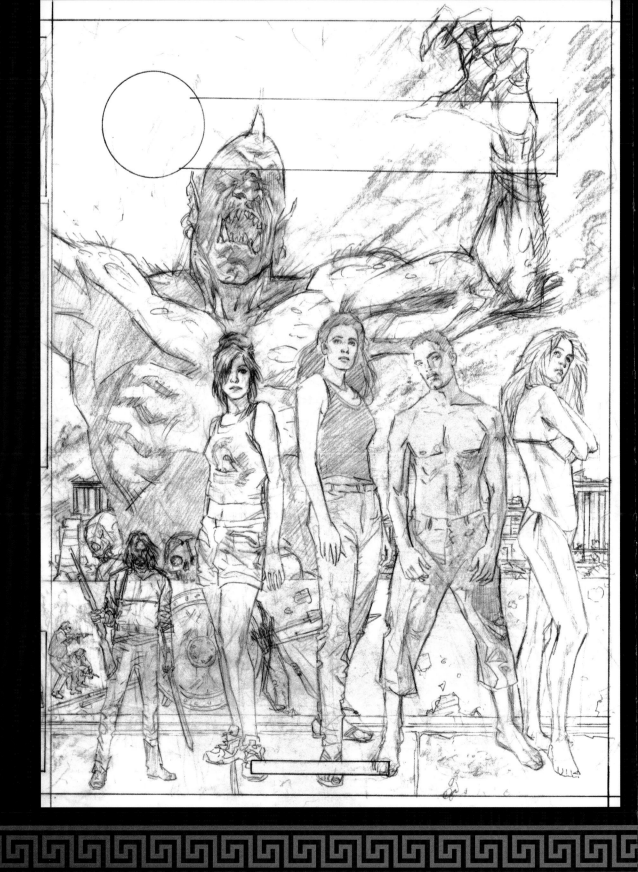

PENCIL COVER FOR BOOK 1, UNUSED

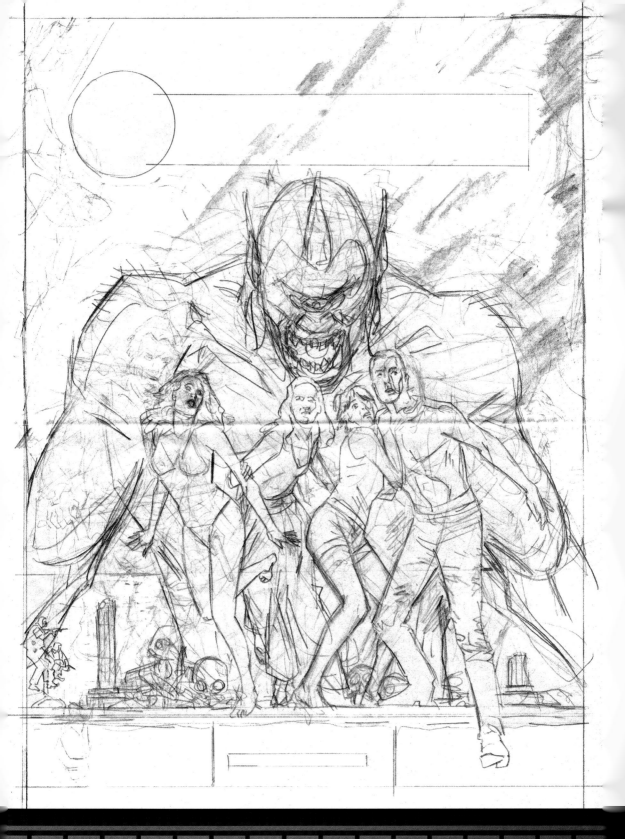

ANOTHER PENCIL COVER FOR BOOK 1, UNUSED

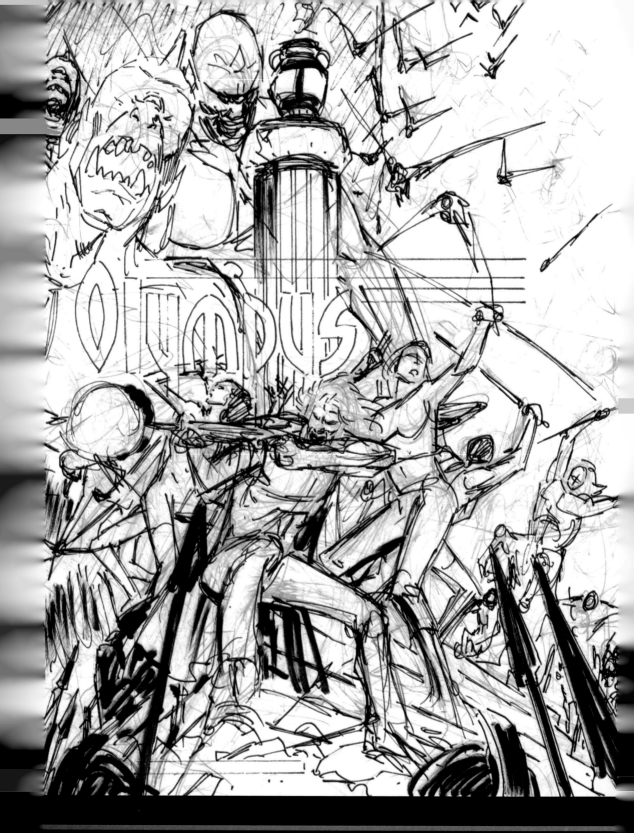

CONCEPT WORK FOR COVER OF BOOK 2

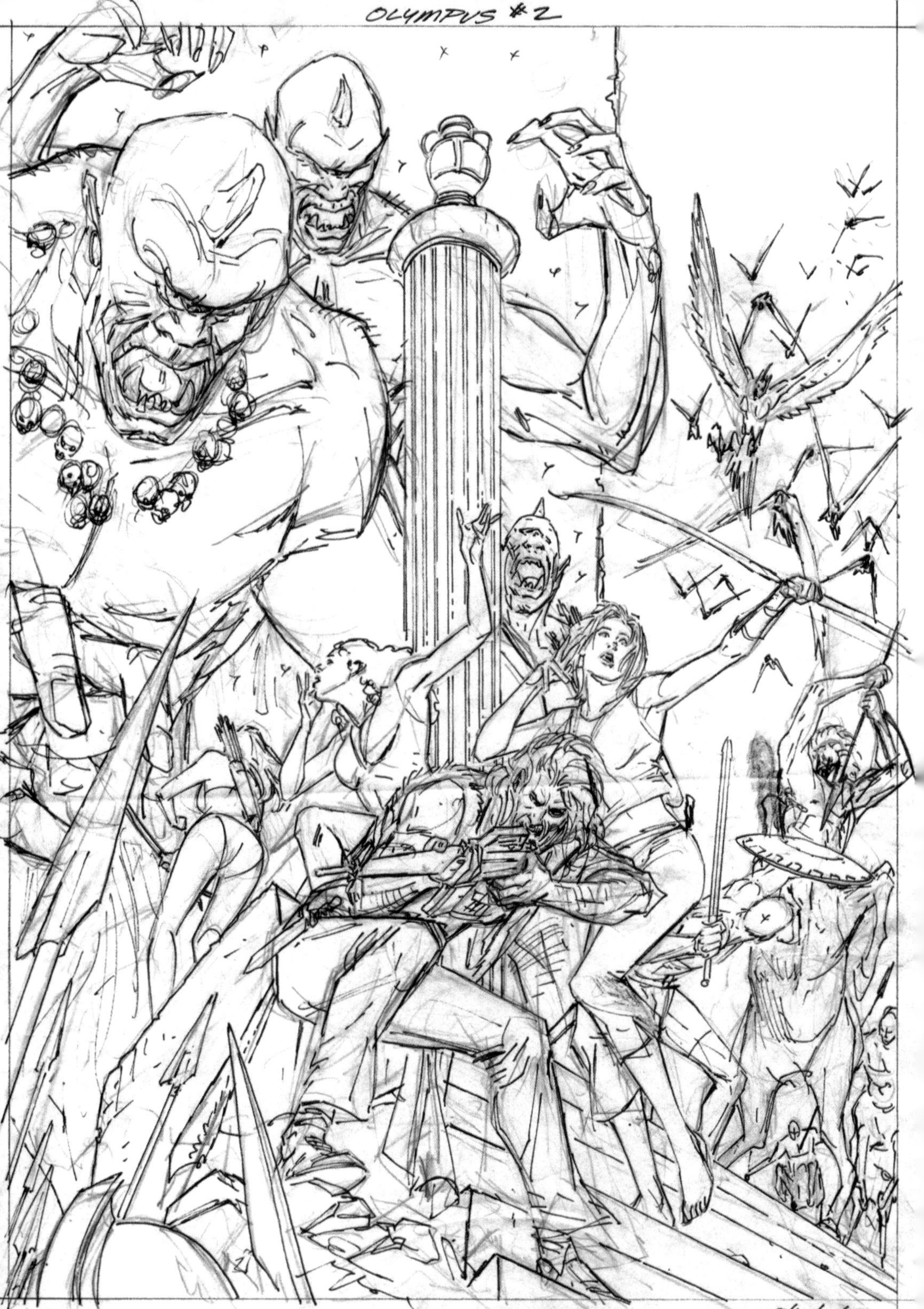
OLYMPUS #2
9/16/04

PENCIL COVER FOR BOOK 2

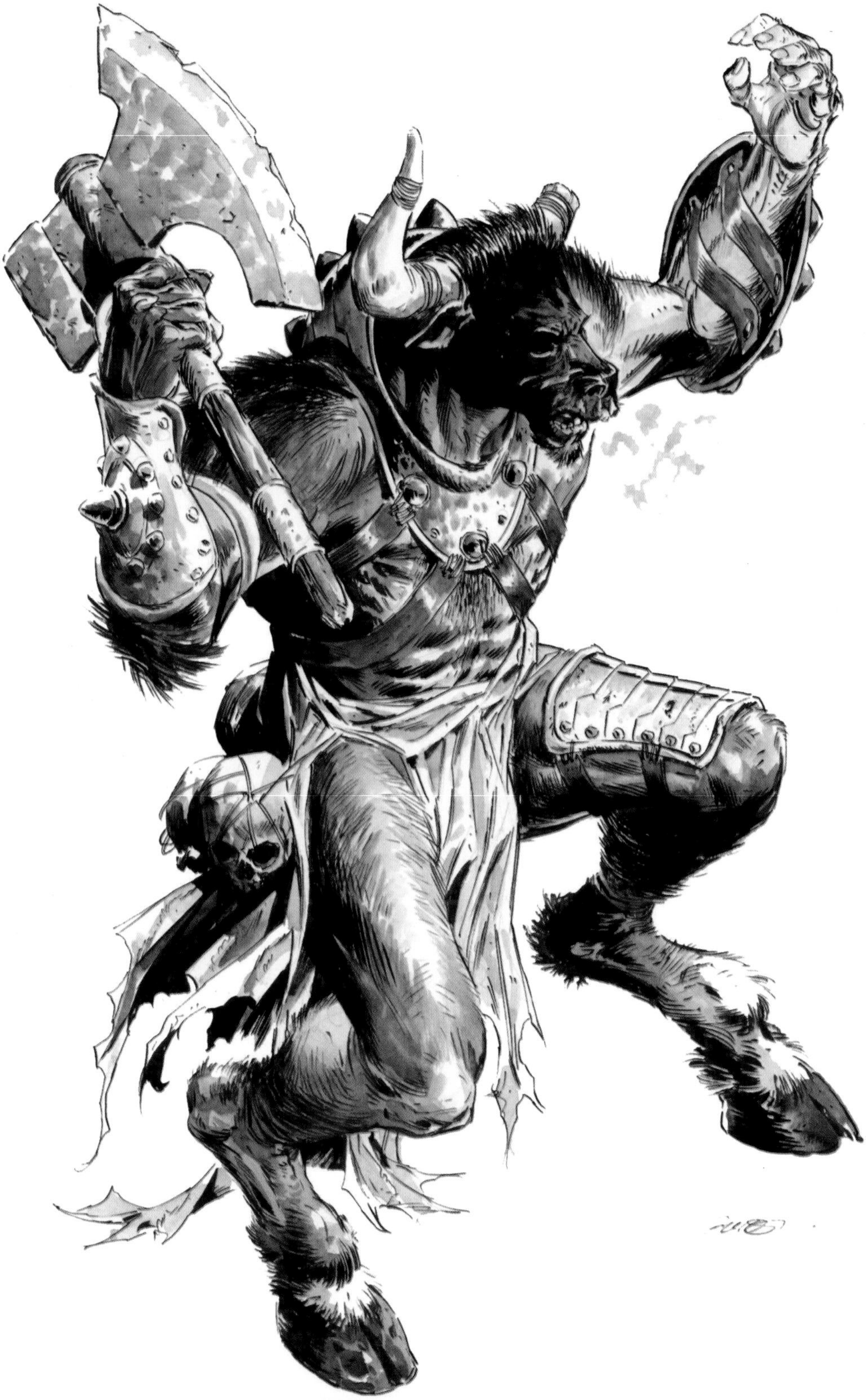

EARLY MINOTAUR ILLUSTRATION

ANOTHER EARLY CYCLOPS ILLUSTRATION

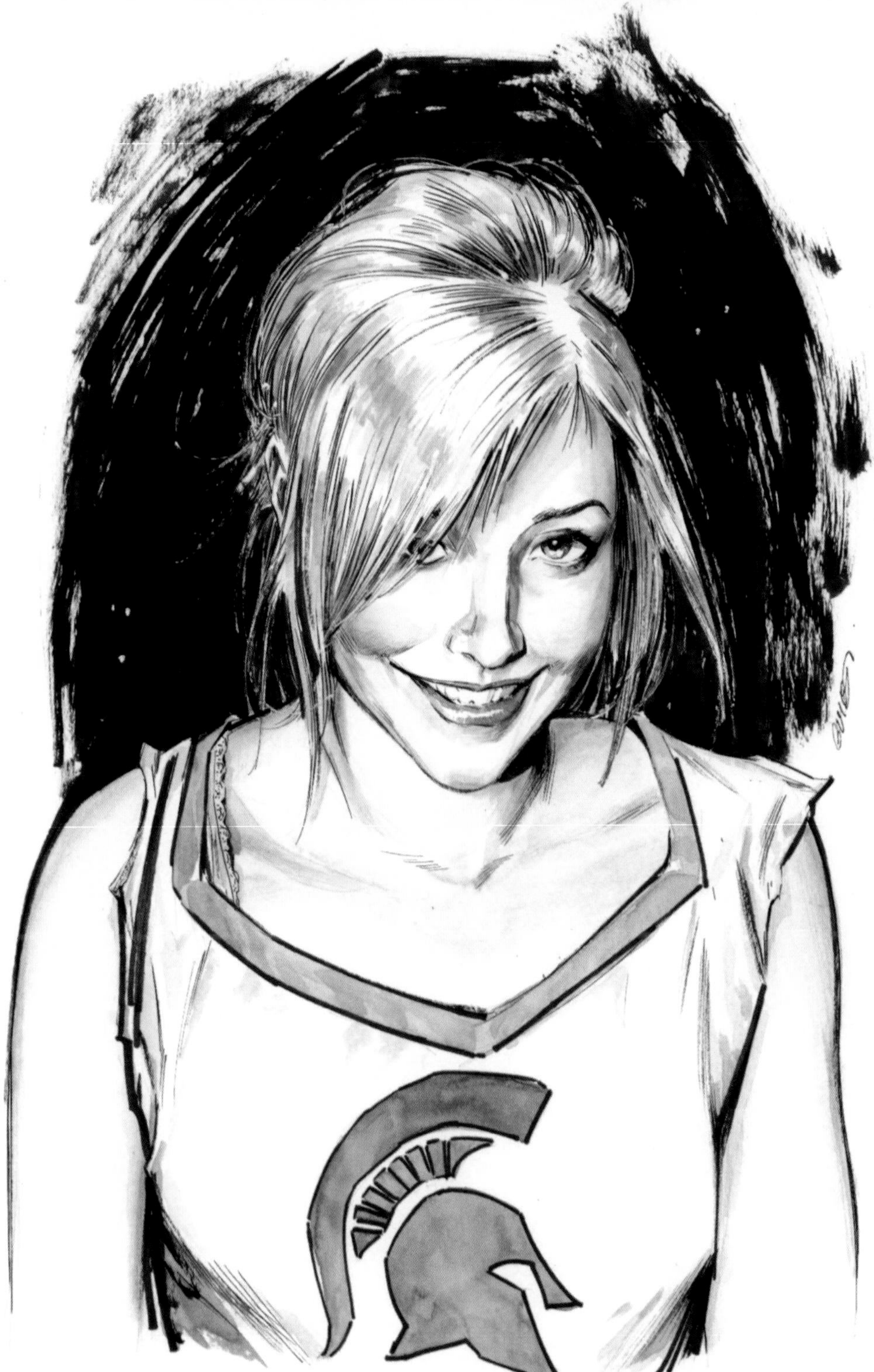
REBECCA MOORE

REBECCA MOORE CONCEPT ART

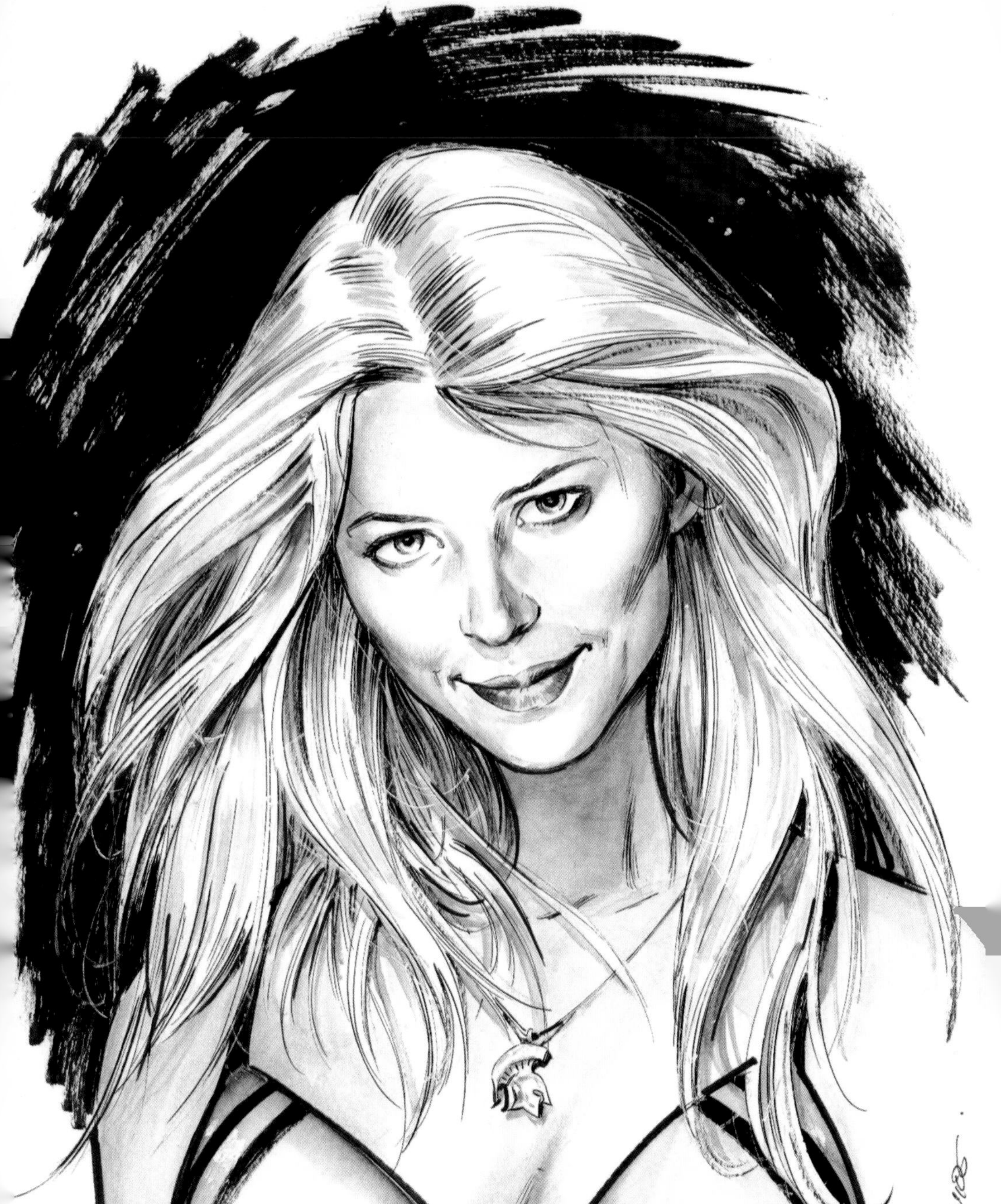
SARAH MOORE

SARAH MOORE CONCEPT ART

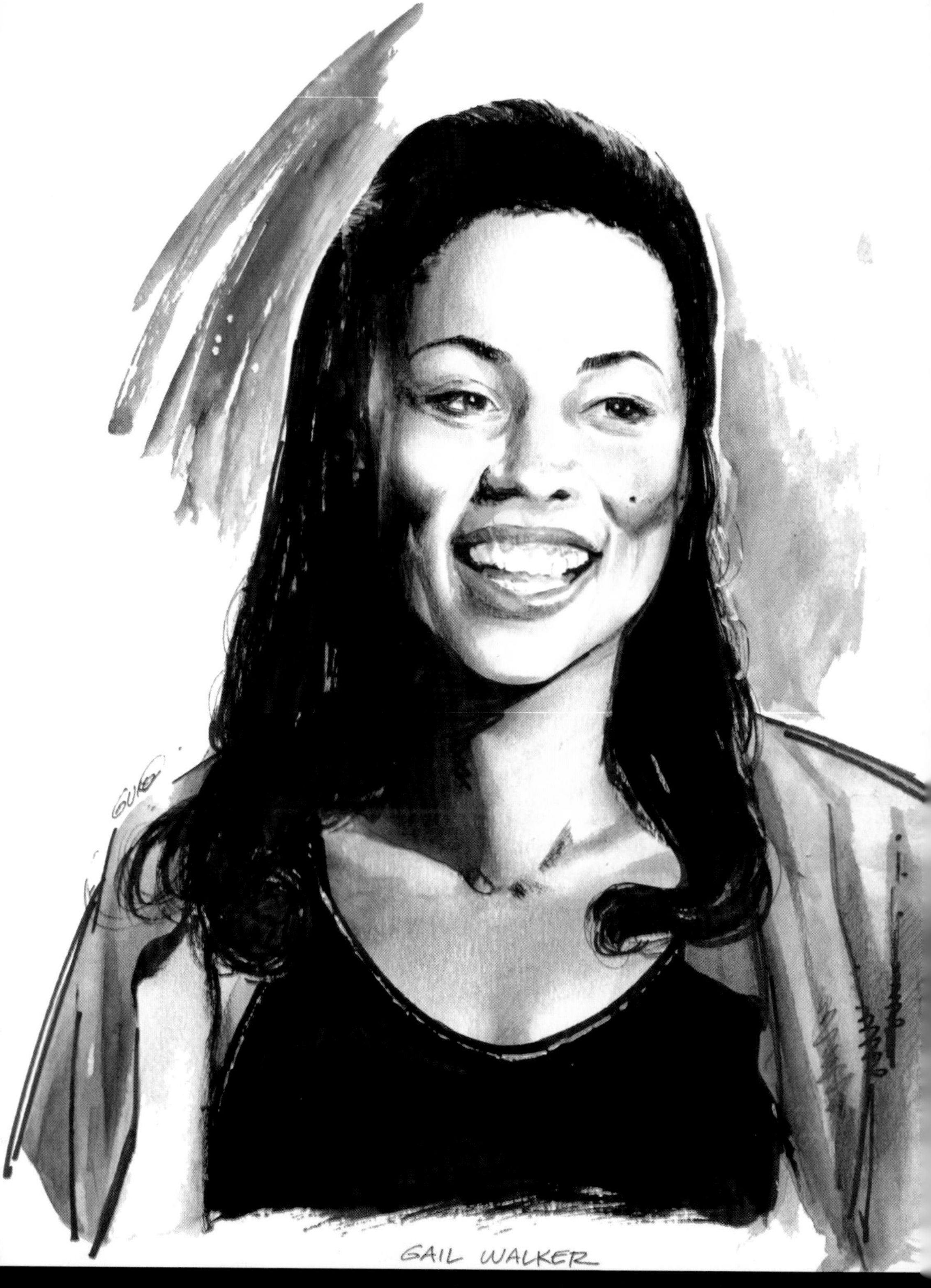
GAIL WALKER

GAIL WALKER CONCEPT ART

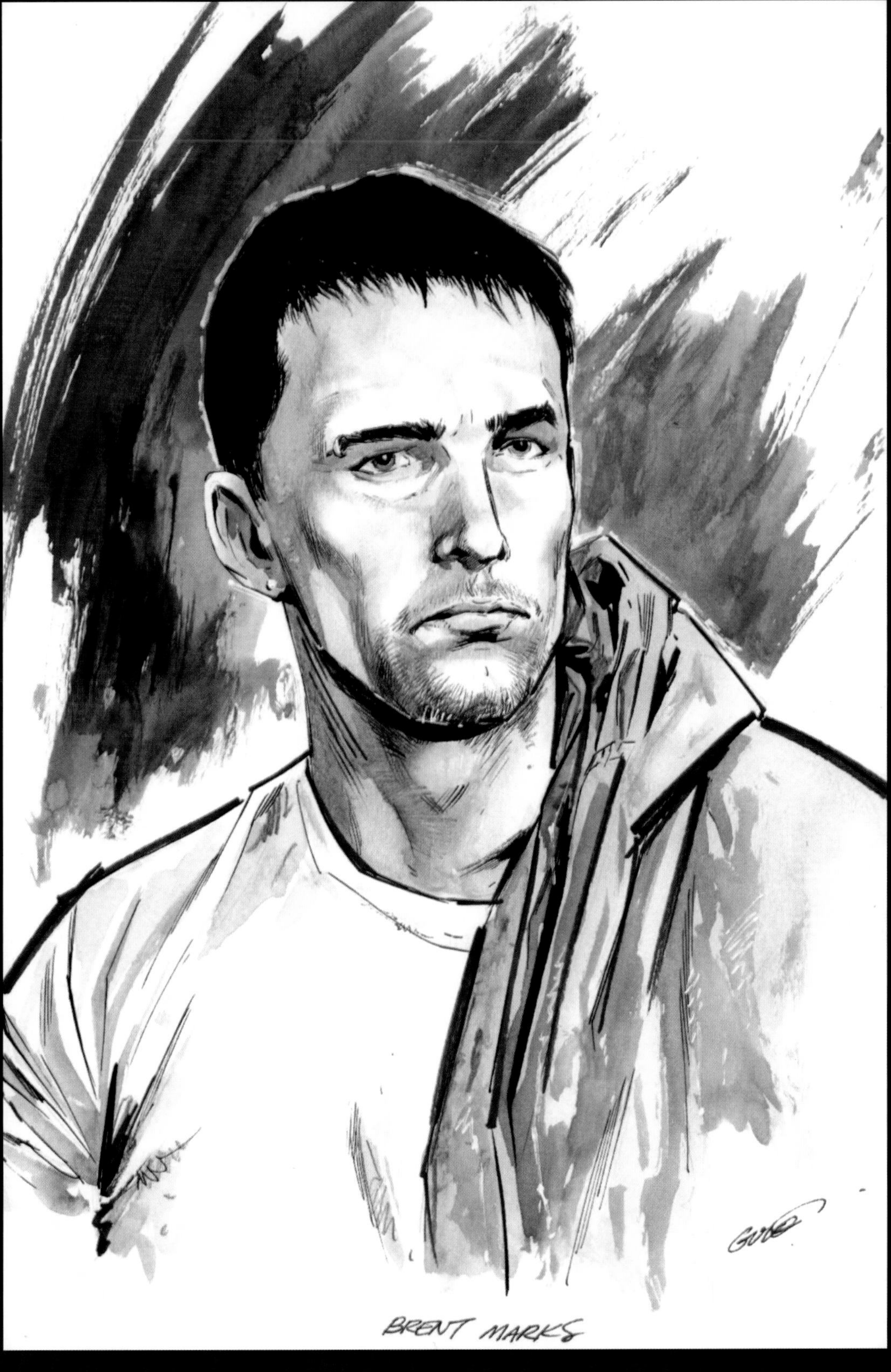
BRENT MARKS

BRENT MARKS CONCEPT ART

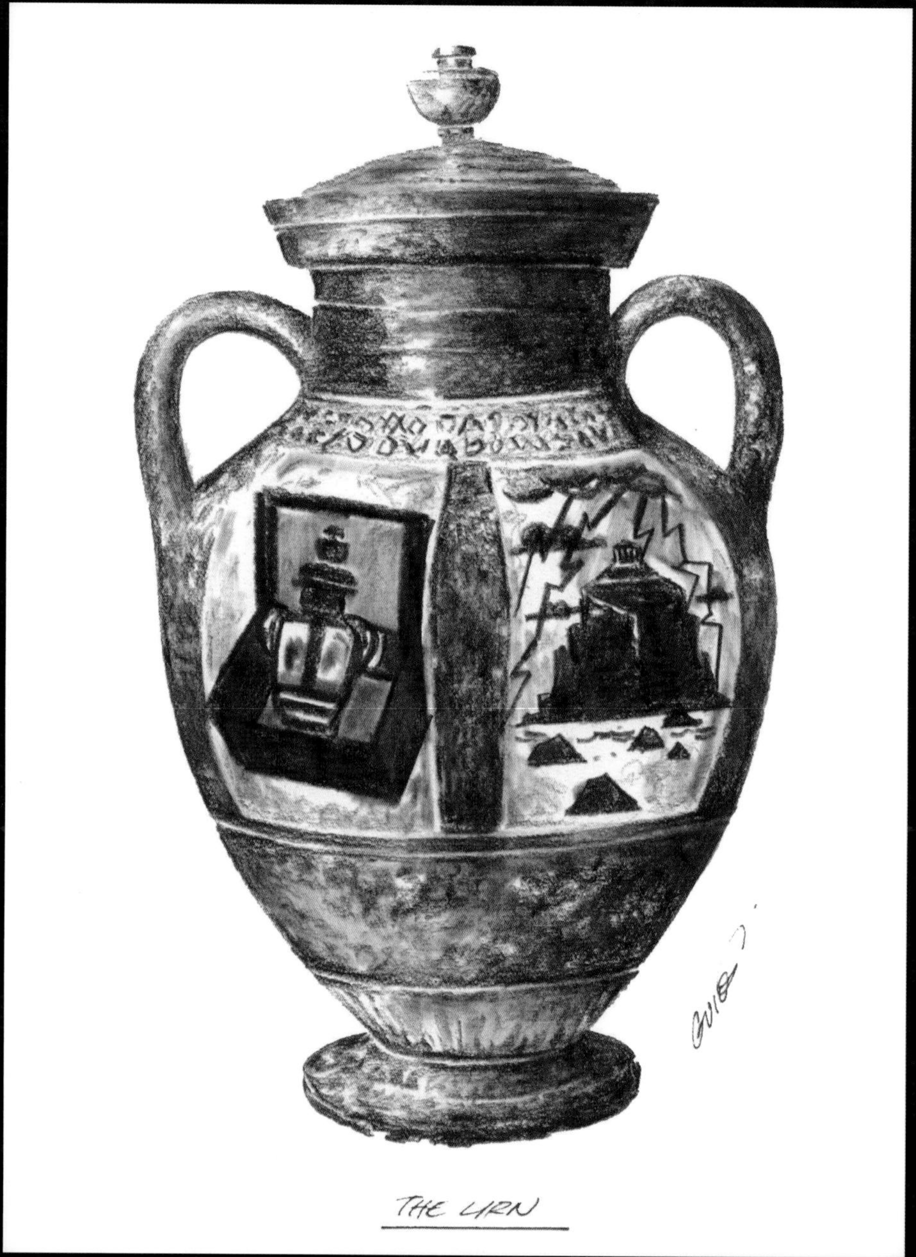
THE URN

THE URN CONCEPT ART